C

MW01104248

DEDICATION

....

Traitors in Treblinka is dedicated to the millions of victims of Nazi oppression who had their homes, possessions, and very lives stolen from them. The world will never know the extent of our loss. How many composers, scientists, leaders and inventors were lost to the crematoriums? Our tragedy is ongoing and unending.

PROLOGUE

....

What follows is a personal account of confronting horror. Scenes of cruelty, suffering, and explicit sexuality may not be suitable for young readers.

Individual experiences in this story, in fact, reflect the degradation of an entire society, previously among civilization's most advanced. Implicit in the story, then, is the question: What brought about the collapse of values and decency within Germany?

In the last Chapters 56, 57 & 58, I touch on the debilitating hyperinflation of the post-World War I Weimar Republic, and its undermining of the trust, civility and work ethic of the German people.

The scenes of the story involving sexuality are not there only for romantic interest; they express a Master Race policy of the Nazi government. Perfect Aryan children were to be "produced" without regard for marriage or normal courtship. This program, *Lebensborn,* is further explained in Chapter 58.

Now, in the centennial year of my life, I am remembering and recounting the time my friend Ezekiel and I were ordered to visit the death camps in Poland. We were sent to these places of inhuman horror by our boss at the secret Army Rocket Research Facility in northern Germany near the town of Peenemünde.

General Dornberger* was in charge of this very secret rocket research and testing facility. His primary concern was the health of his Jewish slave-labor workforce who were constructing, testing, and finishing the secret V-I and V-II missiles. The general was determined to know why his Jewish technicians and laborers were lasting only a few months before getting ill and often succumbing to sickness or exhaustion.

The general was under a lot of pressure from our Führer to produce a reliable missile for the Reich.

I remember our orders read: "discover why our Jewish prison-workers are dying of disease or exhaustion after only a few months at our facility." The General appointed Ezekiel and me to fulfill the mission of discovering what was happening to our Jews in the

---

* Major General Dr. Walter Robert Dornberger was a German artillery officer whose career spanned two wars. He was captured by the armed forces of the United States in WW I and spent almost 2 years in a French POW camp. He rose to the rank of Major General as the leader of the Wehrmacht secret rocket base at Peenemünde, in northern Germany during WW II. After WW II General Dornberger was brought to the United States along with 1600 other German engineers and scientists to work for the United States Government rocket development program under the secret intel code, "Operation Paperclip."

From 1950 to 1965 he worked for the Bell Aircraft Corporation rising to the level of Vice President. He was a major contributor the X-15 project and very instrumental in advancing the United States in space exploration. Following retirement, he returned to Germany and died on 27 July 1980 in Baden-Württemberg. He was 95 years old.

two labor camps supplying most of our laborers: Treblinka and Auschwitz.

It has been over eight decades since those unforgettable and horrifying visits to the death camps and I beg the readers' forgiveness. Forgiveness for being an unwilling participant in the most corrupt criminal conspiracy to ever be perpetrated on an unsuspecting nation. My beautiful country, Germany, was brought to near total ruin by greedy and self-serving politicians and their criminal henchmen during the 1930s and 40s.

I was an unwilling participant because I looked very Aryan. At age sixteen I was six feet four and a half inches tall with sandy blond hair and steel blue-grey eyes. My biggest problem, and the problem that saved my life, was that I was Jewish. My mother's family was one hundred percent Jewish, and my dad was Swedish- Christian. Although I never thought too deeply about my faith growing up, I found it most interesting to be comfortable attending either church or synagogue.

I always tried to be attentive to the teachings of the Bible and the written Torah. Many of the prayers I had learned in my early years attending our synagogue and church helped me and my childhood, and life-long friend, Ezekiel Leven, get through the terribly sad and difficult years of the Holocaust.

In the last few months of 1943, Ezekiel and I were ordered to the concentration labor camps to find an answer to General Dornberger's question. The General was determined to know why his Jewish technicians and laborers were only lasting a few months before they became ill or succumbed to disease or exhaustion.

These few months were painful and dangerous for Ezekiel and me. Whenever I thought about our time at Auschwitz and Treblinka, I had trouble breathing and even seeing clearly through watery eyes for several years. It was the most heart-breaking period in our lives. To this day I find myself shaking and weeping at the thought of the murder of so many children and innocent victims of the Nazi occupation forces.

My life-long friend Ezekiel and I severely underestimated the risk these camps posed to us. We really had no idea we were heading toward imminent danger. In addition, neither of us realized the Gestapo* was on to us until it was almost too late. Writing about these times is very difficult; but this is our story.

---

*   Gestapo is an abbreviation of the German name for Geheime Staatspolizei translated as the (Secret State Police). On February 10th, 1936, the Nazi Reichstag passed the "Gestapo Law" which included the following statement: "Neither the instructions nor the affairs of the Gestapo will be open to review by the administrative courts." This meant the Gestapo was now above the law and there could be no legal appeal regarding anything it did. Gestapo Headquarters on No. 8 Prinz Albrecht Strasse, Berlin, brought fear and trepidation to German citizens who could often hear the cries and screams of those unlucky enough to be questioned by the Gestapo.

INTRODUCTION

....

The commanding officer of Germany's very secret rocket training group Major General Walter Dornberger had a problem. It was a simple problem but with a rather complex solution, with dire implications if handled incorrectly.

In the 1930s, before the start of World War II, the Nazi top-secret rocket program was based on the northern coast of Germany on Usedom Island in the Baltic Sea. This Army research facility was so secret, most people in the German Army knew nothing about it. Even senior officers in the Wehrmacht knew nothing about what was going on in this northern outpost. The German public was completely unaware of the cutting-edge advanced research being accomplished at this military facility; most folks were not even aware there was a military base at this location.

In 1936 on April second, the German Ministry of Aviation paid 750,000DMarks to the town of Wolgast for the entire northern half of the Island of Usedom in the Baltic Sea. This peninsula became the home for the secret Army Research Center for developing rockets for military use.

The German High Command was able to investigate rocket research because this form of armament was not specifically prohibited or even contemplated by the Treaty of Versailles which ended the Great War (WW I). This loophole in the treaty allowed the Nazis to secretly develop the V-I and V-II missiles as weapons of war without violating the Versailles Treaty.

General Dornberger's principal problem was that he didn't like or ever want to work for the head boss at SS Headquarters, Reichführer Heinrich Himmler.*

The General considered Himmler and indeed his entire SS organization a para-military organization which at best provided the Wehrmacht and the German people very little protection or benefit for the vast sums of money the Reich was spending on developing it. Even more concerning to the General, the SS perpetuated what seemed to be a thug-like and club-like atmosphere that was only one step above the SA (Brownshirts) and the Gestapo, the National German Secret State Police.

Originally the Schutzstaffel or SS was designed in 1925 as a protective squadron or echelon for our Führer, Adolf Hitler. In the 1930s Reichführer Himmler had set up and staffed the labor

---

*   Heinrich Luitpold Himmler, a former chicken farmer, was the main architect of the Holocaust and the Lebensborn program. He became head of the SS in 1929 and developed and organized the concentration camps throughout the Third Reich. He was greatly feared by friends and foes alike. He was captured by the Russians while trying to flee the country after the war. He was turned over to the British at their headquarters in Lüneburg, Germany in May 1945. Upon examination by a British medical doctor, Himmler kept jerking his head away when it came time for an oral examination. Under threat of a forced oral examination, Himmler took the cowards way out and crushed a potassium cyanide pill and was dead in 15 minutes on 23 May, 1945. The man responsible for the murder of six million Jewish, Romani, Russian Prisoners of War, and countless other men, women, and children was 45 years old.

camps that supplied the slave labor for the rocket manufacturing at Peenemünde. The commandants of these "camps" were the SS.

After the British bombed the secret missile development base on Peenemünde in August 1943, labor from the Dora Concentration Camp was used to build and maintain the gypsum mine in Nordhausen near the geographic center of Germany. The research and manufacturing of the V-I and V-II missiles was moved to the gypsum mine to avoid the range and detection of the Allied and Russian bombers.

It was the Dora Camp that supplied most of the slave labor to build-out the gypsum mine for rocket development and manufacturing. The protective-custody leader and Commandant of the Dora Camp was a monster named SS-Obersturmführer Hans Karl Moeser.*

These labor camps were built in Germany, Poland, and all-over Eastern Europe. A particular criminal element in the SS called the SS Death's Head Division was tasked with guarding and running these labor or concentration camps.

The Rocket Research Center had to be moved from Peenemünde, on Germany's northern coast, to the gypsum mine in Thuringia, Germany. Mittelwerk (Central Works) near the town of Nordhausen was chosen for the site. The British had discovered the research center on Peenemünde and bombed it on the 17th and 18th of August 1943. The new manufacturing and

---

* In December 1945, an American Military Tribunal sentenced Moeser to death. At his hanging his last words were: "The same way, with the same pleasure, you shoot deer, I shoot a human being. When I came to the SS and had to shoot the first three persons, my food didn't taste good for three days, but now it is a pleasure. It is a joy for me."

assembly plant for the rockets had to be far from the reach of the Russian and Allied bombers.

The concentration camp inmates that Himmler would send the General at the Army Research Rocket Center in Peenemünde and Mittelwerk to manufacture the rockets were very talented slave laborers. The workers included electrical engineers, mechanical engineers, teachers, electricians, jewelers, clockmakers, and all sorts of technically skilled people. The problem was almost one hundred percent of the workers sent by Himmler from the camps were sick, malnourished, and exhausted.

By the time these skilled Jewish workers mastered the manufacturing process for the V-I and V-II missiles, they were literally completely spent. They rarely lasted more than two or three months. If they didn't die of diseases picked up at the camps, they died of injuries because their bodies couldn't take the rigors of rocket manufacturing and army life at the research center; even though the food and living conditions were much improved over the dire conditions that existed in the labor camps. There was speculation many prisoners died due to the abrupt change of an improved diet.

The labor situation at Peenemünde became desperate. So many Jewish laborers were getting ill, that General Dornberger finally decided to send out two men to investigate the concentration or labor camps. He could not replace his very talented labor force fast enough to build and test the "wonder weapons" he was developing. The general wanted to see what could be done to improve the health of the slave labor workers he was getting to assemble his rockets.

The General decided to send one of his tall SS First Lieutenants, Jenz Ramsgrund, and one newly indoctrinated Wehrmacht scientist, Vitali Carapezza, to look into what was going on in the labor camps. These men were to head the investigation into the nutrition, health care, and typical accommodations at the different labor or concentration camps.

The general directed the investigation to begin at the camps where the rocket base received many of their workers: Treblinka, 60 kilometers north-east of Warsaw and Auschwitz in southern Poland. General Dornberger had no idea the camp at Treblinka was not a labor camp at all, but indeed a death camp built specifically to liquidate the victims of the Warsaw Ghetto in Poland. These victims had been living peacefully with the other city residents until the Nazis invaded their country in September 1939.

What the general also didn't realize was his SS First Lieutenant had a Jewish mother, and the newly Wehrmacht indoctrinated scientist wasn't really Vitali Carapezza at all, but the First Lieutenant's boyhood friend, who also happened to be Jewish, Ezekiel Leven.

In spite of the danger their secret Jewish identities posed, both men were eager to investigate the labor camps and find out what was really going on within those barbed wire walls. Jenz mentioned to Vitali when they were alone, "Zeke, we just might be the best choice the General could have made. You might say we are 'uniquely qualified' to get an 'up-front' and accurate report to General Dornberger."

1

The School Years

My name is Jenz Ramsgrund. I was born in Düsseldorf, Germany, in 1920 on the 16th of September. My mom was a German Jew, and my dad was a Swedish Christian. Although I grew up in Nazi Germany, I never considered the Nazi political party a threat to our country until my 15th birthday in 1935.

My best friend in grade school was a fellow Jew named Ezekiel Leven. We had known each other since the first day of the first grade of school in our hometown of Düsseldorf, Germany. Ezekiel changed my life. Of course, I didn't realize it at the time, but Zeke was to become a major influence in the way we thought about and survived the coming dark days of history known as the Holocaust.

Both Zeke's parents were Jewish. His mom, Mrs. Leven, was a dear lady who kept a wonderful home in an upscale section of Düsseldorf. His father, Dr. Leven, was a prominent thoracic surgeon at the University Hospital in our city.

After the Summer Olympics in 1936, the restrictions on Jews in Düsseldorf and throughout Germany became increasingly difficult for all Jewish families. There were book burnings of writings from prominent Jewish authors; Jewish physicians found it increasingly difficult to practice medicine at most hospitals in the Reich.

Even workers at my dad's plant, which had been consolidated into I. G. Farben, had experienced instances of anti-Semitic activity against some of their staff members. One of my dad's colleagues had been dragged out of his office on some pretense, beaten, and was never seen again. When my father went down to the local Gestapo office in Düsseldorf to inquire about his colleague, he was told to never come back and to never inquire about the individual again.

My dad did call back using an assumed name two weeks later. When he inquired about his colleague from Farben, there was no notice or record of him ever being arrested or held by the Gestapo. It was a very sad time for the worker's family.

I was quite large for my age. I could never seem to get enough to eat. Even at the end of a meal, I was always a little hungry. In the third grade, I was almost the size of my teachers. My best friend Zeke was a more normal size. Our friendship developed such rapport we could almost intuitively know what the other was thinking. This intuitive thinking was a great help when later in our lives we had to outthink some of the nastiest criminals in all recorded history – the Gestapo.

While I was growing up and attending school, Zeke and I became close friends. We spent most of our time in and out of school together studying, eating meals together, and attending school functions. We even went to each other's church and synagogue. Our parents also became friends. We would go on picnics together in the nearby woods.

On one occasion our families had traveled quite deep into the forest north of Düsseldorf and were enjoying a quiet picnic near a picturesque steam. It was late afternoon and the sun sent slanting shafts of light through the tall pines.

We heard some noises and stomping in the nearby brush and two wild boars came charging out of the brush at us from about thirty meters away. Everyone got up and headed quickly back to the car park. I just stood there amazed at the size and threatening noises of the grunting boars.

As one started to come at me in a loping charge, making what sounded like a high-pitched scream, I just stood my ground and gave it a swift kick on the snout as soon as it got near me. My kick rolled the boar over. The animal seemed surprised and discouraged; both the boars waddled off into the brush.

My parents warned me to never try that trick again. Dr. Leven said the boar can become enraged and quite dangerous. "It's best to leave them alone unless you are armed with a rifle. Your large size perhaps discouraged the animals."

While in grade school, many of my classmates would make fun of me in a somewhat lighthearted teasing way because I was a little oversized. My mom was a German Jew. Although quite tall and athletic, she married someone even taller. My dad was a Swede who grew to a little over six feet five inches. They had met at a conference my father's company had in Sweden just after the Great War ended in November 1919.

Mom was always concerned with the amount of food I could consume. She was forever trying to get me to eat more whole grains and less baked goods. My problem: I was almost continuously hungry. Often, I felt I could eat another meal, directly after eating lunch or dinner. If I skipped a meal or was late in eating at my normal time, I could get a little peckish. My mom was quite relieved when it seemed I had stopped growing at approximately six feet four and a half inches during my mid-teenage years.

Dad had worked for a life sciences company called Hoechst AG during the Great War. The company was trying to develop a medication that would be effective against a raging epidemic in Germany called the Spanish flu. This disease had killed millions of people worldwide and was crippling the work force in Germany. Mom and Dad had met at a company conference devoted to recent research for this viral disease in Stockholm, Sweden, in 1919.

I'm now approaching my centennial year, so I must be realistic about how much of this information I can furnish before I must go to the next phase of my life, or my memory fades completely.

On September 15th, 1935, the political leaders of my country passed what had become known as the Nuremberg Laws. At the time, the new laws meant nothing to me. My parents, however, reacted as if it were the end of Germany as they knew it. The laws were passed at the time I was celebrating my fifteenth birthday, on the sixteenth of September.

These new laws had two essential elements: The first element was the "Law for the Protection of German Blood and Honor." This law eliminated any possible marriages between Jews and Aryan Germans and forbade the employment of non-Jewish German women under the age of forty-five in Jewish households.

The second element of the Nuremberg Law was termed "The Reich Citizenship Law." This law stated that only Germans of related blood could be eligible for Reich citizenship. All others, meaning Jews and Romani people (gypsies), were to be classified as state subjects without citizenship rights.

The Reich politicians, in their "wisdom", decided for foreign policy concerns, to hold off on strict enforcement of these laws until after the Olympic Games, which were scheduled for Berlin in the summer of 1936. That was the summer I met the love of my life at a most unusual place: Hitler Youth Summer Camp.

My parents and teachers in my third year of secondary school urged me to attend Hitler Camp for two very different reasons. My teachers, especially my athletic coaches, felt I had some athletic potential because of my size and quickness, I was almost six feet four and a half inches tall and had very quick reflexes. My long legs were a real benefit for running school races in any type of track competition.

My parents, however, both thought it would be wise, if not mandatory, to attend Hitler Camp to help cover up my being Jewish. Even though I was quite tall, had sandy blond hair, and steel blue-grey eyes, they urged me to hide my strength and quickness by appearing awkward and letting others at the camp often win in any test of strength or endurance. In addition, they told me never to discuss religion or politics at camp.

My dad also cautioned me to never, even unintentionally, hurt any of my fellow campers in sporting or wrestling events. This was a curious request because the focus of my training at Hitler Camp was hand-to-hand combat: how to render the opposition helpless or dead. When I think about the training today, it was actually quite useful, as Zeke and I got older.

After the Summer Olympics in 1936, more and more signs of anti-Semitism sprouted up around our city of Düsseldorf and throughout Germany. It looked like Hitler could develop and extend his hatred and disrespect for Jews since the Olympics were over and the world's attention wasn't focused on Germany.

Ezekiel and I had to be very careful. Even walking around downtown Düsseldorf could be dangerous. Often, Jews were accosted, searched, and beaten by the Brownshirts and other unsavory elements of German society who were fervently anti-Semitic.

Fortunately, for me, Ezekiel was very smart. He had a sixth sense about dangerous situations; though not cowardly, he knew how to avoid trouble. He was determined, kind, and, introspective. I was proud and honored to have him as a friend. It was almost as if my outward physical strength matched the hidden steel of his inner strength.

2

Hitler* Youth Camp – Summer, 1936

Ilsa and I met while swimming at a lake adjacent to our Hitler Youth Camp. I had gone down to the lake with a fellow camper, Dieter, after a long hike with a heavy pack. We were hot, drenched with sweat, tired, and hungry. It was a cloudless, warm, mid-summer day. Our thinking at the time was a nice refreshing swim in the cool lake water would clean us up and refresh us for dinner. We really didn't consider or even think about any possible repercussions from the camp counselors. Why would we? Germany was a free country and this was summer camp!

We certainly were not searching for members of the opposite sex. As I recall, most of my thoughts at Hitler Camp revolved around getting enough sleep and getting enough food, during all of our exercise and combat training. I was almost continuously hungry. If I didn't eat enough, I sometimes would get a little overzealous in some of the competitions with other campers. My dad's warning would continually remind me: *"Be careful not to injure your fellow campers."*

---

* Adolf Hitler was Time Magazine's Man of the Year in 1938.

While swimming, Dieter and I were interrupted by one of the counselors from the nearby Women's Camp. When a woman came into the water fully clothed from her hiding place behind the bushes, Dieter became completely flustered by her beauty, backed out of the water, and ran back up to the camp dining hall. This was the first of several encounters I had with this very lovable and truly kind woman named Ilsa, who was a counselor at the female version of the Hitler Camp known as the Hitler Youth Camp for Young Women. Ilsa and I were clearly attracted to each other at this first meeting.

On our second "chance" meeting at the lake, Ilsa brought her friend Gretchen to meet me. At first, I was disappointed that I would not be able to spend any private time alone with Ilsa. However, her friend Gretchen seemed very comfortable meeting me.

In fact, both young women were openly direct in their sexual attraction to me. Soon, to my surprise, we three were sexually intimate. Gretchen, very forward, was not at all embarrassed about making love to me, while Ilsa helped me through any discomfort I had been feeling. These experiences were not at all what I expected at Hitler Camp while undergoing combat training.

If memory serves me correctly it was on our fourth or fifth meeting down by the lake in the summer of 1936 when I was in for a complete surprise. I had skipped dinner at the Hitler Camp dining hall in order to meet Ilsa and Gretchen at our private little beach for a "swim" in the late afternoon privacy of the lake.

When I think back on those days, whenever I thought about Ilsa, I completely lost my appetite for food. Although I never shared my love life at Hitler Camp with my parents, my mother probably would have been happy at least there was something limiting my food consumption! Mom was always concerned about the possibility I was eating too much. She was continually worried I might get too tall or overweight.

Since I had been with Ilsa and Gretchen on other occasions, I was getting to feel quite comfortable with both beautiful women making love to me. They were both very caring and loving young women. Although they were both a few years older than me, our age difference didn't seem to mean too much or bother them at all.

Even though I had explained to both women that I was only sixteen, because I was tall, they both probably felt I looked older. On this late afternoon, the sun was still quite high, but the birds were singing their evening songs in the meadow. The sky was bright blue with a few puffy clouds; the air was warm, and a slight breeze rustled the carpet of flowers in the meadow. As I approached the beach in my Hitler shorts and t-shirt, I found, to my complete surprise, three women swimming in the lake.

At first, I was a little surprised, even chagrined. I knew all three of them could not be there to see me. Well, I was wrong! As I approached the beach, Gretchen called up to me. "Hello, Jenz. Isn't it a perfect afternoon for a swim?"

Ilsa followed with, "Hi Jenz, it is wonderful to see you again. Come on in, the water feels terrific."

Both responses from my friends made me feel more comfortable; it looked like they were there to enjoy the cool lake water on a warm summer afternoon. Then they introduced Gretchen's friend.

Gretchen spoke right up, "Jenz, this is our dear friend, Erika."

Since all three girls were mostly submerged in the lake with only their heads above water, I really couldn't see any of them very well. As I kicked off my shoes and shirt and cautiously entered the water, all three of them stood up and walked toward me.

Ilsa volunteered, "Erika is one of the senior counselors at our camp and wanted to meet the handsome man that Gretchen and I have been meeting down here at the lake."

"Oh," was all I could say. My fear was that my voice might leave me entirely. I did manage to get out a few words.

"It... it's... a pleasure t...to... meet you, Erika." I was starting to stammer, so I decided to keep my mouth shut and not embarrass myself further.

She came over to me and shook my hand. I was relieved when she had formally greeted me... that is until she placed her other hand on my chest and said, "My friends told me you were a very good-looking man, but I had no idea." It seemed odd to me at the time that she hadn't let go of my hand.

Also, she had to be a little older than Gretchen and Ilsa, but equally as tall and beautiful. She had shiny blue eyes that seemed to dance when she talked. I found out later she was almost thirty years old! She then pulled me closer, and whispered in a low voice,

"It is **very** nice to meet you."

I looked around and thought about exiting the lake in a hurry, even though I hadn't even swum one stroke. I muttered something about being late for dinner, "if I didn't get back to the camp."

Then I stated more firmly,

"If I don't get back up to the camp for dinner, my counselors will write me up and it won't look good on my camp record."

That's when Erika re-affirmed in a low sexy voice, "Oh Jenz, you do not have to worry about being late for dinner, we are all counselors at the woman's camp, and I am the senior counselor-in-charge."

At this point, I kept trying to not think about how her hand on my chest was affecting my insides which had somehow started to tingle. I thought to myself, *I wonder if she always talks with such a low whispery voice.*

I started to slowly back out of the waist-deep water. I stopped when I realized that my privates were enlarging, and I didn't want anything showing. Ilsa could sense my unease and awkwardness and came over to reassure me.

"Oh, Jenz," Ilsa cooed. "Please do not be bashful, Erika doesn't mean to be too forward or aggressive. She is a wonderful leader and example for our Hitler Youth."

In my mind, I tried to justify how "being a wonderful leader and example for our Hitler Youth" had anything to do with my current predicament.

Ilsa put her hands around my neck pulled me down to her level and gave me a friendly kiss on my cheek.

"And besides," she whispered in a sexy voice in my ear, "we have agreed that Erika can be first this afternoon!"

"Oh, Ilsa," I started to protest. "I will embarrass myself."

That's when she put her hand down underwater and massaged my swelling privates. I was tingling all over with her kind touch.

As I got older, Ilsa's very presence in my life became magical for me.

Ilsa held one hand and Erika the other as they directed and pulled me out of the water toward the mossy glade. Gretchen reassured me,

"Jenz, we will all be very kind to you; please do not worry about embarrassment."

As they led me to the glade, my legs felt wooden and would only go where they were leading me. Erika spoke to me in her low sexy, whispery voice, "Jenz, let's sit down and relax. Please - tell me all about yourself."

I couldn't tell her anything. I could hardly talk. Words wouldn't come to my mouth. I was worried about my swelling privates and tried to look at anything else other than the three beautiful girls in their bathing suits surrounding me in that wooded glen. The moss felt cool and spongy to sit on.

That's when Gretchen said, "Jenz, let's get you out of your wet Hitler shorts." She and Ilsa pulled them off as they stretched out my legs; they slipped off without a struggle. I was powerless to resist. I couldn't even say anything except in a hoarse voice... "O... Okay."

Erika was rubbing my neck and back while whispering in a low voice in my ear, "Jenz, you handsome man, do you mind if I'm first?" She was kneeling behind me, but then put her arms around me and was rubbing and messaging my chest from behind.

At the time, I had no idea my chest was so sensitive to a woman's touch. I felt a fire glowing inside of me.

I tried to answer her, but all I could mouth out was, "Oh... Okay, ...but, I don't want to.... embarrass you."

What I meant was I felt foolish and didn't want to embarrass myself. Here I was completely naked on a mossy glade with three beautiful women surrounding me in their bathing suits.

Erika probably read my thoughts. She asked in that low voice, "Do you mind if I slip out of my wet bathing suit?"

She could probably tell that I was a little uncomfortable....and nervous. I really wanted to crawl under a rock - or run-up to the camp for dinner. I just couldn't move. *My chest and privates were tingling so much that I felt I should cover myself.*

She said, "Jenz, look at me."

I glanced toward her.

"Aren't I appealing to you?"

"Oh yes!" I replied quickly. *Her beauty was thrilling to me.*

"Have you ever been with an older woman?"

"I... I've only b... been with Ilsa and Gretchen," I stammered. "Although I'm tall, I'm only sixteen years."

"Please, you have to relax, and let me make sure you enjoy yourself." She whispered in that low sexy voice. *At this point, I wasn't sure if it was Erika's hands on my chest, or the low sexy voice — anyway, my insides were aflame.*

"Girls, help me make Jenz relax." She then gently pushed me down into the cool spongy moss and started kissing my stomach and gently pinching my chest with her thumb and forefinger.

Ilsa was kissing me on the lips and cheek while whispering in my ear, "Jenz, you have to learn we are just young women who are trying to help you relax."

I was anything but relaxed. My privates were swelling out of control, my entire body was tingling. I was hugging and kissing Ilsa while Erika was kissing my stomach. Nobody was touching my privates, but Gretchen had removed her bathing suit and was rubbing the inside of my thighs.

When I thought I couldn't take it anymore, Erika whispered, "Would you like to be inside me?"

"Y... Yesss..." was all I could say in a halting, hesitant voice.

With that, she kneeled across me and slid me into her. There was no weight on top of me. Just the wonderful feeling of gently pulling and pushing on my member. Gretchen had moved from my inner thighs to my testicles and was giving them a gentle massage with little light pinches.

When I started to thrust, all three of them said in unison, **"Don't move!"** Then Ilsa whispered, "Let us do the moving for you."

13

Erika was playing hard to get with me. As soon as I came close to exploding inside of her.... she would stop moving and told me, "Relax Jenz, you are doing just fine. You feel great but I want you to enjoy yourself!"

After a short time, she started moaning like a wounded animal, I thought I might be hurting her. I couldn't hold back any longer, my whole body started vibrating and shaking. I thrust once... twice... and exploded into Erika. She let out a long, low, sexy whimpering noise. I wasn't sure if she was uncomfortable or possibly hurt. I heard her girlfriends giggling as I must have blacked out.

I opened my eyes and Erika was looking directly into mine. Her eyes were dancing. She asked, "Did that help you unwind after a busy day?"

"It couldn't have been any busier," I mumbled. "But yes. I'm so relaxed, I doubt if I'll be able to move for a long time."

That's when Gretchen said, "Excellent, Jenz. I don't want you to move, let us massage you until you recover. Remember, I'm next!"

"Oh... Gretchen... I don't think I will be able to move until tomorrow."

"Jenz," Gretchen volunteered, "You just don't understand the recuperative powers of young men." She grabbed me around the neck and gave me a very long and luscious kiss. Her tongue was darting in and out of my mouth.

Ilsa told me, "Jenz, just relax. Let us massage your aching muscles." She proceeded to kiss me on the chest and pinch my nipples with little soft bites.

Erika was massaging my legs and kissing me on my inner thighs. She whispered in her low sultry voice, "Jenz, I know you will feel very good as I work my way up your legs."

Well, she was right. When she started licking my privates, my brain immediately snapped out of its lethargy. I began tingling all over. My privates started swelling uncontrollably. I started to get up, but Gretchen gently pushed me back into the moss.

Gretchen gave me another very loving kiss and whispered in my ear, "Darling, it's my turn, you can't go anywhere right now, just don't move."

As I started to protest, Gretchen got on top of me and slipped me inside of her and whispered, "Now that's much better, isn't it, Jenz?" I couldn't say anything but nodded my head slightly to say yes. She started very slow rhythmic movements on top of me whispering in my ear, "This is what our Führer wants for us."

Since Gretchen's head only came up to my chest, Ilsa was kissing me and whispered, "Jenz, please don't move, let us do all the moving for you. Erika was gently messaging my privates and occasionally squeezing ever so slightly.

Gretchen started a little fuller rhythmic movement on top of me. She increased her movements slightly. Every time I started to thrust, Ilsa would say, **"Stop!"**... and Gretchen would stop her movement and place her hand on my chest. As soon as I stopped thrusting, she would resume her rhythmic motion. It was pure torture for me.

After a few minutes of this torture, I got so excited I couldn't control my body any longer. I rolled her over, so she was on the cool moss with me on top of her. I kept thrusting until I exploded into my dear friend Gretchen. I collapsed and rolled off her. She was crying.

"Oh, Gretchen, I am so sorry. I don't know what possessed me. I lost complete control of my senses. I certainly didn't mean to hurt you!"

Gretchen shook her head, "Oh... Jenz, you didn't hurt me, these are tears of joy. You felt wonderful inside of me. Thank you for your loving-kindness."

I was completely out of breath. My heart was racing. I felt like I was floating on that cool bed of moss in the glade.

That's when Ilsa kneeled beside me and whispered in my ear, "I hope you haven't forgotten me, Darling."

"Dearest Ilsa," I mumbled through trembling lips. "I could never forget you or the kindness of your friends. I know our Führer has encouraged lovemaking with Aryan men, but are you sure this is what our God wants for us? *I had never learned this from the teachings in our church or Schule in the synagogue.* Although I love your friends, you are the only one for me - dear Ilsa, you have my heart!"

"Oh Jenz," She whispered in my ear. Her eyes were damp with tears. "You are the only one for me. I promise I will never share you with my girlfriends ever again. I want you, and you alone, forever."

She turned and asked her friends, "Girls, I will see you back at our camp. Jenz and I need to be alone to talk."

Gretchen and Erika slipped back into their bathing suits and left us in the glade.

Ilsa and I just held each other for the longest time. The sun was almost down; the heat had gone out of the day. The merlin birds sang in the distance. The flutter of nighthawk wings could be heard close to the glen.

For the first time that day I felt truly relaxed. Ilsa apologized for her girlfriends saying, "I'm sorry they acted so forward toward you; from now on, I want you for myself!" She then hugged me and gave me a very passionate kiss.

My insides started rumbling. I wasn't sure if my attraction for Ilsa was reigniting my passion or, if I was hungry since I had skipped dinner.

Ilsa answered that question for me by whispering, "Let's hold each other forever;" she then slipped me inside of her.

We just rocked back and forth and mumbled to each other. She asked if we could write to each other when the school year started. I told her I would like that. Hitler Camp was almost over. School was starting next month. I was getting sleepy.

Ilsa kissed me awake, she was dressed in her bathing suit. She got up and disappeared up the path that led to the women's Hitler Youth Camp. I got up and dressed very slowly and limped back to the dining hall at the Hitler Camp to see if there was any leftover supper. The only light came from a half moon and millions of stars; it was a memorable evening. I had a little trouble walking, but then started thinking that maybe my friends had taken advantage of me down by the lake. Even though I might have felt they had slightly abused me, I had a very big smile on my face, all the way up the hill.

A rather strange incident occurred during the last week of Hitler Camp. I was asked to go to our camp leader's office. His office was in a little cabin across from the dining hall area. Although nervous, I showed up there right after our afternoon calisthenics program.

"Good afternoon, Sergeant," was my greeting to the enlisted Wehrmacht officer. I gave the sergeant a half-hearted Hitler wave of a salute, and asked, "Why have you summoned me here this afternoon?"

"Come in, Jenz. You have done well here this summer. Have you considered a career in the Wehrmacht?"

"Not yet, Sergeant.

"I'm only sixteen years old and would like to study engineering at the Technical University in Berlin. If I can get a Wehrmacht deferral, I will start my engineering classes after next year."

"Oh," remarked the sergeant. "You want to be an engineer for the Reich?"

"I would very much enjoy working where I might do the most positive good for Germany," I said quickly.

The sergeant then surprised me with, "Jenz, you seem to be Schutzstaffel material. I am going to put you on a watch list for the SS. They could well be in touch with you while you are studying at the university."

"Thank you, Sergeant, is there anything more for me?"

"No, Ramsgrund, but congratulations. Very few are put forward to the SS from this camp. Your marksmanship and hand combat skills have been exemplary. I'm sure you are aware of the SS motto: 'Loyalty is my Honor.'

"You appear to be the Nordic racially pure type the SS is looking for to join their ranks. You should also understand the SS has to ensure you marry only a suitable woman, and do not dilute our racially superior code of honor."

"Yes, Sergeant. I am aware of the strict discipline in the Schutzstaffel." *My thought at the time was: I certainly did not want to dilute my race with anyone having anything to do with the Nazi Party.*

My most important lesson from my time at the Hitler Youth Camp was my enduring love for Ilsa. However, a most useful skill, I was later to learn in earnest, was my ease of ending a man's life. Gestapo members who were disrespectful to my Jewish friends quickly found out how efficiently I had learned killing skills at Hitler Youth Camp.

3

Incident on Königsalee 26, Bucherer's Jewelry Shop, Downtown Düsseldorf

Late in October 1938, Ezekiel and I had been in the central library in Düsseldorf studying for an exam in physics. Ezekiel and I always studied together for a couple of important reasons. Since Jews were not allowed in public schools in Germany at this time, Zeke stayed current in his studies by following the work I was doing in school. The second reason, which I am a little embarrassed and reluctant to admit, was Zeke always had a much firmer grasp than me on the concepts in mathematics and physics. He was always better at explaining how to solve difficult problems and issues; he was much more thorough than my calculus instructor.

Both of us had ambitions to be engineers for Germany. Our best hope for a premier education in engineering was in Berlin at the Technical University. Zeke's only recourse for attending any public university in Germany during those dark days of growing Nazi oppression was to become anything but Jewish. At this point in our studies, I had figured out how to make him Aryan.

Various decrees and the grave danger of personal harm from the Brownshirts made it impossible for Jews to be out on the streets at night in Germany. I had been able to get credentials for Ezekiel that made him Aryan. He had an Italian passport and driver's license telling the world he was Vitali Carapezza. This would allow us to study in the library and for Ezekiel to study with me at the Technical University in Berlin next year.

I hate to admit it, but Ezekiel was like a live-in tutor. Most of the concepts that I found confusing in physics or mathematics were easily explained to me by Zeke.

It was getting on toward ten in the evening, and the central library closed at eleven. My brain was starting to turn to mush, and I asked Zeke, "Have you had enough?" He said, "Sure, Jenz, but I can keep going if you can."

It was late enough for me, and we still had to catch a bus to our section of Düsseldorf. I suggested, "Let's get a snack on the way to the bus stop."

As we left the library, there was a surprising number of people milling about the city. Zeke quietly announced, "They look like Brownshirts; let's use some caution." The temperature had to be near freezing; the wind had a little bite to it.

As we walked toward the bus terminal, it looked like a few of the Brownshirt thugs were vandalizing some of the shops along Königsalee Street. I whispered to Zeke, "It looks like someone has broken into the old jewelry shop!"

Bucherer's,* an old-line jewelry shop with origins back in the 1880s, was halfway down Königsalee street. Flash-lamps danced

---

* Bucherer's Jewelry Shop survived the Nazis and has several locations world-wide. They specialize in fine jewelry and high-end watches.

inside around in the back of the store. The front door was slightly ajar.

There were several alarms going off on the street, but no authorities were coming. It was difficult to determine which shops the alarms were coming from.

I told Zeke, "The Brownshirts are probably intimidating for the local police."

As we approached Bucherer's, we could see movement inside the shop. In addition to the front door being ajar, someone was moving behind the counter.

Zeke whispered, "Maybe the owner is injured or in some sort of confrontation with the troublemakers."

Reluctantly, I pushed open the door. Two young Brownshirt thugs were behind the counter helping themselves to a tray of expensive watches.

"Hold it!" I yelled. **"Get out of here!"**

The larger of the two individuals brandished a knife and exclaimed, "What are you going to do, call the authorities?" He was tall, around five foot eleven inches, with a wiry build. His face was contorted into a sneer as he yelled at us. **"You get out if you know what's good for you!"** He was very angry with our interference with their criminal plans.

He came around the end of the counter, directly toward me, and held the knife in front of him in a threatening position about eighteen inches from my face. He knew the police would not interfere with the Brownshirts in the burglary of a Jewish-owned shop.

I tried to tell him, "If you leave now, you won't get hurt!"

"I'm the one holding the knife, you idiot!"

I thought to myself, he does present a good argument, but then I thought, he has no idea how fast my hand can move – especially in the dim light.

I quickly grabbed his knife hand at the wrist, and then pulled and twisted his arm at the elbow. I heard an audible click! I wasn't sure if I had broken his arm or just dislocated his elbow. His knife bounced harmlessly off the floor.

"Aaaa!" he bellowed. "You broke my arm!"

His companion was shorter, probably around five feet seven inches, but slightly overweight; he tried to throw a punch at my face. I grabbed his fist as it was flying at my head and gave it a sharp twist backward.

Ow! He bellowed. My wrist!

Snap!

I heard the wrist bones break. Both thieves were disabled. They held their broken arms with their good arms while moaning curses and complaints as they fled the store.

Zeke and I pulled the door shut and walked out into the frigid evening. We were met by an icy blast of wind as it came down Königsalee Street. No one seemed to pay any attention to us, and the goons were nowhere in sight.

As we neared the bus station, there was a distinct lack of people at the bus station on a bitter-cold late fall evening. There were no police anywhere in sight, only the distant blaring sounds of the multiple alarms going off in the frigid air.

My Introduction to the SS

It was almost two years later, while a student at the Technical University of Berlin, when I received a note from the SS informing me of an appointment at their headquarters the next day. The note made my roommate very nervous.

Vitali Carapezza and I had been boyhood friends since the first day of school in Düsseldorf. Vitali's real name was Ezekiel Leven. He was a fellow Jew, and we were life-long friends.

Ezekiel's name change helped to cover up his Jewish heritage. Having an Italian last name and credentials allowed him to attend the Technical University in Berlin. Even though we were both Jews, I looked Aryan because although my mom was Jewish, my dad was Swedish. I used my dad's last name: Ramsgrund.

Ezekiel had developed and even improved his Italian accent and could use it whenever he had a need for it. His apprehension was evident because he asked, "Are you actually going into the SS Headquarters for this appointment?"

"I'm not sure I have a lot of choices, Ezekiel. Not showing up could be even more dangerous for both of us. I will dress up and look quite presentable and try to remember my military bearing from Hitler Camp. *Although we had eliminated several members of the Gestapo over the past two years, I don't think the Gestapo or the SS were aware of who we were.*

"Do try not to think about or dwell on the damage we have done to the Gestapo over the past year, Zeke. Every member of the Gestapo we have eliminated was a traitor to a free and noble Germany. Furthermore, before they were members of the secret Gestapo police force, they were probably common criminals.

"Ever since my discussion with the sergeant at the end of my summer at Hitler Camp I had been reading a bit about the SS or Schutzstaffel and its leaders."

"Have you been able to find anything positive to say about the SS?" asked Ezekiel.

"Not really," was my succinct answer. "Perhaps the SS is slightly less thuggish than the Brownshirts or Gestapo. Although I'm not sure if 'less thuggish' is a very positive trait. Originally, the SS started out as an elite guard for our Führer, but they seem to have grown into a group of enforcers for Herr Hitler, Himmler, and the rest of the dastardly scoundrels running our government.

"The SS had an interesting and checkered beginning to their history, Ezekiel. It was formed in the early 1920s to originally counter the violent and bloody actions of the Brownshirt movement. The organization initially seemed like a glorified bodyguard detail for our Führer. Hitler created the SS and had its members dress in distinctly black uniforms modeled after the Italian Fascists' uniforms.

"The Gestapo and the SS share space in a building at No. 8 Prinz Albrecht Strasse near the center of Berlin. This address brings terror to the hearts and minds of most God-fearing Berliners.

There has been talk of citizens being harshly questioned and even tortured in the basement chambers.

"Ezekiel, the biggest problem is the Brownshirts. Hermann Göring* has control over these thugs and has prohibited the local police from interfering with them when they are out on the streets.

"It is getting dangerous for Jews to be out after dark, so we have to be very cautious. We cannot afford to be stopped and searched by these criminals. Let's go directly to the bus stop, get away from the center of town, and get back to our apartment to plan how to outwit these cowards. I will travel to the center of Berlin tomorrow to meet with the SS people and find out what they want."

It was toward the end of my second year of engineering school when I received orders to report for SS training at one of the many labor camps sprouting up in Germany. Since the SS was charged with overseeing and guarding the labor or concentration camps throughout the country, my first assignment led me to a camp where the prisoners were treated with utmost cruelty. The Dachau labor camp was originally built in and around an old munition factory by Heinrich Himmler in 1933. It took me exactly 24 hours to realize I could never live with myself pretending to be part of the SS organization at this or any of the labor camps.

Before my paperwork had been processed, I wrote a letter to the head SS office in Berlin asking if my engineering skills could

---

* Hermann Wilhelm Göring as Commander-in-Chief of the *Luftwaffe* rose to become the second most powerful man in Nazi Germany. His power began to wane when his air force could not prevent the bombing of German cities by Allied bombers, and he could not adequately re-supply the *Wehrmacht* at Stalingrad. He died from self-ingestion of cyanide the day before he was to be hanged by the Nuremberg Court on the 15th of October 1946.

be better utilized by the Reich anywhere in the country. Within a week the camp commander summoned me to his office.

"Lieutenant Ramsgrund," he began in a harsh and quite stern voice, but then calmed down, "it appears the powers to be at SS headquarters have decided to use your skills elsewhere. Although I am not accustomed to being overridden in such matters, I am holding orders in my hand for you to be transferred to a Wehrmacht base somewhere in northern Germany. I was unaware we even had a Wehrmacht base in such a remote location, and I have no idea why we have a facility in such a desolate area. However, these orders are countersigned by Himmler's deputy and carry the full weight of our Führer.

"You are to report in a little over a week. You may stay in your quarters here until you arrange for transportation to someplace called Peenemünde."

"Oh! Thank you, Herr Commandant, but I will leave immediately. The week will allow me to visit family and perhaps arrive at my new duty station early."

The corpulent base commander struggled to stand but returned my Hitler salute. "As you wish, Lieutenant. Good luck with your new assignment in the wilderness." He then almost collapsed as he slumped back down into his chair.

My Hitler salute had my best effort at almost a touch of enthusiasm. Even though I was unaware of what might await me at the next duty station, it had to be better than this prison of horrors. I was thrilled to be going almost anywhere - especially to a place where I might be able to utilize my engineering skills.

I spent the next week fending off the Gestapo and visiting my family and the love of my life, Ilsa. In addition, it took me a little time to figure out the location and transportation to the Wehrmacht base at Peenemünde.

I had some satisfaction eliminating a Gestapo headquarters building in Hamburg, and hopefully throwing the Gestapo off my parents' trail. I was able to make the destruction of the Gestapo building look like an accidental gas explosion. It was almost as if the Gestapo had little to do but ferret out Jews, honest businessmen, or anyone who disagreed with the Nazi goals of pure German Aryan blood.

My knowledge of the German Secret State Police or Gestapo had been limited. I inherently knew they were an enemy to law-abiding Germans, but I had no realization of the depths of their depravity.

5

Peenemünde, The Wehrmacht Secret Research Center

My trip to Peenemünde was interrupted by the Gestapo on two occasions, but fortunately, I was able to get to my duty station on time. It didn't take me long to get familiar with the important work being done at this remote army base. It was the research center for the development of secret missile weapons. Once I saw some of the problems the engineers at this army base were trying to solve, I discussed with Herr Frits Gosslau,* the chief engineer of the V-I programs, the possibility of bringing on another aeronautical engineer to help with problems with the guidance system.

"Herr Gosslau, I had an acquaintance at the Technical University in Berlin who might be able to be of service to the Reich with this particular problem."

---

* Fritz Gosslau graduated with a doctorate from the Technical University in Berlin in 1926. His Ph.D. study was on cooling piston-driven aircraft. He was the principal engineer who developed the V-I flying bomb. The world's first guided missile. After the war, he continued to develop improvements in piston engines. He died in Bavaria in 1965 at age 67.

"What are you suggesting, Lieutenant?"

"I had a classmate at the Technical University who is proficient in calculus and physics; he is studying aeronautical engineering. One of his areas of expertise is guidance systems for aircraft."

I wanted to whet the chief engineer's curiosity, but I had to be careful not to appear overly enthusiastic.

"Just who is this individual, Lieutenant Ramsgrund?"

"His name is Vitali Carapezza. He is originally from Italy but speaks fluent German. He is one of the top students in physics at the university."

"Give me the spelling of his name and the name of his department head. I will have him checked out."

I felt Vitali would check out fine if it wasn't the Gestapo doing the checking.

"Yes, Sir! I will write his contact information on an internal memo for you later this morning."

A few days later, Dr. Gosslau came to me and gave me orders to go and get Vitali to join the engineers at the secret rocket research center. Although both of us were Jews, our cover stories were strong, as long as no one looked too closely into our past. I knew Vitali would be nervous, but I figured we would both be safer hiding in the confines of the secret army base.

Two weeks later, I brought Ezekiel into the base at Peenemünde. He had to go through indoctrination, swear allegiance to our Führer, and learn how to wear a Wehrmacht sergeant's uniform.

"I feel really uncomfortable in this uniform, Jenz." Ezekiel confided in me at dinner the next evening.

My reply was rather cryptic. "Can you think of a better disguise to protect our Jewishness? And remember, Vitali, you are not a Jew anymore. You are an Italian citizen working for the Reich."

"Well, you make a good point, Jenz. It may save us from some anti-Semitic reactions from the Brownshirts."

The following weeks and months Ezekiel and I did everything we could think of to slow down the development of the V-I and V-II missile systems. We had to be very careful using complex mathematical formulae and physics to come up with ways of altering the guidance systems for the V-I and V-II rocket systems. We could not afford to be discovered.

The most basic alterations of the fuel for the V-I and the fin guidance system for the V-II seem to be the least detectable and least dangerous methods of slowing down the development and effectiveness of both missiles.

One afternoon, head of the Army Research Center, Dr. Walter Dornberger, came and spoke to the engineers. He expressed specific concerns about the Jewish workers who were building, testing, and improving the V-I and V-II missile systems.

At first, Ezekiel and I thought the worst. Had our subterfuge been discovered? Had anyone discovered we were actually Jewish?

Fortunately, no. Dr. Dornberger was very concerned about the health of his Jewish workers.

"I am speaking to you this afternoon about an issue of great concern," the general began.

"This secret facility on the North Sea has been in operation for the past four years. As you know, in addition to the approximately two hundred scientists and engineers, we employ almost three hundred laborers from the labor camps in Germany and the Eastern Territories. Many of these prisoners are highly skilled. We have electrical engineers, electricians, clockmakers, jewelers, finished carpenters, and metal workers.

"These prisoners are an essential part of the testing, assembly, and shipping of these missiles to our field officers. During our struggle with the Allies, these missiles may gain increasing importance as weapons."

One of the Air Force officers raised his hand. "Is there a problem with these prisoners, perhaps the discipline is too lax?"

"No!" replied General Dornberger. "The problem is they are dying at an alarming rate; almost as soon as they arrive, they start getting sick. I have assured Reichsführer Himmler we are not mistreating these prisoners. They are receiving proper discipline and berthing, and they eat essentially the same diet as our enlisted soldiers.

"They are dying from systemic or infectious diseases or exhaustion. Some of them collapse on the assembly lines; some even the first week they are here. Others cannot even lift parts as small as 10 kilograms."

"Are they infected when they arrive at our base?" asked one of the scientists.

"The Reichsführer has assured me the prisoners are reliable and healthy when they leave the camps. He has given me a list of the camps we draw from and orders for two of our staff to visit any of these camps with only one stipulation: we must maintain absolute secrecy of anything we see or hear at any of the labor camps. Violation of this order is to be met with the most severe punishment: an immediate firing squad.

I raised my hand to ask a question. I was rather tentative about my question after the mention of the firing squad.

"Yes, Lieutenant, what is your question?"

"Approximately, how many of these camps are in our country and the conquered territories?"

"Herr Himmler has assured me there are over a thousand labor camps with six of them designated as extermination camps. He claims we should be able to get talented prisoners from any of them."

This was the first I had heard of 'extermination' camps and a hush fell over the room. Evidently, many of the other scientists and officers hadn't heard of these camps either.

"Are any of these facilities close to our research center here at Peenemünde?" I asked. *The general seemed relieved someone would ask a question after the defining silence after the word 'extermination' was used.*

"Let's see," answered the general while looking at the map Himmler had provided.

"Yes. It looks like Treblinka isn't too far. It is located about 65 kilometers northeast of Warsaw. From what I understand, many of the Polish Jews from the Warsaw Ghetto are imprisoned there. Herr Himmler has explained to me the method of removing Jews from our country and the conquered territories is called 'Operation Reinhard.'* This operation, as explained to me, is designed to remove Jews from German lands and re-locate them to the East in conquered areas of Russia for farm work.

"As you all know we are very busy here at the research center and under a lot of political pressure from Reichsführer Himmler and our Fürher to perfect these weapons. In addition, it is important we produce them in record numbers for the defense of the Fatherland.

---

* "Operation Reinhard" was named after an infamous criminal Nazi, Reinhard Heydrich. He was assassinated by the Czech underground in May 1942. Heydrich was one of the cruelest Nazis in WW II. This Nazi convened the "Wannsee Conference" near Berlin on January 20th, 1942. On this date, Heydrich informed all the relevant officers in Nazi Germany of the "Final Solution of the Jewish Question" as decided by Hitler: the deportation, murder, and extermination of all the Jews in Germany and the Conquered Territories.

"Recent developments include testing a missile for underwater launch and from the surface by submarines. In addition, we have on the drawing boards and in the design stage the A-4 missile capable of traveling to targets in Russia, Japan, and even the United States, if necessary.

"If there are no further questions, I would like to ask for volunteers for a small team of officers to go to a few of these internment camps to find out why our Jewish laborers are not up to the task of building our missiles."

My hand slowly went up when I saw no one else volunteering.

"Sir," I started reluctantly. "Since I have been to both Dachau and Auschwitz and have seen how the SS run their labor camps, I will volunteer and write up a report. However, I may need at least one other person to accompany me in order to find the facts about our laborers. I would need orders allowing freedom of movement and access to the camp doctors in order to have accurate information. I would also need to have free access to the commandant of each labor camp I would visit."

"Thank you, Lieutenant. We can spare perhaps one other person.

"While you are inspecting the labor camps, I am ordering you to recruit from the camps you visit a few specialists from a list I will entrust to you before you depart. We will need at least another ninety to one hundred fifty men or women in order to get this research center up to optimum production. After development and testing, we will require another two or three thousand workers to produce these weapons in the quantities our Führer requires.

"I will produce a list of the workers we will need for now. You will have your orders within two days."

"Thank you, General."

6

Our Trip to Treblinka

Thankfully, Zeke had volunteered to accompany me on the inspection of the labor camps in Poland. He was the only person I could truly trust in the entire Peenemünde secret Army facility. Although both of us were continually worried about being discovered as Jews, we felt our bold impersonation of the SS and Wehrmacht were our best cover. Zeke and I discussed the trauma we might experience while visiting these labor or concentration camps.

"Zeke, are you sure you will be okay visiting these appalling and disgusting prisons?"

"I'm sure I would like to know where my parents wound up. I have no illusions as to the extent of the cruelty the Nazis will exhibit toward decent Germans."

The next week the Luftwaffe provided us with a flight to Warsaw. Although our orders were thoroughly checked, a carbon copy was taken when we landed at the Warsaw-Okecie Airdrome. It was a routine flight and took only about two and a half hours. Except for the exceptional loudness of the aircraft engines, it seemed like a routine flight.

A car and SS driver, Lance Corporal Heine, met us at the plane. His second sleeve insignia indicated he had over six years of service. His uniform was crisp and well-fitted. Although the answers to our questions were glib and short, he seemed polite with good military bearing. He mentioned it would take approximately ninety minutes for the drive to the Treblinka camp.

It was a beautiful warm late spring day, so we rode with the windows down.

"Corporal," I asked very politely, "How is the progress going in the ghetto?"

Although my question was innocent enough, it prompted a rather contemptuous retort. I knew our forces were trying to remove all the Jews from the part of Warsaw known as the Jewish Ghetto.

"Lieutenant, we should have the rest of the Jew vermin cleaned out by the fall. Our forces have the ghetto surrounded and we have erected a sturdy wall around the entire area. It is just a question of starving them out or carting them off to Treblinka."

Zeke and I just looked at each other. The blood was draining from our faces. My first reaction was anger, but I caught myself and replied, "Excellent, Corporal. Where are the detainees being held?"

"The ones who are strong and can be of value to the Reich are kept at the Treblinka Camp for work for a limited amount of time. All the rest are euthanized immediately. Those who are chosen to work usually are euthanized in three to four months."

We rode in silence for a while. Zeke finally spoke up. "How are the detainees being killed, Corporal?"

"I think many of them are dead before they even leave the transports, Sargent. Several hundred Jews, including women, children, and very old people are packed into each cattle-transport

35

car on the train. Often, they are left at the railroad siding at Treblinka without food or water for a full day or more. There is very little fresh air and the bodies rot and mix with the fecal material and urine since there are no bathroom facilities on the transports."

I carefully worded my next question to avoid conflict of any kind. "Corporal, what happens to the able-bodied Jews after they leave the transports?"

"Oh," replied Heine, "Some of them are even reluctant to step onto the platform and have to be whipped, beaten, and yelled at by the guards. There is usually a large barking dog present to help add to and create confusion and panic. This helps hurry the Jewish vermin to the selection area. The whole idea is to instill a feeling of dread and terror into the prisoners."

"What is the purpose of creating all the confusion and consternation?" asked Zeke.

"Compliance!" remarked the Corporal. "All the Ghetto dwellers have been informed to leave the ghetto and board the trains in order to transport them to the east for farm work. They are told to bring only what they can carry."

"So, we are basically lying to them?" questioned Zeke.

"Of course," emphasized the Corporal. "If the vermin knew they were going to their death, they might rebel and be even more difficult to root out of their homes. In addition, it might cause interruptions in the orderly method of euthanizing them and ridding them from the Reich."

"Do some of them complain or resist?" I asked in a nonchalant manner.

"Not usually, Lieutenant. If they do, they are whipped by the Ukrainian Guards. The dogs are trained to bark and bite the Jews. The transportees are immediately herded into the selection area."

"The dogs are actually trained to bite the Jews?" was Zeke's innocent question.

"Oh, yes!" replied the Corporal. The deputy commandant of the camp, SS Oberscharführer Kurt Franz, has a personal pet, a rather ferocious hound named Bari. He is trained to lunge and bite the Jews in their genitals. He is very effective.

"In addition, there are two large signs to complete the deception. The first is as the prisoners enter the camp. The first sign proclaims in Polish and German:"

"Jews of Warsaw, Attention!

You are in a transit camp, from which you will be sent to a Labor Camp. In order to avoid epidemics, you must present your clothing and belongings for immediate disinfection. Gold, money, foreign currency, and jewelry should be deposited with the cashiers in return for a receipt. They will be returned to you later when you present the receipt. Bodily cleanliness requires that everyone bathes before continuing the journey."

"Keep in mind Lieutenant, the entire entry area to the camp is neat and clean with flower gardens and often music to greet and calm the unwary deportees.

"The women and children are immediately sent to the undressing barrack on the left, and the men are sent to the undressing barrack on the right. They must deposit all their valuables with the cashier at the end of the shed."

"Do the Jews willingly go into the undressing barracks?" asked Zeke.

"Yes, Sargent, they usually do. If they hesitate, they are whipped or beaten with a metal bar or cudgel."

"It seems altogether harsh and inhumane," was all I could say.

"Oh, no, Lieutenant. You will see how well organized and orderly the entire process is handled. There is a large sign at the end of the barracks in Polish which completes the deception:

"Attention!

Fold all your clothes. Everything you have brought with you must be left where you undress except for money, valuables, documents, and shoes. Hold your money and valuables until they are collected at the window. Tie your shoes together, and leave them in the places marked. You must come to the baths and vapor room entirely nude."

I then asked a question about the willingness of the Jews to enter the gas chambers.

"Corporal, do the Jews always just walk into the death chambers without hesitation?"

"Lieutenant, I have never been allowed into the camp to witness any of the actual procedures. All my information is second-hand from escapees or SS Death Head officers from the different camps.

"From what I understand, if the Jews show any hesitation they are whipped, or beaten with iron bars. If the men try to avoid entering the gas chambers, they are summarily shot dead on the spot."

"Corporal, this is a little concerning for me and my sergeant. We had hoped to obtain some healthy, strong men and women workers for our facility at the Army Research Center."

"What are you working on at the facility, Lieutenant?"

"Most of the work is in conjunction with our war effort. But we require a reliable and healthy workforce."

"Well, shortly, you and your sergeant will be able to see the prisoners for yourselves. We are approaching the first guard station for entrance to the Treblinka camp. I should tell you, most of the guards are Ukrainian, and they have a mean and nasty disposition. If they are at all lax or forgetful in any of their duties, they are immediately shot."

As we slowed for the guard station, the guard unshouldered his rifle and aimed it in our direction until he saw our uniforms. I showed him a copy of our orders and he waved us through.

The guard did warn us to approach the entrance with caution. "Sir, there have been some difficulties with the last transport which arrived this morning. Many of the men resisted going into the undressing barracks and had to be shot. Unfortunately, some of the women and children were also killed in the melee."

Zeke shot me a sideways glance. I thought to myself, what sort of hellhole are we about to enter. I asked the driver, "Corporal, I realize the Reich has many of these labor camps, is Treblinka any different from the others?"

"Well, yes. Treblinka has been set up as an extermination camp to rid the Jews from our precious country and the conquered territories. We indeed have three of these extermination facilities, although I believe Treblinka is the largest."

"What are the others, Corporal?"

"The SS has set up Death Camps at Belzec in the south near the town of Lublin; Sobibor in the forest near the village of Sobibor; in addition to here at Treblinka.

"You have to understand, Lieutenant, when we came to liberate Poland in September 1939, there were over 400,000 Jews living Warsaw alone. Getting rid of the Bolshevik criminal Jew is a big job for our leaders in the Wehrmacht. Think about how many Jews live in all the small villages and towns throughout Poland and the new territories. We have had to organize and utilize the local police to help round up all these criminals."

It was all Zeke and I could do to prevent ourselves from breaking down and showing our outrage. I gave Ezekiel a sideward glance and squeezed his arm for reassurance. Both of us were going to need to stay strong for this visit.

Entering Hell on Earth

The railroad depot at the gate to Treblinka was awash with blood and bodies. I told the driver to wait for the sergeant and me to return. I took the car keys to ensure his loyalty and our ride back to Warsaw. This was not the place for two Jews in German uniforms to be discovered.

It was late morning, and the warm sun was beating down on the railroad platform congealing the blood and gore. The sight on the platform turned my stomach. I was surprised both of us could keep from retching.

There was a company of slave laborers carting off the bodies and washing down the platform with buckets of water. I approached the guard who looked like he was in charge. He was wearing a Ukrainian Army uniform. He was barking orders and held a whip in his right hand. He had been whipping one of the prisoners when I approached him.

I held up my hand and motioned for him to stop. **"Guard,"** I said with some authority in my voice. **"What is going on here? You know these procedures are supposed to go smoothly."**

Many of the laborers had blue armbands, designating them as a Platform Workers *(Bahnhofkommando)*. These were trusted prisoners overseen by the SS. Their duty was to empty and clean the transport cars as quickly as possible and transfer the transportees to the SS man in charge.

"Yes, Lieutenant." The guard snapped to attention. "I understand. But many of the men on the transport wouldn't go quietly into the camp's selection area and had to be shot. Unfortunately, some of the women and children were killed or wounded in the disturbance."

The SS officer in charge of the prisoner disembarkation process came over to Ezekiel and me and introduced himself as *SS Oberscharführer* Kurt Bolender.*

"All of us here at Treblinka are concerned, Lieutenant, many of the Jews and other undesirables are learning this camp is not a transit camp but the end of the line for them – a death camp.

"What can I do for you, Lieutenant?"

"We are here to see the Commandant. I have orders from Reichführer Himmler." I opened the packet which displayed our orders.

---

* Oberscharführer Kurt Bolender joined the SS Totenkopfstandarte, (Death's Head) unit in 1939. His initial position was in the euthanasia program where he excelled at his duties. He was known for throwing babies, children, and the sick directly from the freight transports into the trolly with a load that went straight to the Lazarett (infirmary), where they were immediately shot or thrown into pits to be cremated. In 1961 he was recognized while working as a doorman, with false identity papers, at a German nightclub. In December 1965, before the conclusion of his trial in Hagen, West Germany, Bolender committed suicide by hanging himself in his jail cell.

The officer glanced at them and saluted with his response. "Yes, Sir. Please follow me."

"Just a moment, Officer. I need to dismiss our driver."

I motioned for Ezekiel to follow me to the automobile. When we were away from the SS Officer, but not too close to the car, I leaned close to Zeke and cautioned him: "Zeke, this could be much worse than we ever imagined. We must be very cautious not to outwardly display any emotions. Be careful of facial expressions or any outward reactions to the horrors we may encounter."

"I hear you, Jenz. I already feel like being sick to my stomach."

"Driver," I announced as I handed the Corporal the keys. "Thanks for the ride, we will find our own way back to Warsaw."

Zeke and I followed the officer into the camp.

As we entered the facility, both Zeke and I were impressed with the cleanliness of the walkways which were bordered with flowering plants. We both noticed an odor we couldn't quite place. It might have been a cleaning solution or a disinfectant.

"Officer, what is that odor?"

"I'm used to it, so I don't really smell it anymore. It could be a combination of the vapors from the gas houses or the incineration of the corpses."

"Oh," I asked naively, "do you have a lot of fatalities at this facility?"

Officer Bolender proudly answered, "Close to one hundred percent! There is no time off for good behavior." His last statement was said with a bit of a chuckle.

"However, some of the stronger or more fortunate prisoners are allowed to function on work details or in the kitchen for a short period of time."

As we walked into the camp there were several men sweeping the area the officer called "the square." It was surrounded by barbed wire.

"Here is the location for the separation to take place."

"What happens here?" I asked.

"Well, let me show you to the Commandant's office. You will meet our deputy commander SS Oberscharführer Kurt Franz. Our Commanding Office SS Oberscharführer Franz Stangl is an expert in euthanasia but is away at another camp at the moment."

Officer Bolender knocked and walked into a plain stripped-down office just inside the gate. He introduced us to the deputy commanding officer, Kurt Franz.

The deputy commanding officer was nothing like I had pictured. He was cordial to Zeke and deferential to me. He had an almost cherub-like face and spoke like a well-educated officer. He was physically in excellent shape – not overweight or slovenly.

"Good morning, gentlemen. What can I do for you on this beautiful day?"

"Hello, commandant. We have orders from Herr Himmler to locate and procure suitable workers for our Army Research Center in northern Germany."

I displayed our orders on his desk for him to read.

After reading our orders without comment, he exclaimed.

"Excellent, Lieutenant! You are welcome to view all parts of our operation here. I think you will find it very efficient. We had a transport come in about an hour ago and the deportees have undergone separation and are now in the undressing centers. Lieutenant Bolender will show you whatever you need to see.

"Unfortunately, some of the deportees were uncooperative and had to be shot, but for the most part everything is back to normal now."

"How," I asked, "did you secure the cooperation of the deportees?"

"The Ukrainian guards usually shoot the ringleaders in the head. The rest usually submit to beating with the iron bars or the whipping. My hound, Bari here, often helps by barking and biting the Jews in the genitals." A brief smile spread across his baby-like face.

My goodness, I thought, that hound is the size of a small cow. "Lieutenant Bolender, please show our guests our efficient method of liquidation after the deportees enter the undressing sheds."

"Yes, Sir!

"Right this way, gentlemen."

We walked right into the women's undressing shed. There was some weeping and general confusion as the women were trying to undress and reassure their crying children. Many of the women were asking questions about their circumstances but were being yelled at by the shockingly belligerent female guards.

A male Ukrainian guard was shouting at the women and children to fold their clothes neatly so they could be disinfected.

"Please keep your valuables or money. You may turn them in to the cashier and get a receipt at the end of the shed," he bellowed.

There were several hundred women and children in the over-crowded undressing area. Because of my size, I might have been intimidating to many of the women and children. They seemed to duck out of the way as Zeke and I followed Officer Bolender through the shed. We tried to keep our eyes looking down. Many of the women were quite beautiful.

One of the young women grabbed Zeke by the arm and asked, "What is happening to us? Are we already lost?"

A woman guard stepped out of the shadows and began whipping the young girl unmercifully.

The guard yelled, **"Stop bothering the sergeant, prisoner!"**

Zeke grabbed the whip and yanked it from the guard's hand, **"I will take care of disciplining the prisoner, guard."**

Zeke threw the whip down and turned to the female prisoner and helped her off the floor. He grabbed her under the left arm and as he pulled her gently to her feet he whispered, "Please stay strong young miss I'm afraid all Germany is lost. Please follow the others to the next station."

I could tell Zeke was shaken by the guard whipping the beautiful young woman. There was a cut where the whip had been slashed across her back. But to his credit, the expression on his face remained stoic and unchanged.

Zeke and I followed Officer Bolender to the next building. About twenty male prison workers were lined up behind several tables.

"These are the Gold Jews *(GoldJuden)*," announced Officer Bolender. "They are mostly former jewelers, watchmakers or bank clerks. They are here to sort the money, jewelry, or any valuables they can steal from the prisoners.

"Of course, when their work is finished and the transports stop coming from Warsaw, they will all be killed."

"Why is that?" offered Zeke.

Bolender shot back, "Everything we do here at this death camp is very secretive. We cannot allow everyday Germans, or the rest of the world to know what is going on here. We are liquidating all the vermin and Jews from the conquered territories very efficiently. You must understand, Sergeant, this is a huge, and very important undertaking."

There were several hundred women and children in this crowded room. Zeke asked, "Why are some of the women lying on the tables?"

"Oh." Replied Bolender, in a very matter-of-fact tone, "These *GoldJuden* are doing cavity searches including their genitalia for hidden valuables."

"These searches seem pretty thorough," remarked Zeke.

"You have no idea!" Bolender shot back. "Wait until you view the next couple of stations. Some of these Jews are very inventive and sneaky."

Zeke just shook his head.

I gave him a sharp look and whispered, "Zeke, remember, even though all this is overwhelming, we cannot afford to show any emotion. Just remember everything we see here today. Our first-hand visit could be important for future generations of law-abiding and decent Germans."

Zeke nodded his understanding as we walked into the next building.

This building contained almost twenty men with scissors. These men *(Friseurs)* were in the process of cutting off the women's hair.

I asked Officer Bolender, "Why is it necessary to cut off the women's hair?"

The men were cutting off the beautiful hair of all the women, including the children, and tossing the hair into large suitcases.

"This has been routine in all the camps since earlier this summer," replied Bolender. "The women are told it is to ensure the effectiveness of our de-lousing program before they are transported to their next duty in the East."

"What would the Reich possibly do with this much hair?" asked Zeke.

"After the hair is cleaned," Bolender offered, "It is threaded on bobbins and converted into industrial felt. The felt product is made into slippers for submarine crews and felt stockings for the Reichsbahn. Some of the human hair is also used as upholstery for furniture."

There was a lot of screaming and crying in the building. It was truly heartbreaking to see people so utterly distressed. *I thought, if Zeke doesn't lose control, I surely would.*

Officer Bolender bragged, "All this screaming and confusion will be over shortly. As soon as this group enters the tube, there is no escape. The tube runs directly to the gas chambers. This group will all be dead in 30 minutes."

It was then I realized the hideous suffering of the victims on the journeys in the stinking, over crowded cattle cars was nothing compared to the horrors on arrival at the Treblinka camp.

8

Saving a Few from the Gas Chambers

Zeke took me aside as the first of the nude women were being herded and whipped to enter the tube leading to the gas chambers.

He whispered, "Couldn't some of these women be of use to the general at Peenemünde? Perhaps some of them could work in the kitchens, do administrative work, assemble the rockets, or be part of a cleaning crew? They could be valuable to the Reich."

I brought Officer Bolender over after nodding my approval to Zeke. I had to talk in a loud voice to be heard over the cries, screaming, and general confusion.

"Sir," I began. "Some of these women might be useful at our research facility on Germany's north coast. Our orders from Herr Himmler read that we may transport some of the prisoners found at these camps back to Peenemünde for use to the Reich."

"Take your pick, Lieutenant! Be quick about it. Once they enter the tube, I cannot save them."

Zeke looked at me and asked, "How are we supposed to pick out those who will live?"

"Here, put my SS uniform jacket over the young woman you picked up off the floor and take the next five people in line and bring them over to me."

"What if they have children with them?" queried Zeke.

"Bring them along, of course." I talked loud enough so Officer Bolender would know exactly what we were doing.

Zeke took my coat with the SS designations on the collar and approached the totally nude woman who had been whipped and just had her hair cut off. She was crying softly and speaking to the female child behind her.

"What is your name, Miss?"

"I am called A…Adiya." She was startled by the attention from the Wehrmacht sergeant amid all the confusing yelling.

"Oh," Zeke replied, "God's treasure."

"How would you know what my name meant?" replied the young woman. "Unless you are…" She looked surprised and shocked.

Zeke held up his hand for her to stop talking. He kept trying to avert his eyes by looking down, and not looking at the incredibly beautifully-figured woman before him. Her breasts and everything about her was perfectly proportioned. It was difficult for him to keep looking away.

"Miss," Zeke placed my coat over the shivering young woman, "would you and the next five women in line, please come with me?"

As Zeke covered her, he kept trying to look down or away to avert his eyes from her very full body. He felt enough shame for both of them.

You could tell this young woman really wanted to live, she was around eighteen years old and had her whole life ahead of her. Her eyes were brimming with tears.

"May my younger sister come also?" she asked in a pleading voice.

"Yes! Please hurry! Come this way."

Six women and a child around ten years old followed Zeke around one of the tables over to Jenz and Officer Bolender and me. They were all frightened and whimpering.

Jenz, in a very quiet voice, told the women not to pay any attention to whatever came out of my mouth next.

In a loud voice, so others, including Bolender, could hear, I started shaking my finger and shouting at the women, **"You women are enemies of the Reich! You have been chosen for a special assignment. Go with the sergeant; retrieve your clothes and belongings and prepare for a long train journey."**

"Vitali," I quietly instructed, "Take the ladies to their belongings and pass through the kitchen so they may pack some food for their journey to Peenemünde. Please accompany them on the transport train back to Warsaw and board the next available train to the rocket base. Here is some money to cover the cost of transport and here is a copy of our orders in case you are questioned. Please secure some hats or kerchiefs for the women out of the piles of clothing. I will meet you at the camp at Auschwitz in a few days."

Vitali ushered the six ladies and a young child out of the haircutting room and back to the next building to retrieve their clothing.

One of the Ukrainian Guards stopped them. "Where are you going, Sargent? These women are scheduled for the showers!"

He raised his rifle and pointed it at our small group.

With the guard's comments, the women became almost hysterical. A few started crying.

"Ladies, calm down. My name is Sergeant Carapezza. Please stay close to me and show no emotion until we are out of this hellhole."

"Out of my way, Guard. These women are on special assignment for the Reich; I have orders from Reichsführer Himmler!"

Zeke was stopped again at the main gate, but he then left the camp with the women who had been scheduled for death, I said a silent prayer to myself:

Father God, watch over Ezekiel and indeed all the men and women in this prison of horrors. Please embrace them in your heavenly arms, ease their pain and suffering, and keep them all close to you.

As I turned around to leave the hair-cutting room, Officer Bolender approached me, "Lieutenant, would you like to see the rest of the camp and how we 'encourage' the vermin into the chambers?"

"Okay," I replied.

9

The Killing Machine

Officer Bolender and I walked outside and observed a line of very reluctant and terrified women being whipped and prodded with iron bars down a sandy pathway leading to a large, enclosed building.

"Bolender," I began, "Is all this violence necessary?"

"It depends," he answered tentatively. "Most of these women think they are going to a shower area. We even have showerheads installed on the ceilings of each gas chamber. Most of the people are relatively cooperative until the last few vermin are packed into the chamber. When they realize they are so tightly packed into the chamber there is no possible room for bathing, nor are there any drains in the floor, they start to panic."

"Some of the condemned have to be whipped or shot. A fresh coating of sand must be swept over the path to cover up the blood after each transport goes through. We call the path the 'pathway to heaven'."

"Is there any way out for these souls?"

"Never" replied Bolender. "The doors of the gas chambers are locked and hermetically sealed. The tractor engine starts up immediately and the monoxide gas is pumped directly into the chamber. Most days we can liquidate an average of three to four thousand of the Jews daily. Some days many more of these undesirables are extinguished."

Officer Bolender seemed almost cheerful as he described how Germany was efficiently liquidating all the Jews from the Reich.

My depression was tensing all the muscles in my back and head. I tried not to clench my teeth too hard. My facial muscles were bulging. My headache was going to be massive.

The weather was now slightly overcast with a chill in the air. The tractor engine started up and I could hear muffled screams from the gas chamber. My emotions were at the breaking point.

"Would you like to watch their terror through the thick glass viewing window?" asked Bolender.

"No, Bolender. I have seen quite enough."

"Our mission here at Treblinka," he continued, "is to eventually euthanize all the vermin from the conquered territories. A model of this camp will be used for eventually liquidating all the Jews from the East including Russia."

"It sounds like you folks here at Treblinka will be in business for quite a while."

I tried to speak in a conversational tone as I looked on to the gas chambers. These killing machines were murdering my Jewish friends, neighbors, and probably the intellectual elite and some of the most skilled leaders and technicians from the Reich.

I was sure these officers and guards at Treblinka and throughout the Reich had no idea of the cultural, scientific, and human resources lost to the rest of the world these deaths would represent.

"Well." After a considerable pause, Bolender continued, "We are trying to be as efficient as possible. Our goal is to remove five to six thousand ghetto inhabitants each day. However, that requires three or four transports each day. Some of the Jews in the Warsaw ghetto are putting up some resistance as their fate is getting known."

"Does our Fürher and Herr Himmler have knowledge of the Jewish resistance in the Warsaw Ghetto?"

"Oh, yes," replied Bolender, with a touch of glee. "If the Jews don't come out peacefully, and they cannot be starved into submission, our forces just go in and shoot anyone resisting arrest. If the rabble tries to hide from our men, they are burned out of their homes and shot on the spot."

"It sounds very efficient and complete." Although I was seething inside, I tried to maintain my composure. I had to raise my voice over the screams and crying of the Jewish women and children being whipped and forced into the gas chambers. The scene was brutal and heart-rendering. I was afraid at one point I might fly into a rage or just collapse from sadness.

"Who developed this 'efficient' method of" - *I paused because I almost said murdering* – "eliminating the Jews?"

"Our second in command is SS Officer, Kurt Franz.* He has had extensive experience with euthanasia at other camps like Auschwitz.

"Deputy Commander Franz had originally suggested we use the strong disinfectant, Zyklon B, also known as hydrogen cyanide, as a method of killing the Jews quickly. However, our camp commander, Franz Stangl,** felt the monoxide gas was sufficient, even though it took longer for the Jews to die. Commander Franz had the gas chambers rebuilt in order to accommodate more Jews.

---

*   Kurt Franz epitomized the worst the SS had to offer. He was the cruelest and most feared of all the SS Guards at Treblinka. He used to ride around Treblinka on his horse and took delight in whipping and shooting the prisoners. His dog, Bari, a Saint Bernard was the size of a young cow, and was trained to bite the genitals or the backside of the unfortunate detainee. His favorite torture was to kick to death new babies arriving on the transports. Having your children destroyed before the parents' eyes was the cruelest form of genocide.

Franz was recognized while working as a cook and arrested in Düsseldorf on December 2nd, 1959 and sentenced to life in prison. At his trial, witnesses agreed not a single day passed when he did not kill someone. A search of his home found a photo album of Treblinka with the title, "Beautiful Years." He was released in 1993 for health reasons and died shortly afterward.

**   Commander Stangl was responsible for re-organizing Treblinka into a more effective killing machine. He beautified the grounds with flowers and flowering bushes to conceal its' main purpose. He would often wear a white uniform and carry a whip. The prisoners nicknamed him the "White Death." After the war, he escaped to Brazil until he was tracked down by Nazi hunter, Simon Wiesenthal and arrested on 28 February 1967. He was sentenced to life in prison and died in Düsseldorf prison on 28 June 1971.

Our new gas chambers are capable of liquidating twelve to fifteen thousand Jews per day."

"Have you ever had to load the gas chambers to that capacity?" I asked with some trepidation.

"We need three or more transports each day to reach our capacity. Transports arrive from all over the Reich: Holland, France, Romania in addition to Germany, Poland, Czechoslovakia, and Hungry. We are starting to get more from the Eastern Territories including Belarus, Silesia, and Russia.

"Our Führer has notified all the death camps we should expect many more transports after the fall of Stalingrad."

"What are you expecting after Stalingrad?" I asked.

"Oh, the Jews and most of the population of the city will be eliminated. The men will be shot by the Wehrmacht and the women and children will be transported to our death camps here in Poland. Sobibor and Belzec's death detention facilities will handle any surplus.

"Our Führer feels that a victory at Stalingrad will cut off the oil supplies to Russia from the oil fields in the south and ensure our total victory in the East.

"What is your interest in our workforce here, Lieutenant?"

"Our facility in northern Germany needs able-bodied skilled workers for our research facility. We need machinists, engineers, and electricians as well as general workers to staff our facility.

"Many of our workers at Peenemünde have not been with us long because of sickness, malnourishment, or exhaustion – or all three. I will need to screen the male detainees from your transports to find healthy people with these skills."

"Why don't we screen the last male transportees," Officer Bolender suggested. "They will be coming out of the undressing area as soon as the gas chambers are cleaned and readied for their arrival."

"Why do the chambers need cleaning?" I asked in my naiveté. I was completely clueless and shocked by Bolender's answer.

"After a gassing, the chambers are awash with feces, urine, sweat, and blood. Most of the blood comes from the prisoners. As they realize they are being gassed, they try to claw their way out by the door. This frenzied panic usually lasts from eight to twenty minutes before they are all dead. We usually wait another few minutes in order to ensure each group is completely deceased."

"What do you do with the bodies?" I asked.

"All the dead are carried to the burial pits and burned or covered with lime and sand between each layer. You must understand, we have a big job here. We have to rid the Reich of thousands of Jews and other criminals every day. Herr Himmler has required us to complete the elimination of the Jewish Ghetto in Warsaw by the end of next summer."

"Would you like to see the burial pits and 'Lazarett'?"

"You will have to tell me, what is the 'Lazarett'?" *I was a little reluctant to ask, because it was like the Polish word for infirmary.*

"Yes. Of course. The 'Lazarett' is the execution site where unruly prisoners are stood up against a sandbag wall and shot. You never want to visit this part of our camp unaccompanied."

His comment sounded a bit like a warning. I hoped he hadn't guessed I was Jewish. I kept up my bravado with another comment.

"Let's take a look at the incoming group of male deportees and see if our facility could use any of them."

As we walked back through the reception area another transport was pulling into the station.

I asked, "Officer Bolender, what will you do with all the folks on this train that just pulled into Treblinka?"

"We never unlock the doors of the boxcar transports until the group before them has been completely gassed. We cannot allow a great number of anxious prisoners wandering around the camp. We just do not have the space for them."

"Isn't there any place in the camp where they can wait to be processed?" I asked.

"Unfortunately, they have to wait in the boxcars. They are so tightly packed, no one can sit or lie down. They have to wait until we have room for them."

"How long is the average wait?"

"Oh, sometimes they have to wait in the boxcars all day. It is particularly difficult for us in the summer. The Jews are without toilet facilities or food for several hours."

"How is their waiting in the boxcars difficult for the camp?" I asked the officer.

"Ramsgrund, you wouldn't believe the smell! Particularly in the heat of the summer. The mixture of sweat, fecal material, and urine is overwhelming. There is very little ventilation in the boxcar transports when they are not moving. Many of the Jews are dead or near death when we can finally unlock and open the sliding doors to the railroad cars."

The entire unloading and processing of the Jews sounded horrible and unthinkable. How could anyone contemplate treating another human being with this cruelty? I wouldn't have believed it if I hadn't seen it in person.

As I walked around the Treblinka camp, a feeling of abject loneliness crept into my very soul. The horror surrounding me was pervasive. I asked myself: *could God know about this place?*

10

Male Selection for our Research Center in Peenemünde

Officer Bolender and I went into the men's undressing area. He kept his hand on his pistol – probably in case of difficulty. There were three Ukrainian guards with rifles at the ready also in the building. No one was being whipped or disciplined, but there was considerable unrest, complaining, loud talk, and shouting.

Some of the men were shouting, **"Where have you taken our wives and daughters?"**

The answer was always the same shouted by the Ukrainian Guards. **"You will meet up with them shortly after the fumigation process."**

I was crying inside. I knew how important families were to the Jewish household. This separation of families to be murdered was the cruelest method of genocide. It is universally met with revulsion.

Bolender drew his Luger pistol and aimed it at the ceiling and shouted for the men to be quiet. Without discharging his weapon, everyone quieted down. I came forward and made the announcement:

"Men of Warsaw," I began, "I'm Lieutenant Ramsgrund. Reichsführer Himmler has given me orders to bring certain qualified men back to our Wehrmacht Research Center to help with the construction of innovative weapon systems for our heroic war effort against the Allies and the Russians and all enemies of the Reich.

"To be qualified for this work, you must have a background in engineering – either electrical or mechanical or as a master machinist or electrician. Furthermore, you must be able to demonstrate your knowledge to me before we leave this facility. If I find you are not being truthful with me, there will be consequences.

"Do I have any such qualified men here now? Please step forward and keep your clothes on until we have made a determination."

I stepped back and looked over the men. Out of two or three hundred men in the room, a handful stepped forward. I encouraged them to come with me and we found a table in the small building adjacent to the women's undressing area in the hair-cutting room. A total of fourteen men followed me into the room. I asked them to pull up chairs around one of the tables. Officer Bolender stood in the door with his hand on his pistol.

I had to speak in a loud tone because of all the murmuring and complaining.

"Men," I started my introduction, "I have orders from the highest authority to bring qualified Jews to our Wehrmacht Research Facility in northern Germany. I am specifically looking for engineers, electricians, and machinists. You must be in excellent health and physical condition.

"If any of you have come over to this room under false assumptions or credentials, or you are in poor health, you are

**ordered to return to the men's undressing area, and you will
receive no consequential or additional punishment."**

I waited a few minutes while the group collectively made up
their minds to chance going to another facility.

One man raised his hand and tentatively stood up.

"Sir." He spoke in a halting German language with a decidedly
Polish accent. Although he was a little hard to understand, I got
the essence of what he was saying.

"My name is Horace Breitman. I am a machinist, but you
addressed us as men of Warsaw. I am from Belarus. I did not want
to mislead you, if you were under the impression, I was from the
Warsaw Ghetto. My family lived approximately one hour east of
Minsk before the German invasion of Russia. After the invasion,
we moved west to the Lublin district of German-occupied Poland."

I answered as carefully as possible. "I am looking for qualified
men who have a skill needed by our research facility in the north
of Germany. Where you are from is not important for the needs
of the Reich.

"Breitman, if you are skilled in machine parts manufacturing,
assembling, and fabricating, you could be valuable for our research
center.

"After I have checked on the qualifications of each man
here, you all will be sent back to Warsaw on a transporter with
two Ukrainian Guards. These guards will take you by train to
Peenemünde, in northern Germany and on to the research center.

"Breitman, you remain behind after everyone is escorted to the
kitchen area and then to the transports. I would like a word with you."

Most of the color drained from Breitman's face. He looked
like he might pass out. I did tower over the Polish machinist, but
I didn't realize he was so nervous and fearful.

I couldn't blame him. His future was disturbingly uncertain in this horrible place.

"Have, have I done something wrong?" The poor Jew was shaking and stammering.

"Not at all, Breitman. I want to know how you wound up in the Warsaw Ghetto."

11

Killing the Elderly and Children

Just when I was thinking nothing could be as atrocious as this hell-on-earth called Treblinka, Breitman's story led me to believe there was even more dreadful news to come.

Horace Breitman was a highly trained machinist. He had done many projects for different companies in Poland, Russia, Belarus, and for the Reich.

He explained he was quite friendly with one of the local reserve police captains who had come from Hamburg, Germany, to his home in Belarus to assess the "Jewish problem."

Breitman explained, "I had become friends with one police officer. Major Wilhelm Trapp had become friendly with our family because our fathers had served together in the Great War. I'm not sure he even knew I was Jewish; he never asked. My father's family was originally from just south of the Stockholm area in Sweden.

"In addition to our familial connection, I had done some small project machine work for the major when he had trouble getting parts for some of his equipment and vehicles."

"Were you able to maintain your friendship with Major Trapp as our troops conquered and swept through the Eastern Territories?" I asked.

"For the most part, yes," Breitman answered. But then a very strange emotion started to overcome the machinist and he almost fell into a vacant chair.

"Are you going to be okay, Breitman? Tell me what is going on!" I shot back with a little force of command behind my voice. "There will be no consequence for you."

"Lieutenant, do you really want to hear my story?"

"Yes, go ahead, Breitman. Enlighten me."

"Well, the whole sad story began on a Sunday afternoon early in November 1941. Major Trapp had stopped by our home in Belarus to ask some questions about the Jewish section of the town of Slutsk, Poland. Although a reserve officer in the Hamburg police force, his detachment was assigned to the Eastern Territories to help with a solution to the Jewish question in the Central Government of German-occupied Poland."

It was a warm, late fall day, and I had all the windows open for ventilation. The major seemed upset about our conversation, and I offered him some coffee-cake my wife had baked, and something to drink. I offered tea, but he snapped back, "Do you have any schnaps?"

I poured about two ounces into a small glass.

"Thank you." He downed it in one gulp.

"What is troubling you, Major?" I inquired.

"It is this whole 'Operation Reinhard' business, the major responded. I have had orders from Heinrich Himmler through his district commander, Odilo Globocnik,* to make the entire Central Government area of German-occupied Poland free of all Jews by the end of 1943.

"I was ordered to make the Lublin district *Jewdenfrei* by the first of January, 1943. My orders were specific to start in the town of Slutsk, south of Minsk in Belorussia."

"There must be thousands of Jewish people living in the Lublin district and throughout the Eastern Territories," I replied. "Where would they all go?" I asked.

"Please don't misunderstand me, Lieutenant. All the Jews from these areas are to be liquidated. If they couldn't be shipped to concentration camps, they were to be immediately shot."

"How does our Reichsführer or Major Trapp plan on eliminating thousands of these Jews?" I asked, hoping I wasn't going to get an answer I dreaded.

"Well, Lieutenant, the major started to rock back and forth in his chair and tell me the details of what went on in Slutsk south of Minsk. By the end of the Major's description of the proceedings in Slutsk he was carrying on and crying so much I had to close the windows."

"The major complained on the morning of 27 October 1941, a reserve Police First Lieutenant with a Battalion from Lithuania

---

* Odilo Globocnik met with Himmler on 13 October 1941 and proposed eliminating Jews in the conquered areas of Poland with assembly-line efficiency in concentration camps using gas chambers. Globocnik was a violent Nazi who rose to command all the Polish extermination camps. He was so unstable he terrorized his own concentration camp commanders. Globocnik committed suicide by biting on a cyanide capsule when tracked down and arrested by British troops on 31 May 1945.

backed up by the SS came to him and ordered the major to liquidate all the Jews in Slutsk in two days."

"What happened," I asked with trepidation.

At first, the major said it couldn't be done. Major Trapp complained, "If all the Jewish tradesmen were liquidated, vital enterprises in the city would be immediately paralyzed."

However, the Lithuanian commander of the reserve battalion emphasized he only could spare his men for two days. He had two days to cleanse the Jews from Slutsk before he had to move on to other villages in the area. He wanted the entire city *Judenrein,* or cleaned of Jews, before he had to leave.

"The city of Slutsk at the time had approximately 12,000 inhabitants. One third of these folks are Jewish," complained Major Trapp. "Most all, indeed all of the inhabitants are living in harmony without causing any trouble for their neighbors."

The major then related to me what happened in a very soft, almost whimpering and crying voice:

"All the Jews were pulled out of the factories and forced from their homes at gun-point. They were loaded onto wagons and driven out to the forest in groups of twenty to fifty men, women, and children. The Jews were then ordered to remove their clothes and valuables and lie naked face down on the cold earth. The auxiliary police then shot them in the back of their head."

"I am a family man," sobbed Major Trapp. "Initially, I could not bring myself to shoot innocent people, especially women and little children."

The Lithuanian lieutenant chided me. "Major, if you do not have the stomach for this work, my men will carry out the sentence. Of course, I will have to report your lack of bravery to my superiors."

Breitman continued. "Trapp was a reserve policeman from Hamburg and had no desire or inclination for further advancement in rank.

"Trapp told the Lithuanian he couldn't even watch, but he heard the screams, crying, and gunfire on his way back to the village.

"Any of the Jewish men who resisted, according to Trapp, were shot in their homes or on the street. The elderly, who couldn't walk to the wagons, were shot in their beds. Children, including very young children, along with their mothers who were trying to protect them were immediately shot. Corpses were lining the streets of the Jewish Ghetto and on the city streets. There was blood all over the sidewalks. It was utter chaos. There was shooting everywhere.

"I don't think Major Trapp will ever be the same. He had never witnessed anything so cruel and inhumane, even in the Great War.

"He had a military background and said he could not bring himself to be part of this beastly action."

I then asked what I thought was a reasonable question.

"Breitman, was there any consideration for Jews who might be useful for the Reich?" My suggestion would be to save these folks for working in industries that are going to be critical for Germany to win this war.

"Lieutenant, if you were Jewish and from Slutsk, you were dead. There were also a lot of White Russian people in the city who were brutalized, clubbed, and eliminated by the execution squads."

"Does Reichsführer Himmler know of these Judenrein procedures of important workers in the Eastern Territories?" I was trying to understand the source of so much hatred and anger. Even though I had witnessed all kinds of anti-Semitism, even in Hitler Youth Camp, this seemed abominable and completely wasteful.

"The Reichsführer has to know, but perhaps not the effects of the drain of critical workers on the war with the Russians," commented Breitman.

"I will message General Dornberger to get further workers for our research center in Peenemünde. I will want you to accompany me tomorrow to Sobibor. I need your fluency in Polish. From there I will need an introduction to Major Trapp.

"If you help me accomplish the procuring more Jews for the research center, you will be completely free to go back to your home and family in Belarus."

"My family," Breitman said softly, "has already been murdered in the Treblinka camp."

"Will you be able to carry on for them?" I questioned.

"I will do it for my family and the many other families in Belarus."

12

The Sobibor Death Camp

It took Breitman and me a day to make our way to the Sobibor Concentration Camp by automobile requisitioned from the Warsaw Command. My uniform and orders from Reichsführer Himmler got us through all the checkpoints on the way to the eastern part of Poland governed by the Reich.

As we approached the camp, the area looked like a peaceful farm in the middle of a meadow. The camp area looked almost like a perfect rectangle approximately four or five hundred by six or seven hundred meters. The buildings even had the vague look of a farm with village buildings. The only unusual look was the surrounding barbed wire fencing and watchtowers. The wire perimeter fence had pine branches intertwined with the barbed wire to limit the visibility of the inside of the camp. The camp looked very peaceful as we approached.

It was a picture-perfect day with only ominous dark clouds overhanging the probable area of the crematoria. There was no wind but there was a faint unpleasant odor in the air.

I warned Breitman. "Do not show any emotion or facial expressions displaying dissatisfaction, disbelief, or outright rage at what we might encounter at this camp facility."

"Thank you, Lieutenant. I appreciate your trust."

I wanted to trust Breitman. His background was not too dissimilar to my own. I just couldn't be sure he wouldn't let my secret be known under torture or carelessness.

We went directly to the commandant's office. Franz Stangl, the current SS officer in charge, was not in his office, so I presented my orders to the deputy, Oberscharführer Hermann Michel.*

This officer radiated pure evil. His deep-set eyes and expanded forehead made me think of a pre-historic relic who could possibly be only part human.

The Oberscharführer, however, was pleasant enough after he viewed Himmler's orders, and even offered us a brief tour of the facility. I introduced Breitman as my aide.

"Gentlemen," he started as we walked out of the area where the incoming Jewish prisoners were kept. "Our duty here is to euthanize as many Jews as they send us. Since Operation Barbarossa began last summer, we have had many transports from the East coming to our facility."

He grabbed a white coat as he was leaving his office. We entered the separation area and he put on his white coat and stood on a table. The white coat gave the poor Jewish prisoners the idea he was a doctor. He spoke in a very kind and understanding voice to the captured audience: ***"People, please calm down. You are all being resettled in the Ukraine. You will be doing productive***

---

* SS Oberscharführer Herman Michel worked at the Sobibor Death Camp because of his extensive experience in the T-4 Euthanasia Program. His experience was gained at the Hartheim Killing Center where physically and mentally disabled people were put to death by lethal injection or by gas. After the war Michel fled to Egypt where he disappeared.

*farm work and will be valuable for Germany. Please go to the
undressing rooms and leave your clothing in a pile for complete
disinfecting. Your valuables will be returned to you after the
showers and delousing. Thank you."*

He spoke in such a reassuring, gentle, and refined voice, his
nickname was "The Preacher." The prisoners had no idea they
were being tricked into going to the gas chambers.

"Even more concerning," he addressed us, "we are getting more
and more transports from as far away as France, the Netherlands,
Bulgaria, and Croatia. Our staff is working at capacity. However,
we have an expert in euthanasia coming soon in order to expand
our gas chambers."

"Who is coming, Oberscharführer?"

"His name is Christian Wirth,* Lieutenant. He is also known
by the thousands of Jews coming through the camps as 'Christian
the Terrible,' 'Christian the Cruel,' and by many of us as the 'Wild
Christian.' He is an expert at mass extermination of the Jews,
Russian prisoners of war, and gypsies who come to our facility."

"Wirth started out as a reserve police captain but found his
calling in euthanizing people. He began by killing the weak and
the handicapped by lethal injection; but gradually he found more
and better ways of liquidating hundreds of Jews at one time.

---

*   It was Wirth whose guidelines and policies toward prisoners gave
the Ukrainian guards and SS men in the camps the authority and
encouragement to create a reign of terror and misery for the Jews.
He epitomized the worst debasement of Nazi authority. Christian
Wirth was killed in May 1944, by Yugoslav Partisans while traveling
in an open car near Trieste in northeastern Italy. He was 59 years old.

"Our gas chambers here can only hold up to two hundred Jews at a time, but I hear his death chambers in Auschwitz can euthanize up to two thousand Jews at a time.

"I understand from your orders, Lieutenant, you are looking for technically trained Jews for a research facility?"

"Correct, Oberscharführer Michel. Our facility needs machinists, electricians, and engineers. Assembly and experience working with small parts would also be helpful. Breitman here is a technical expert in machinery and is helping me with the candidates."

"What is it you are building at your facility, Lieutenant?"

"It is all top-secret weapons development work for the war effort, Oberscharführer, not to be discussed outside of the research center. Knowledge of the German language would be helpful.

"Are you experimenting on humans for the Reich, Lieutenant?"

"Never! Our interest is in weapons development. I apologize, but further discussion is not permitted."

"How can we at Sobibor help with your efforts at the Research Center in northern Germany?"

"It would be best for us to interview a few men and women from the transports as they come into your camp. I would like technically trained people who would prove valuable for our efforts. However, they must be in good physical health.

"Many of our current laborers at the center cannot remain healthy under the strain of weapons development because of the time constraints our Fürher has placed on our project."

"Come over to the selection area. The last transport prisoners have not been sent to the undressing station, yet. You may interview prisoners directly in the separation area."

Officer Michel explained to us that the Sobibor Camp was divided into three distinct areas. The Forward area of Camp I included the unloading area for deportees, living quarters for Ukrainian Guards and SS personnel, and different shops and kitchens for maintaining the camp. The Camp II area was needed for the undressing area and storage of valuables and clothing removed from the prisoners. The third part of the facility, the Camp III area, was for the gas chambers, combustion engine area for producing the monoxide lethal gas, and prisoner barracks. This area also contained the mass graves and outdoor crematoria.

"It's all designed to run very efficiently, Lieutenant. Remember, we are under pressure from Herr Himmler to euthanize thousands of deportees from all the villages, cities and towns of the conquered territories and from all over Europe."

"It sounds like an impossible task," I commented.

"Yes, Lieutenant. Let me take you over to Camp II and the collection area where you can choose some candidates for interviewing.

"I must caution you, Lieutenant, be careful not to let these folks know they are being led to their deaths. These Jews can get very uncooperative, if they know they are about to die.

"Our purpose is to get the prisoners to hurry through the undressing and hair-cutting area in order to move them into the gas chambers. Often, we tell them to hurry because the shower water is getting cold. Occasionally, we must whip and beat them in order to get them into the chambers – especially if they have any idea they are being led to their death."

Under my breath, I said a silent prayer for my fellow Jews who were being deceived and murdered at an alarming rate. How could I ever forgive myself if I couldn't help to bring an end to this monumental crime. What could Zeke and I do? If we were discovered, we would be shot immediately.

It was getting late in the day. Breitman and I could sense a certain tension in the air. The Oberscharführer said something about the end of day count was approaching and several of the SS and Ukrainian guards were not present at their duty stations.

I asked what I thought was a comment about guard reliability.

"Where are the SS men guarding the new arrivals from the transports?"

"Many of the men," offered the Oberscharführer, "pick out the best-looking young women from the transports and suggest they trade sex for their lives."

"Are any of the women saved by these encounters?" I asked.

"Never!" The Oberscharführer spit out the words. "After the sex in the officer's quarters, they are led immediately to the gas chambers."

I said a silent prayer for these poor completely innocent women. Not only were they being unjustly and brutally murdered but abused and debased for the pleasure of these criminals.

"However, this is very strange," said Michel. Although all the Jews are within the wire enclosures, there are no Ukrainian Guards or SS men in the selection area."

Just then we heard gunfire from the distant part of Camp II.

"Gentlemen!" shouted the officer. "Something very unusual is happening. Please leave as quickly as possible for your own safety."*

As Breitman and I started for the front gate and back to our automobile, we could look over our shoulder and see armed men coming from the entrance of Camp II.

As we entered our car, we could hear multiple gun shots from within the camp. Machine gunfire erupted from the guard towers.

Breitman asked, "Do you think it is an uprising of some sort?"

"I'm not sure," I answered, "but let's drive a few kilometers down the road and see what develops."

---

* On the 14th of October 1943, at 4 pm several prisoners took part in an uprising and hundreds of their fellow Jews escaped. Eleven SS Guards were killed. The successful uprising was planned by a Jewish Red Army POW, Lieutenant Alexander Pechersky.

After the war, Lieutenant Pechersky was not allowed to leave Russia by the Russian Government. So, he was unable to testify at the Sobibor Trial at Nuremberg, or the Eichmann Trial in Israel. He died in Russia in Rostov-on-Don on the 19th of January, 1990. He was 81 years old.

13

Saving a Family

We drove until we came to a forest area and parked by the side of the road. It was a quiet and peaceful area without any thought of conflict and murder. There was a gentle breeze whispering in the pines and songbirds chirping their songs in the adjacent meadow.

I removed my hat and talked with Breitman. "Look, Breitman, if any people from the recent transport come this way, we are going to try to save them."

"Sir." The machinist had a curt reply. "These Jews have had the most traumatic experience of their lives. They may not be totally comfortable with a uniformed SS officer offering them safety."

"Breitman," I stated firmly, "that is where you are going to be indispensable. You will have to encourage and convince whoever comes this way to let us lead them to safety. Speaking to them in their native language should help."

"Sir, I will try; but there are no guarantees. I have experienced the trauma these folks have been through. Do not be surprised if they would rather take their chances in the forest!"

We waited almost thirty minutes before a group of five men came running along the edge of the meadow.

Breitman got out of the automobile and flagged them down. However, as soon as the lead escapee got within thirty meters of the car, he recognized the SS insignia on my uniform and called out to the others. They immediately scattered into the forest like frightened animals.

"Breitman, we may have to try a little different approach. These poor souls were being whipped and beaten this morning by men wearing this identical uniform. I'm going to fold my coat and place it in the back seat."

As I was talking, a group of 40-50 escapees came running through the meadow heading for the woods.

Immediately, Breitman jumped out of the car and yelled to them. Like a herd of sheep, they headed for the car. As they approached the automobile, I stepped out of the driver's side to greet them.

I'm not sure if I looked intimidating, because of my size, or perhaps a little too Aryan with my sandy-blond hair and steel-blue eyes. Or, as they approached the car, they might have spotted my uniform coat in the back seat.

Whatever the reason, almost all the escapees scattered for the woods at the edge of the meadow. One small group stayed behind. It was a husband and wife and two small children. The little ones were probably about five to eight years old. They looked terrified and completely exhausted.

The man got on his knees and begged. "Please, sir. Have mercy on my family. My children cannot run any farther from the hell of the Sobibor Camp. We have not eaten in two days and have been beaten and whipped by the Ukrainian guards at the camp."

Breitman was translating for me as I held up my hand for poor escapee to stop.

"Young man," I started. "What is your name?"

"My name is Jacob Wiernik; my wife is called Hanel." He was trembling and shaking. He did seem to understand my German dialect.

I asked Wiernik to stand. He had difficulty standing and seemed very unsteady on his feet. It was a bit problematic because I still towered above him. His nervousness was evident. He could barely make it to his feet. Standing there in front of Breitman and me had to be painful for him. His wife and children looked frozen with fear.

"Look, Wiernik. You and your family are in a very precarious situation. The local Polish population consists of mainly rural farms. The farmers, for the most part, are somewhat anti-Semitic and totally terrified of their Nazi occupiers. It would be very doubtful if the local population would be at all helpful in sheltering, feeding, or hiding your family. As a matter of fact, they could well turn you in to the local police for a cash bounty or as assurance for protection."

"What am I to do?" queried Wiernik, blinking nervously, eyes downcast.

"I will tell you that your chances in the forests are very sketchy. You could come upon militant partisans, vengeful farmers who would probably get a reward for turning you in, or bandits who could kill you and your family."

"Is there any hope for my family?" Wiernik's wife began to sob.

"Yes. But you have to trust Breitman and me."

Wiernik looked at his wife who still shaking with fear but nodded in the affirmative.

"What would you have us do?" he asked in a quiet, timorous voice.

"I will remove my uniform coat from the back seat and wear it. You and your family need to squeeze into the back seat and do exactly what we tell you."

"I will do what you ask," said Wiernik. "But you have to understand how difficult it is for my family to be in an automobile with an SS* officer. I know they will be very frightened."

"I know you folks will do the best you can; if we are stopped, try not to appear frightened. There will be police, Wehrmacht soldiers, SS guards, and possible Gestapo** looking for all of the escapees from Sobibor."

"Where will you take us?" asked Wiernik.

"Breitman and I are on our way to Auschwitz. We will stop in Warsaw, Chelm, or Krakow and procure Aryan work papers for you. This way, you will have a chance to blend into the general population without fear of being sent to a concentration or death camp."

---

*   Schutzstaffel (Abbreviated SS). Originally was established as Adolf Hitler's personal bodyguard unit. It would later become both the elite guard of the Nazi Reich and Hitler's executive force prepared to carry out all security-related duties, without regard for legal restraint. The "Death's Head" division of the SS performed all the security-related duties for the concentration camps.

** *Geheime Staatspolizei,* abbreviated *Gestapo,* was the name for the Nazi Secret State Police. It was formed in 1933 by Hermann Göring and later transferred on April 20th, 1934, to the head of the SS, Heinrich Himmler. See p. xii.

14

Stopped and Searched by Local Police

We had been traveling south for about twenty minutes when we came to the first roadblock obstruction. At first glance, it appeared that two local police officers had parked a motorbike and an automobile across the road blocking it entirely.

As we approached, I observed only one of the men was dressed as a local police officer. The other man was in a civilian suit. He was tall, almost six feet with a forehead that slanted backward and a too short lower jaw. My guess was he was most probably Gestapo. In my mind, I thought of him as "rat-faced."

As we slowed to a stop, I pulled slightly to the right to get partially off the road. I added a warning: "Wiernik, please keep your children quiet. Do not respond, even if the authorities ask you a question. I will do all the talking. And most importantly, do not get out of the car, even if ordered to do so. I may ask you to get out of the car in a commanding voice; however, do not get out of the car under any circumstances. Is that clear?"

It was obvious. The family crammed into my back seat were terrified. I just prayed they would follow my orders to remain in the automobile and stay quiet. The sun had set and the twilight brought a gathering gloom to the landscape. There was a forest of tall pines on both sides of the road.

The police officer approached our automobile and I rolled down the window. When he saw my uniform, he stiffened and asked, "Sir, where are you headed?"

"We are on our way to Lublin. Officer, what is the problem?"

"There has been an uprising at the Sobibor Camp, Lieutenant, and several of the Jewish vermin have escaped into our beautiful country," was the police officer's comment.

"Here are my orders, Officer. As you can see, we are traveling at the behest of Reichführer Himmler, and we need to get on our way."

"Of course, Lieutenant, your papers look in order, you are free to continue your journey."

"Hold on, Officer. Let me see those orders!" Rat-face had quickly approached the car and had drawn his weapon.

I politely handed him my orders and in a quiet voice ask if there was any problem with the Reichführer's orders. I also calmly inquired, "and who are you?"

"I am the local Gestapo agent, Lieutenant. We are hunting for escaped criminal Jews from the Sobibor Camp."

"Agent, I am really sorry; but we haven't seen any criminal Jews today."

I hadn't had anything to eat since breakfast and I could feel my anger rising a notch. Perhaps my stomach was growling just a little. My mother always told me my pleasant demeanor suffered a bit, if I hadn't eaten in a while. I could just imagine what was going through the minds of the folks in the back seat.

"Lieutenant, I would like to inspect your automobile. Everyone out of the back seat," commanded the rat-faced Gestapo agent with a less-than-polite tone to his voice.

However, nobody in the back seat moved!

Rat-face was getting red-blotchy skin around his neck. I could tell his blood pressure was rising. He commanded again in a brusque and much louder voice, **"Everyone out of the back seat, now!"**

As he was ordering the family out of the back seat, he brandished his weapon much too close to my face.

I addressed the Gestapo agent in a very polite and almost caring tone, "Sir, let me get them out of the back seat for you. And please, do not wave your pistol near an SS officer's face again."

"People, please get out of the back seat and exit the automobile."

As I was issuing the order, I turned around in the seat and winked at the frightened and terrified family behind me.

Nobody moved.

I addressed the Gestapo agent. "Sir, I will remove them from the back seat."

While talking in a quiet and calm voice, I opened my door slowly, and stood up beside the automobile. The Gestapo agent seemed surprised at my height. I don't think he expected anyone imposing to challenge him. I felt it gave me a critical advantage. I then slowly closed my driver's side door.

As I went to open the rear door of the automobile with my left hand with my hand on the door handle, I instead brought my right fist down in a swift and decisive blow on the agent's gun arm. I heard a distinct snap of a broken wrist bone; the weapon fell harmlessly to the ground.

The look of shock and surprise on the agent's blotchy face was complete. He gave a short cry of surprise and did not see the side of my clenched fist slam against his carotid body in his very red neck.

I was pretty sure I had broken his neck; his head snapped violently toward me as his body lurched in the opposite direction. He fell limply to the ground without uttering another sound.

The look of shock and alarm on the policeman's face was classic. He was aghast and started to cry out in panic.

I grabbed the officer around the neck in a chokehold and twisted his chin in a violent jerk in the opposite direction from where he was facing. He died instantly and fell to the ground in a heap with a broken neck.

I'm not sure who was more surprised. Breitman's eyes were as big as saucers. I wasn't sure the family in the back seat was even breathing.

I asked Breitman, in a soothing and completely calm voice, "Would you mind helping me get this trash into the boot of their automobile?"

He instantly came to life and jumped out of the car and asked, "Where did you learn to fight like that?"

"Hitler Camp," was my response; Breitman looked shocked and surprised. It was difficult for me to suppress my glee with a fleeting smile.

I think the stunned family in the back seat was breathing again.

Breitman and I loaded the two very dead officers into the trunk of their car. I drove it a short distance into the woods. Breitman pushed the motor bike in behind the car and into the brush.

"Are you just going to leave them in the woods?" asked Breitman.

"I think it would be best," I replied. "The local police will probably think the escapees were to blame.

"Since most automobiles carry siphons, let's top off our tank with the petrol in their automobile and motorbike."

15

Getting Aryan Papers

We had been driving south for about two hours when Breitman asked where we were headed. I got the feeling he was anxious to get back to his hometown. Although his immediate family had been murdered by the Nazis, he still had friends, possible relatives, and an employer who probably needed him.

We were blessed because we passed no further police checkpoints in our journey.

I made the announcement so the frightened family in the back seat would know our intentions.

"We are headed for the city of Krakow; it is about four or five hours south of where we are now."

"In Krakow I will go to the SS main office and message my sergeant to meet me at the Auschwitz-Birkenau Labor Camp.

"In addition, I will procure Aryan work papers for you and our friends in the back seat. The work papers should protect you from further roundups. When you find work, please stay out of the Jewish ghettos. Remember, the local police will not be your friends. The local authorities routinely work with the local Gestapo and the SS.

"If you have questions, please ask them now."

"Sir," came from a woman's voice in the back seat. "Why is a member of the SS helping poor Jews? All the SS officers we have encountered have done nothing but torment and murder our families. When the Gestapo broke into our home, they said we would be shot if we did not comply immediately and go to the square near the railroad station. They shot several of our neighbors – even their children when they resisted. They herded us like cattle onto box cars on the transports.

"The German police packed us so tightly into the rail cars, there was no place to sit down. There were no toilet facilities or food or water. Breathing in the locked box car was difficult because there was only a small window rimmed with barbed wire for air.

"When we arrived at the Sobibor Camp, the SS men whipped us and forced us into a large, barbed wire enclosed area. Several of our neighbors, especially the elderly adults, died on the transports. Then we heard shooting, shouting, and general confusion from within the camp. That is when we ran for the forest. My children were completely spent when you told us to get into your automobile."

"Unfortunately, Miss, your story is being repeated all over Germany, Poland, and the New Territories. Anti-Semitism has infected the German people. Many good Germans oppose anti-Semitism and the maltreatment of Jews. But if they complain to the authorities, they will find themselves in the same labor camps as their Jewish neighbors."

Hanel Wiernik then spoke up again. "Sir, you are being very kind to my family, and believe me, we owe you our lives and enduring gratitude. But why are you doing this?"

"Mrs. Wiernik," I started, "not all Germans are anti-Semitic. Our leaders and their followers, especially the Gestapo, are probably the world's worst criminals. The men in the SS are probably no better."

"But," Mrs. Wiernik persisted, "please tell my family why you saved us?"

"It is complicated, dear Wiernik family. Let me try to explain while I ask you a question.

"What is your profession?"

"I am an accountant," explained Mr. Wiernik.

"Thank you, Wiernik. How many potential accountants, physicians, engineers, scientists, and world-renowned composers, artists, and craftsmen do you suppose the Nazis crammed into those cattle cars?

"I will tell you the answer, Mr. Wiernik. The world will never know! How many people have been murdered who could have discovered medicines for curing many of the diseases that directly affect the German people or other populations in all the countries in the world?

"How many men, women, and children have been murdered who could have become wonderful leaders of their city, town or country?

"How many children have been murdered who could have become great composers, the next Wagner or Mendelssohn?

"Or philanthropists! No, Wiernik family, the Nazis have no idea of what they are forever destroying.

"My sergeant and I have orders from our German Research Center in northern Germany to find laborers from the camps to help with our weapons research."

"Will you need any of us at the Research Center, Lieutenant?"

"No, Mr. Wiernik. I will go directly to the local command center in Krakow and get Aryan work papers for your family and Mr. Breitman. It is my strong suggestion you disappear into the city, find meaningful work, and thank our God; He has spared us so far from the worst nightmare of the Nazi regime."

16

Nazi Command Center, Krakow, Poland

It was late afternoon by the time we arrived on the outskirts of Krakow. Our first stop was at a small hotel where everyone could get a meal and water. I knew the children had to be quite hungry, but they were being very quiet in the back seat. I will have to admit, I wasn't in the best of humor; I'm sure Breitman was also hungry. We all had to wash up in the washroom.

The sky was a lead-gray overcast and it was late in the evening. There was a chill to the brisk wind; it rather matched my mood.

Although the older woman at the hotel desk didn't look too happy to be serving an SS officer or any of us so late, she led us to the dining area and we had a decent meal of mushroom soup, bread, and cheese. I knew food was scarce in Poland, and was grateful this rather dilapidated-looking hotel had something for us to eat.

"We will stay here for the evening and go into Krakow tomorrow morning."

Mrs. Wiernik asked, "Why are we going to this particular city in Poland, Lieutenant?"

"Krakow is one of the few major cities in the Central Government, under Nazi occupation, which has not been completely destroyed and flattened by the Wehrmacht."

"Is it safe to be in this particular city?" asked Breitman.

My response was stern and emphatic. **"No!** There are no cities under the occupation of the Nazis in the Central Government safe for anyone, particularly Jews.

"Many Jews have been rounded up and cordoned off in the ghetto area south of the city of Krakow. And many have been shipped off to the Plaszow slave labor camp. Please do not think of any area in Poland safe for Jews."

"Do you have any suggestions where we should go, if we can obtain our Aryan documents tomorrow?" asked Mr. Wiernik.

"Stay away from the Jewish ghetto! You may be drawn to the houses of worship, but they could be a trap for capturing unwitting Jews. I know of at least one instance where the temple was burned to the ground with the worshipers locked inside. The Brownshirts burned to death over one hundred men, women, and children in their lust to rid the town of Jews. Anyone attempting to flee the burning temple was shot and killed. Some of the congregation hung themselves or slashed their wrists rather than suffer the fate of being burned to death."

The next morning, Mr. Wiernik asked what I thought was a very reasonable question.

"Lieutenant, there has always been a bit of anti-Semitism in Poland for as long as I can remember. When we were forced to board the transport and brought to the Sobibor camp, we thought our journey was an extension and an escalation of this anti-Semitism. We were advised Sobibor was a transition camp. We were told our families would be sent to the East to do farm work for the Reich. Are you telling us the SS were lying to us as they packed us on the transports?"

"It is certainly not my pleasure to have to inform you, Mr. Wiernik, but Sobibor is a *Totenlager!* (Death Camp). You and your fellow Jews were being misled by the local police and the SS in order to gain your cooperation. Had you not broken out of the camp, your entire family would be dead by this time and cremated and buried on the premises. I'm sure, those who did not break out with you when they had a chance, are already murdered and buried by now."

"Mein Gott im Himmel!" cried Mrs. Wiernik. "Is there no place in Poland where my family can be safe and live peacefully?"

"Hiding in the city with Aryan work papers will be the safest place for your family. The Gestapo has offered many of the farmers in the countryside rewards for turning in Jews. The partisans are very wary of anyone they do not know personally. They would kill a Jew before they would chance hiding them and being discovered by the Wehrmacht or the Gestapo."

"I have heard of one German businessman in Krakow who, although he is a member of the Nazi Party, is somewhat sympathetic to the plight of Jews. If you have problems finding work, or if the Gestapo has approached you, consider looking him up."

"Who is this Nazi who does not persecute Jews?" asked Mr. Wiernik.

"His name is Oskar Schindler.* He makes enamelware and armaments for the Wehrmacht. Although his position as a Nazi is in military intelligence and he is a member of the *Abwehr,* he is known in the Jewish underground for saving many Jews from the transports and the death camp at Belzec.

"He appears and has admitted to being a profit-motivated Nazi, prospering mightily off the labor of hard-working Jews. If the Gestapo is in his factory, he comes across as a hard-liner loyal Nazi, with no compassion for any Jews.

"He is known, however, for actually going into the concentration labor camps to rescue his Jewish workers from the transports and the death camps. He is a man you could trust; he will not bring any pain or hardship to your family."

---

* Oskar Schindler was in the Abwehr section of the Nazi Party. He spent all his wealth (several million dollars in today's money) on factory renovations in order to hire more Jews. He produced enamelware and armaments for the Wehrmacht. The rest of his fortune was spent on bribes to Nazi Officials and the Gestapo so they would look the other way when it came time for rounding up Jews and sending them to the death camps. Initially, he hired Jews because their labor was cheaper and his profit greater. After seeing the atrocities inflicted on the Jews by the Nazis, Schindler did everything he could to save as many Jews as possible from the death camps. After the war, he retired penniless in West Germany and was partly supported by payments from Jewish relief organizations. He died in Hildesheim, Germany on 9 October 1974, and was buried in Jerusalem on Mount Zion. He was the only former member of the Nazi Party to be so honored; he was 66 years old.

"We are nearing the Wehrmacht Command Center. When we arrive, please stay in the automobile. Do not let anyone leave the automobile unless it is on fire!

"The other address to avoid at all costs is # 2 Ulica Pomorska Strasse.* This is the command center for the Gestapo in the Krakow district. They could arrest you regardless of your Aryan paperwork. Once you were imprisoned by the Gestapo, it would be too late to help you."

The Wehrmacht Command Center was in the central Krakow police station. It was a low gray building with a hint of decaying Italian architectural consideration. Dark clouds hung over the building that morning like a veil of dread. The Nazi flag was flying over the building as proud defiance of all reason.

---

* # 2 Ulica Pomorska Street was originally built to house students from the Silesian region of Poland. After the Nazi invasion of Poland, it was used as headquarters for the dreaded Gestapo. After 1945, it was used by the Soviet Secret Police, the NKVD, until the 1950's.

17

A Disastrous Encounter
with a Childhood Bully

I parked a little way up the street from the building and repeated my instruction for everyone to stay in the automobile. I gave Breitman a carbon of my orders in case he was questioned by authorities.

The place looked quite similar to other prisons I had "visited" in the Reich. This one had lots of battleship gray paint to go with the cement flooring. The prison was called Montelupich Prison, after the street by the same name.

I hadn't realized the prison had been taken over by the Geheime Staatpolizei or Gestapo until after I entered and started a conversation with the older, chain-smoking woman at the front desk. She had one cigarette in her hand and another still smoldering in the ashtray.

The official but pleasant, gray-haired woman seemed to blend in quite naturally with her surroundings. Her German, however, was excellent and understandable with only a hint of a Polish accent. She was so thin and pale, I thought for a moment she might be an Auschwitz survivor.

"Good afternoon, madam," was my polite greeting. "I would like to talk with the commander, Herr Hahn.* I am here under orders from Reichführer Himmler." I spread out my original copy on her counter.

The clerk looked nervous but tried to give me a satisfactory answer. I noticed a slight tremor in her voice.

"Of course," she answered. "He...he is just finishing a meeting but will be available in just a few minutes. You may wait in the conference room just down the hall; it is the first door on the right."

As I entered the conference room, I noticed a framed letter of commendation on the wall. It praised Herr Hahn for his recent promotion to the rank of *Sturmbannfürher* (Major) in the *SS*. In addition, the letter complimented his work with the *Einsatzgruppe*, a paramilitary killing group, and his position as Chief of the *Sicherheitdienst (SD)* or the intelligence branch of the SS, and *Sicherheitpolizei (SiPo)*, security police for the occupied city of Krakow.

It made me realize this Nazi was a very dangerous man.

As the Sturmbannfürher entered the conference room, I got up and gave him an enthusiastic Hitler salute.

He waved back and remarked, "What brings you to our city, Lieutenant?"

---

* Ludwig Herman Karl Hahn was a cruel member of the Schutzstaffel (SS). After the war he disguised himself as a farmworker then as an insurance broker. Journalists uncovered his true identity in 1960. He was convicted of deporting Jews from the Warsaw Ghetto to Treblinka. After all his appeals he received a life sentence in 1973. He died in Ammersbeck, near Hamburg in 1986. He was 78 years old.

"I am here under orders from Reichführer Himmler, Sturmbannfürher." I spread out my orders out on the conference table.

"I need three Aryan work permits for Jewish laborers I am taking for the secret Wehrmacht Research Center in northern Germany."

"What is going on at your research center, Lieutenant?"

I didn't want to appear disrespectful, and I needed cooperation to get the Aryan work permits. I decided to give him a little knowledge of what was happening in Peenemünde.

"Sir, everything I am about to disclose to you is top-secret and must not be discussed with anyone. Do you understand?"

"Of course, Lieutenant! I am no stranger to the penalties of loose talk, even among friends and colleagues."

"I can tell you this much, Sturmbannfürher. We are designing, building, and testing new weapons. These weapons have a range of several hundred kilometers and can be loaded with very powerful warheads.

"As you can tell from my orders, I am in the process of visiting some of our labor camps in order to find Jews with special engineering, electrical, or mechanical skills to help us with this endeavor."

"What about our own engineers and scientists?" asked the major.

"Unfortunately," I continued, "many of our scientists have been sent to labor camps or are involved with the war effort in another capacity."

"How many Jew laborers do you need?"

"Over time, we will need several hundred. I am going to meet my sergeant at another camp next week to find out who else might be available. Today I need work permits for three individuals."

The major brought me out to the reception area and directed the gray-haired woman he called Yael to write up the Aryan work papers.

I surmised the woman to be Jewish from her Old Testament name.

The major then asked Yael to summon one of his guards to show me the prison while she was preparing the documents.

After a couple of minutes, a smartly dressed guard called Gerhard came from a door to the rear of the reception area and introduced himself. The guard looked surprised to see me, but it was probably because of my size. I am quite tall at six feet four and a half inches.

"Gerhard," commanded the Sturmbannfürher. "Please show the lieutenant our efficient prison, but bring him back in thirty minutes for his documents."

"Ja, sicher, jawohl, Herr Sturmbannfürher."

As Gerhard led me down the hall to a flight of stairs leading down to the prison, he gave me a rather quizzical look. His facial expression didn't make too much sense to me at the time. We went down another flight of stairs to rows of small cells lined with stone. The area was below ground, unheated, and was cold and damp.

Gerhard asked, "Lieutenant, what part of Germany are you from?"

This question seemed a little personal, but I assumed he was trying to be friendly to a senior SS officer.

The guard was showing me the inside of one of the cold, damp, godforsaken cells when I answered, "Düsseldorf, Gerhard, why do you ask?"

With my reply, he stepped quickly outside the cell and slammed the barred door shut, turning the key and locking me inside.

"What are you attempting to do, Guard?"

"You don't remember me, do you, Lieutenant?"

"I can't say that I do. Are you familiar with me from my hometown?"

"As a matter-of-fact," he shot back in a rather loud and uncultured German slang dialect, **"I remember you quite distinctly from grade school. You were the tallest boy in our class. You broke all my fingers on my right hand defending one of your dirty 'Jew-boy' friends. It was after I got out of the hospital when I learned you were also a dirty Jew-boy. Now I have caught you masquerading as an SS Lieutenant!"**

Locked in a Gestapo-controlled, small, damp prison cell by a jailer who was a grade-school bully and enemy and confirmed anti-Semitic Nazi made my stomach growl. I couldn't tell if I was truly hungry again or chagrined at my foolishness for getting into the stone-lined cell in the first place.

I stepped over to the cell door and spoke softly in a low tone so Gerhard would have to approach the bars to hear me.

Out of caution, he didn't get too close to the bars. However, he must have forgotten about the length of my arms.

As I was speaking in a low voice, I was trying to explain to him that I hadn't had a decent meal in several hours and I was less than totally polite on an empty stomach.

While trying to explain to Gerhard my need for a good meal, I quickly jabbed my arm through the bars and grabbed the evil Nazi by his uniform collar. He was a little off-balance because he was trying to take a step backward. A look of shock came over his very surprised and ugly face. I pulled him with all my force into the bars on the cell. **Clang!**

I could tell by the depression of his skull on the bars the guard was totally stunned. His skull might have fractured. I grabbed the key to the cell from his belt, unlocked the cell, and pulled Gerhard inside with me.

I tried to explain to Gerhard, "The 'dirty Jew-boy' you were referring to was my life-long friend and fellow Jew, Ezekiel. Even though we were quite young, I couldn't tolerate you hurting my friend."

He was mumbling something and swearing quite loudly when I placed him in a chokehold, squeezed slowly but quite firmly on his neck, and snuffed the life out of him. He kicked and tried to scream and squirm out of my chokehold.

Alas, it was no use for him to struggle or complain. I did not enjoy killing anyone, but I did adjust my grip a little and let him take a breath.

I then resumed slowly squeezing the bastard's neck until his body went completely limp.

Then with a bit of effort, I eased him up to the upper bunk of the cell where he might not get noticed for several days. I propped up the thin mattress, laid Herr Gerhard on the mesh springs, let the thin mattress cover him and pulled the cover over the mattress where it draped down about a foot. With the near freezing temperature in this cell block, he might not get noticed for several weeks.

I locked the cell behind me and intentionally worked the key back and forth until it broke off in the lock, making it impossible to access the cell in the near future. I retraced my steps to Yael's office.

"Thank you so much for the work permits, Yael. You have been very helpful."

It was clear that she was still intimidated by me and my SS uniform. Even though I did not wear my officer's hat indoors, like so many pumped-up Nazis, she was clearly cowered by my presence.

I asked her to forward a message to Vitali Carapezza at the Research Facility in Peenemünde: *Meet me at the Auschwitz Labor Camp on the 15th of this month. SS Lieutenant Jenz Ramsgrund.*

I decided to perhaps make her feel a bit better when I leaned over and whispered in a low voice in Yiddish:

"There are many *schlub mamzers* (clumsy, stupid bastards) who wear this uniform."

Her look of surprise and shock was immediate. I wished her good day and walked out of the police station.

18

Auschwitz, A Murderous Machine

I carefully examined the Aryan work papers for the Wiernik family and Mr. Breitman. The papers looked in order and I signed them with my name and SS rank at the bottom of each page.

We then took a brief tour of Krakow. I drove them by Oskar Schindler's enamelware plant where cookware and arms were being produced for the Wehrmacht.

Mrs. Wiernik asked, "Is this where we should come if we cannot find employment?"

"No, Mrs. Wiernik. Come to this factory only if you are in trouble or cannot find any employment elsewhere. Your Aryan work papers should be adequate for finding employment and a home.

"I will drive you by the city housing authority where there are probably many vacant apartments available in the city. Almost all the Jews have had to flee to the ghetto or have been transported to the labor camps under the *Aktion Reinhard Operation.*"*

It was getting dark, and I wanted to make sure my passengers were safe for the evening. Since I had to drive north then southwest to the Auschwitz Camp, I drove them to the small hotel where we had taken our late dinner. I paid for their dinner and two rooms for one week at the hotel. I took a room and decided to wake early for the drive to Auschwitz Camp. I bid my fellow travelers goodbye before retiring.

I told Breitman he would have the option of remaining in Krakow or continuing with me to Auschwitz and on to the Research Center. I suggested he would not be safe returning to his home until the war against the Russians was concluded.

He asked, "Would it be okay to return with you to the Research Center?"

I had to inform him of my plans to get more Jews from Auschwitz for laborers to our facility in northern Germany.

---

* "Operation Reinhard" was named after a brutal Nazi, Reinhard Heydrich. This unrepentant Nazi sought all his life to suppress details of his Jewish ancestry. After being dismissed from the German Naval Service for dishonorable conduct toward a young woman, he was appointed by Himmler to SS Obergrupenführer. Heydrich was responsible for the comprehensive draft of the "Final Solution to the Jewish Problem" presented at the Wannsee Conference in January 1942. An assassination attempt was made on his life by Czech soldiers on the 27th of May 1942. Heydrich died from a massive infection caused by the assassination attempt in a Prague hospital on 4 June 1942. He was 38 years old.

"Breitman, I cannot guarantee your safety at Auschwitz. It could be very dangerous for both of us. I am planning on meeting my sergeant there tomorrow."

"I understand," was his comment. "There is really no place in Germany, Poland, or all of Europe, where I would consider myself safe. Since I have already lost my family to the *Vernichtungslager* (Extermination Camp) in Treblinka, I am not worried about the Auschwitz Camp."

It took us most of the next morning to get to the Auschwitz Labor Camp. Although it wasn't far from Krakow, there were many checkpoints. My orders made it easy for us to get into the camp. What I hadn't realized was this concentration camp was now a death camp for the extermination of all the remaining Jews in Europe.

I signed Breitman into the concentration camp as my aide and reserved a room for him and Ezekiel under Zeke's acceptable Aryan name, Vitali Carapezza. The entire camp was huge; it was spread over several hundred acres in the town of Birkenau. The officers and enlisted quarters were not too far from the main gate.

I went into the enlisted barracks with Breitman in order to make sure he and Ezekiel could secure a couple of rooms for a few days. As I approached the clerk at the front counter, I removed my SS officer's hat and stood in front of his desk.

For some reason, the color completely drained from the clerk's face, and he started to shake. He was shaking with such a tremor he couldn't even log in rooms for two guests. He finally gave Breitman the log and asked him to fill in the names.

I asked the clerk, "Kapo, what is the problem?"

"Sir," he replied, "I am not a Kapo. Although I wear the green triangle, I just handle the paperwork for this facility."

"Why do you seem so frightened? You must have had paperwork from officers in the SS before."

"I'm sorry," the clerk continued; he then started weeping and shaking so much I felt embarrassed for him.

"Breitman, let's find your quarters."

We left the clerk, red-faced and still extremely agitated. I felt badly for him but knew there must be more to his story.

As soon as we were outside, I addressed Breitman. "Horace, after you have settled in your room, I want you to return to this front desk area and find out what is going on with the clerk. Here is a copy of my orders in case you are ever questioned. Try to wring out every bit of information you can from this poor soul, because he may be hiding something we should know about events here at Auschwitz."

"I will give him a few minutes to compose himself," Breitman replied. "Then I will quietly ask him about his family and background.

"I will report back to you in about one hour at the central office."

19

Historical Anti-Semitism

Breitman met me in the central office for the Auschwitz Camp a little over an hour later. He was carrying a small notepad with several pages of scribbled notes he had taken while talking with the extremely nervous clerk.

"Lieutenant, you may want to sit down while I give you the clerk's experience he had with his hometown police and Ukrainian guards. This might take a few minutes. The clerk was very reluctant to discuss much of anything with me until I assured him, I was also Jewish and from a small town in Poland near Warsaw. He seemed relieved we could communicate fluently in Polish."

I was gaining more confidence in Breitman's adaptability to interactions with Jews and Aryans as I got to know him. I suggested, "Let's try to find a quiet table in the Officer's Mess near the back of the camp. It is only a ten-minute walk from here."

It was a wonderful spring day with a hint of the warmth of summer all around the edges. The only dark clouds were above the chimneys of the four crematoriums. The chimneys occasionally roared and spit fire into the smoke when the crematoriums were burning up the bodies of my countrymen. If the wind was wrong, the ash covered the camp.

I had to stay strong so as not to fall into a deep depression. In my later years, I wondered how I didn't fall into the rabbit hole of self-loathing and hate.

We took some tea from the self-serve counter and settled in at a small table in the back of the cafeteria. We were pretty much alone in the cafeteria at this time of day. Breitman looked somewhat reluctant to begin, so I prompted him in a low quiet voice. "Tell me, Breitman, what has our clerk so frightened he cannot function with a coherent voice?"

"His name is Samuel Eisen; he's from a small town near Buczacz, Poland. He witnessed the death of many Jews from his hometown.

"When the Ukrainian guards came into his town to round up the Jews, they made many of the Jewish men dig a deep pit in the local cemetery. The guards placed large planks across the pit. The Jewish people caught in the round-up were ordered to strip naked and stand on the planks. Five Jews at a time were ordered and whipped to the center of the planks over the pits and murdered by machine-gun fire; they fell into the pit.

"Surviving Jews were ordered to go down into the pit and arrange the bodies next to one another, packing them in like sardines, so more bodies would fit into the pit. The pit was filled with bodies as well as urine, excrement, and blood.

"Young children were thrown into the pit alive, only to be covered up by more corpses. A Ukrainian guard would throw young children into the pit alive by grabbing them by the neck and shouting: *'Nimm das dreck und schmeiss herein!'* 'Grab the filth and throw it in!' The children would be drowning in the blood and urine.

"After the shouting and murdering were finished, somehow, our terrified clerk was able to climb out of the pit and survive.

He had jumped into the pit as soon as the firing started. He lied about his age when he arrived here at Auschwitz, because he knew everyone under the age of sixteen was selected to go to the left and on to the gas chambers.

"When he saw you towering over him at the front counter, he had a flash-back to his experience in the pit and was unable to speak coherently."

"*Mein Gott im Himmel,* Horace. What makes people so deranged they are able to commit murder with such horrible indifference?"

"I should also tell you, Lieutenant, of another case of unimaginable cruelty."

"Horace, what could you possibly tell me...; what could be worse than children crawling out of a pit of blood and dead bodies?"

"Samuel has a friend, another Jewish survivor, who works with him at the front counter most of the time. He was with him while Samuel was relating his story to me. He agreed with Samuel and said everything related to me was true. But he also wanted to add his own story."

"Not another atrocity, I hope!"

"This young man's name is Jacob Heiss. He remembered the Germans coming into his town of Buczacz and singing '*Spielzeit fur die Kameraden*' ('Playtime for the Comrades'). That night would be filled with shouting, yelling, shooting, and cries of terror for help. The next day there would be dead bodies everywhere. Jacob was spared in the round up because, at the time, he was visiting his mother and his new baby sister in the hospital. His mom had just given birth to a baby daughter. When the Germans came into the hospital, he hid behind a window curtain in his mother's hospital room, but unfortunately, saw everything happening in the room.

"The German SS guards were going from room to room shooting anyone Jewish. When they came to his mother's room, the guard took one look at the Jewish name on the chart, yelled at his mom, and confirmed she was Jewish. He then grabbed his newborn sister by her legs, smashed her head against the cinder-block wall, and hurled her out of the third story window. The guard wanted to be sure the mother witnessed what was happening to her newborn daughter. Then he shot Jacob's mother. One shot in the head. The room resembled a slaughter-house with blood splashed everywhere."

I couldn't control myself any longer. My face was unconsciously contorted in anguish. A tear dropped into my tea. "Horace, these atrocities have to be remembered, written down, and published in a country with a free press. Even with publication, few would believe this abhorrent cruelty."

"Unfortunately," replied Breitman, "Jacob's small town of Buczacz has a long history of cruelty and torture toward the Jewish population. The anti-Semitism goes back centuries for Jews all over Europe."

"What history are talking about? I asked. I have heard nothing of this sort ever happening in my hometown of Düsseldorf."

"I lived not too far from Jacob's hometown. The Jewish population in Poland was subjected to the worst torture and degradation only humans could dredge to the surface of very twisted minds. The history of the Cossack and peasant uprising of the mid-sixteen hundreds documents some of the atrocities.*

---

*   Hanover, Nathan. "The Book of Deep Mire," The Ukranian Rebellion of 1648.

"Some Jews were skinned alive with their flesh thrown to the dogs.

"The most defenseless suffered the worst: some expectant women had their babies cut out of their bellies and were beaten with the fetus. Live cats were inserted into the women and sewn up. Their hands tied so they couldn't remove the cats. It was a most horrible way to die.

"Some young children were skewered and roasted over a roaring fire for the mothers who were forced to watch and then eat them."

I looked at Breitman with an incredulous look on my face. "Where do you get this information, Horace?"

"Unfortunately, it is a well-documented part of our history."

"Breitman, do you believe in prayer?"

"Of course! But do you think God is in this place?"

"I think God is everywhere, even in this hellhole.

"We have to be extra-careful in this camp. Do not trust anyone.

"However, in the New Testament in the Christian Bible somewhere in Ephesians, there is a quote: *'God himself is our peace. We are no longer foreigners, but fellow citizens of God's household.'*

"It is hard for us to have forgiveness in our hearts for the harsh brutality we have heard and seen all around us. I need to do what I can to select almost one hundred prisoners and their families for work at our secret facility in Peenemünde, in northern Germany. If you can help me, I will do everything I can to ensure your immediate freedom as soon as possible after we arrive at the rocket facility with our workers.

"Sargent Carapezza should be here tomorrow. We will begin the worker selection process for our facility in Peenemünde in the morning."

20

A New Transport Arrives at Auschwitz

The next morning, I met with the camp commanding officer, Rudolf Höss* in his office. He scowled while reading over my orders but was pleasant enough in his demeanor to invite me to the next selection process for the just-arrived transport. I told him I would be bringing my sergeant and an aide with me for picking out the slave workers for our facility at Peenemünde.

---

* Höss was noted for his brutal efficiency while Commandant of the Auschwitz Concentration Camp. He was the first to use the powerful and dangerous insecticide Zyklon-B for the extermination of the prisoners. After the war, he avoided arrest by working as a farm worker until he was discovered. At his trial, he claimed he was only following orders and used care in collecting gold rings and gold teeth for the SS, and women's hair for furniture upholstery. In his autobiography, he rejected any notion he was a sadist and claimed, "I am completely normal; I led a completely normal life." Although he repented while in prison, he was hanged by the Polish Supreme National Tribunal at the Auschwitz Camp he used to command on 16 April 1947. He was 45 years old.

Although Höss was persistent in wanting to know what we were doing at the secret facility, I finally recommended he call General Dornberger if he wanted further information about our projects.

"Commandant, I need healthy technicians and their families. We require engineers, machinists, jewelers, or anyone used to working with small parts. Women prisoners can work in the housing and cafeteria facilities, and they are usually terrific in small-part assembly. We cannot accept anyone who is ill, but they must be trained in their respective technical fields."

The Commandant requested, "Meet the camp doctors at the platform for the selection process at one o'clock this afternoon."

"But, Commandant, isn't the transport already at the siding?" I asked.

"Yes. Of course, Lieutenant. But we find if we keep them waiting without food or water in a sweltering enclosed cattle car for a few hours, the prisoners are much more compliant about being led to the gas chambers. If you think about it, the gas chambers offer relief for them. We are actually doing these Jews a favor."

I thought to myself: *This Nazi is completely immune to the discomfort, pain, and degradation these families must be suffering. These innocent men, women, and children are packed like sardines into a cattle railroad car with no space for toilet facilities, fresh water or even breathable air. If I could have gotten away with squeezing the life out of this bastard's neck, I would have easily and joyfully completed the task right there in his office.*

"Commandant. Won't these prisoners be adversely affected by the lack of water?"

"Of course, Lieutenant! These vermin will be very ready to accept our orders when they are let out of the transports. You might say the prisoners become eagerly compliant."

My immediate thought was this Nazi deserves to be tried and executed. My answer to his swagger, "Excellent, Herr Commandant! I will be near the platform after lunch."

I met Zeke and Breitman at their quarters and they joined me near the rail siding before the first transport was unlocked.

After meeting Horace Breitman, Vitali assured me, "Jenz, all of the women we transported to Peenemünde are secure and safe. Do you remember the young woman, Adiya? She was the one I picked up off the floor after she had been whipped by the guard. I placed your uniform jacket over her to protect her and hide her nakedness and shame after the bastards had cut off her hair."

"Of course, I remember her. Didn't she have a younger sister?"

"Yes, Jenz. Her sister's name is Chasha. I think it means 'to be merciful' in Yiddish.

"She is working in the kitchen along with three of the women, including her older sister. The other women have adapted to assembling hardware for the V-I bomb.

"One lady is working in the lab since she had some experience with chemical engineering. She is actually working on improving the gas-fuel mixture for the V-I engine."

"Excellent, Ezekiel. Thanks for delivering these women to safety.

"Now let's see if we can be successful here at the Auschwitz Camp. What we are attempting here could be extremely dangerous for all of us. We have to assume an attitude of harshness, rigidity, and utter contempt for these prisoners – while attempting to save as many as possible."

"They must be getting ready to unlock the first transport," Breitman suggested. "Many of the guards with the Totenkopfverbande patch (SS-VT) or Death's Head units, are congregating on the platform. A few of them have clubs or whips in their hands. One of the guards has drawn his pistol."

"One of the camp doctors is at the table by the platform. I think the selection process happens at the table," suggested Zeke.

"What legitimate physician would participate in something so heinous as the selection process?" asked Breitman.

I cautiously answered, "I believe his name is Mengele. He is an SS *Hauptsturmführer* (Captain)."

"Doesn't the selection make most women, children, and old people go directly to the gas chambers?" Vitali asked.

"Even pregnant women! Only the physically strong are permitted to live and work under slave-like conditions until they are worked to death.

"You are correct," I added. "Dr. Joseph Mengele* is infamous for his abhorrent genetic research on twins. He has even injected chemicals into the eyes of patients in order to change their eye color from brown to blue. Most of his experiments on prisoners are truly dangerous without regard for the health or safety of his victims. If one twin dies because of his macabre experiments, he immediately kills the other twin."

---

* Joseph Mengele, also known as "The Angel of Death," escaped from Nazi Germany and fled to South America after the war. He lived in Buenos Aries. He fled to Paraguay in 1959 and then to Brazil in 1960. He suffered a stroke and drowned while swimming off the coast of Bertioga in 1979 and was buried under the false name of Wolfgang Gerhard. He was 68 years old. His remains were disinterred in 1985 and positively identified by forensic examination.

21

The Selection Process

I briefly introduced myself and my sergeant and aide to Dr. Mengele as I spread my orders on the table for him to read. He took quite an interest in the secret Wehrmacht base in Peenemünde and wanted to know if we were furthering any experiments on our prisoners.

"Our experiments involve fuels and weapons, doctor. We leave human experiments up to clinicians much more qualified than ourselves."

"If you're interested, Lieutenant, I can show you some of the progress we are making with experiments with twins after this selection. We are still looking for twins or mothers pregnant with twins. I'm hoping some of the work will be groundbreaking. Of course, if our experiment with the twins doesn't work out, we have to euthanize the other twin."

"Isn't it wasteful to have to have to destroy the remaining child?"

"Lieutenant, these are Jews we are talking about!"

"Thank you, doctor, I'm sure your experiments are most interesting."

This officer radiated pure evil. It is a mystery why the German medical profession would let him get anywhere near patients, especially children.

The cattle car gates were unlocked, and the first hapless prisoners tumbled out onto the platform. A prisoner band was playing German marching tunes. The music portrayed an almost festive atmosphere.

Bang!

One of the SS Totenkopf guards shot an elderly gentleman in the head at point-blank range. Blood spattered everywhere and the old prisoner tumbled off the platform. People near the old gentleman were screaming and trying to get away from the guard.

"Doctor, why are we shooting these people even before the selection process?"

"This action is quite routine, Lieutenant, don't let it bother you. This older Jew would have been sent directly to the gas house anyway.

"However, there are three reasons for our initial harsh contact with the prisoners, Lieutenant. First, it lets the Jews know they must follow orders. This cockroach was probably complaining of the severe treatment, without food or water, given to his fellow prisoners during their time of incarceration on the transports. Shooting him in the head, it lets other prisoners know what hard treatment is all about. Second, it lets the prisoners know the consequences of any kind of resistance they might be thinking of fomenting. And third, it makes them so much more compliant when we march most of them to their eternal home in the gas house."

"Why are they being whipped and beaten as they exit the transports, Doctor?"

"Sometimes, Lieutenant, they have been standing for so long in the cattle car, it takes a little prodding to get them moving. When we have several thousand each day to process, we cannot let them linger on the platform. After all, if we aren't careful, this could take hours out of our day."

"Remember, doctor, please ask the prisoners if they have any trade or craftsman skills in engineering or machine parts. Our secret base needs at least 100 skilled men and women for our production facility."

"I will make an announcement on the speaker, as soon as the transports are empty. Get ready, they will start filing by our selection table directly after the transports pull out from the platform. Have your sergeant and aide bring another table for a separate workspace for you."

"I should tell you, Doctor Mengele, because of the very secret nature of our work at Peenemünde, we get the best results if entire families can be routed to our facility. Even young children are put to work under their mother's supervision."

"They don't get too emotional, Lieutenant, when you take them as a group to your northern base?" asked Mengele.

"We can get much more dedication and work from these Jews if they think they have some future by working hard at our base."

"Are you sure you want some women and children? These vermin are usually gassed right away along with the older men.

"Also, do you want Aryan-looking Jews?"

"Our main criteria are healthy-looking families. We cannot take sick or dying Jews that may need the infirmary here at Auschwitz."

"Oh, don't worry, Lieutenant, almost all the unhealthy prisoners are sent to the gas chambers. The infirmary is only for the slave workers here at the camp. Anyone admitted to the infirmary who isn't better in two weeks is automatically killed with the gas."

"Is that method pretty efficient?" I asked.

"**Very!** We are now using a powerful insecticide called Zyklon-B.* It makes sure most of the prisoners are dead within twenty to thirty minutes. With this deadly gas, our chambers can exterminate up to two thousand Jews with each cycle."

My comment was without enthusiasm. "The gas sounds very efficient, doctor."

"It is efficient, Lieutenant, but it does cause a mess. There is a lot of bleeding from the vermin's ears and mouths, plus there is a lot of feces and urine to clean after each gassing."

By this time Vitali, Breitman, and I were ready to lose our lunch, but I forced the comment, "Doctor, please send families over to our table for final selection. We need these workers at the Wehrmacht base in Peenemünde."

It was refreshing just to put a little distance from this evil doctor. The three of us sat at a round table about thirty meters from the elongated rectangular selection table.

It was such a peaceful warm day. It would be a great day to take a cooling swim. I was reminded of my time at Hitler Youth Camp and meeting Ilsa. I missed her terribly. I vowed to make every attempt to get some time off to see her after this assignment. Just thinking about her in my arms put me in a much better place.

---

* Zyklon-B or prussic acid was used initially by the Germans in WWI during gas warfare in the trenches. Prussic acid turns into hydrogen cyanide gas when released. This gas interferes with lung function. Death comes within 30 minutes.

Vitali broke my reverie. "Jenz, I should mention to you, I feel very positively toward the woman we saved from Treblinka."

"Oh, really, which one?" *Of course, I knew, but I was desperately trying to lighten my mood.*

"The young woman the guard was whipping. She seems to have fallen in love with me."

"Are you talking about Adiya?

"Yes. She came with her sister, Chasha."

"She seemed like a beautiful, bright, and very frightened young woman, Vitali; I am very happy for you both.

"But... how do you know she is in love with you?"

I was teasing Zeke a little. I could tell from the way she looked at him after he picked her off the floor after she had been whipped. Even though he had his sergeant's German army uniform on you could tell the way she looked at him there was something special between them.

"As soon as we returned to Peenemünde, she thanked me profusely for rescuing her and her little sister. She knew she was about to go to the gas chamber. I haven't confided in her yet, but I think she suspects I am Jewish."

"We have to be very careful not to confide in anyone, even Breitman or Adiya. Ilsa and I have not even discussed anything about religion. Our country is just too dangerous to be discussing political or religious beliefs."

22

Saving a Few Families from Auschwitz

Dr. Mengele made a brief announcement about the need for skilled workers for our secret research project which seemed to confuse the poor folks getting off the transports even more. The Jewish "prisoners" from the transports weren't sure which way to go. The selectees with families were almost always separated at the selection table but those with special skills moved to our table. Vitali had them line up and we questioned the male members of each family to get an idea of prior work-related skills.

Many of them worked in small shops as cobblers, garment manufacturers, and jewelers. One of the men had been a pharmacist and two were engineers. One of the women taught mathematics at gymnasium.

By the time we finished with the transport, we had enough families to fill three buses.

I informed Commandant Höss we were taking the busses with the Jewish families to our base in Peenemünde, but his drivers would return with the busses immediately after dropping off the slave workers.

119

"Also," I mentioned as an aside to Herr Commandant Höss, "I can assure you, Commandant, these vermin will all be dealt with after our experiments are completed at our secret Wehrmacht base." *In the back of my mind, I was hoping all these poor families would find a way back to their homes and loved ones.*

I informed Breitman in a firm tone, "I want you and Vitali to go over the ground rules and regulations with these families for the trip to Peenemünde and what they should expect once they arrive. Tell them they will be kept on the base and under no circumstances are they to discuss our work there with anyone outside the base.

"In addition, you will add, any discussion of what transpires at this secret facility with anyone will result in an immediate one-way trip back to Auschwitz."

"Yes, Sir!" An agreement from the sergeant and Breitman came in unison.

"In addition, Sargent Carapezza, I need to interview one member of each family at random to see if we have the proper mix for our base. We cannot have anyone who is going to be disruptive, have only marginal skills, or is already ill with typhus."

"I understand, Lieutenant. I will procure the transportation while Breitman organizes the prisoners."

I wanted to find out if any of these prisoners were criminals or potential troublemakers. With so many of our workers at Peenemünde dying of illness or exhaustion, we couldn't afford to bring in outside problems to our secret rocket base.

Breitman, because of his fluency in Polish, and I started interviewing the prisoners who were lined up for the bus. We interviewed these folks back at our small round table. It was out of earshot of the rest of the general confusion, crying, and the cacophony of noise from the selection committee.

I started with one woman who appeared to be alone.

"What is your name, Miss?"

"You may call me Zivia." *

"How did you come to find yourself in this camp?" I asked.

"Lieutenant, I mean no disrespect, but when I was told to go to the left at the selection table with all the other women, children, and old people, I started to the left, and then, when the doctor and guard were looking the other way, I went directly to your table. I knew going to the left was a death sentence, I could not die like a dog in your gas house."

I then asked Breitman to ask where she was from in her native language but to reply in German so I would understand completely.

Breitman asked, "Miss, speaking in German, can you tell us where you are from?"

"I am from the ghetto in Warsaw. The Germans surrounded our ghetto on the 18th of April 1943. The Nazis wanted to give Hitler a little present for his birthday which was on the 20th of April. At six in the morning, the Germans attacked in force and burned, looted, and destroyed our entire section of the city. If people wouldn't come out of their homes to be shot or sent to the

---

* I didn't realize it at the time, but the name "Zivia" had become the secret code name for the entire resistance movement in Poland. I also had no idea this woman was one of the heroes of these brave woman resistance fighters. She died of lung cancer in 1978 at the age of 63, probably from an inveterate cigarette habit. As per her husband's request, only her first name "Zivia" appears on her tombstone. Her son explained, "Zivia is an institution; no further words are necessary."

transports, the Nazis would pour gasoline on their home, put it to the torch and shoot anyone brave enough to leave.

"I saw one mother holding and trying to protect her young child from the flames. A Nazi soldier came along and ripped this sweet young daughter from the mother's arms. He then threw the child to the ground and stomped the tiny body with his steel-toed boots. He then stabbed the writhing little broken child with his bayonet and flung her into the flames.

"This same Nazi beat the mother with his rifle butt and threw her into the street. He laughed as an approaching tank crushed her frail body under the steel treads."

"You have said your name is Zivia?"

"Yes. But truthfully, there are many named Zivia in the Polish Underground."

"Do you have any mechanical, electrical, or machine skills?" I asked.

"Yes," was all she said.

"Will you follow our strict rules at the secret research center and not be disruptive, if I ship you out of this camp?"

"Yes."

In a quiet, but firm voice I told her, "Please get on the bus before the doctor at the selection table recognizes you."

Each family's story seemed more incredible than the family before. I talked with one family member from each group before they boarded the buses. I was satisfied our orders were fulfilled.

I asked Zeke, "Vitali, will you and Breitman be able to get these folks safely to our facility in Peenemünde?"

"Of course!" replied Zeke, "but what about you; aren't you going to return with us?"

I took Zeke aside and in a low voice not heard by anyone but him, "With our Sixth Army in trouble in the east, I'm not sure how long it might take the Russians or the Allies to discover and liberate this camp. I'm going to see whatever I can do to speed up that day."

"Be careful, Jenz. I get the feeling nothing in this camp goes undetected. You could be in grave danger."

"I will be cautious, Zeke. I want to see Ilsa as soon as I get back to Germany. I miss her with all my heart.

"I have a feeling you are pretty anxious to see Ms. Adiya."

I gave him an affirmative nod and a quick wink and added, "I hope her little sister, Chasha is also doing well after the trauma of their lives at Treblinka.

"Please do everything possible to make all of our new workers as comfortable and as well-nourished as you can. Although the buses seem a little dilapidated, I'm sure they will be much more comfortable than the accommodations here at Auschwitz.

"Also, let General Dornberger know about Mr. Breitman. Inform him, because of his linguistic and mechanical skills as a skilled machinist, he is our new aide for dealing with the Polish Jews."

23

Digging in at Auschwitz

The next day I met with Commandant Höss to thank him for allowing us to obtain workers for our facility in Peenemünde. I told him I was going to observe some of the work crews to get some ideas for our disciplinary staff at our base.

There was a shop at the camp where all sorts of uniform parts were traded and bartered for goods and services. The shop had piles of worn enlisted and officer uniforms, some looking almost new.

I traded my uniform jacket for two black SS well-worn shirts and pants. This outfit would help camouflage my real reason for hanging around this hell-on-earth: I wanted to see if there was any possible way of getting the Allies or the Russians here sooner.

News was seeping into Germany in the spring of 1943 of a massive defeat of the German 6th Army at Stalingrad. General Friedrich

Paulus* was encircled by the Russian Army and surrendered to the Russian General Rokossovsky** in February 1943.

All the prisoners in Auschwitz were very anxious to hear any news of liberation. Most of these poor, unfortunate and completely innocent folks had been very successfully dehumanized by the Nazi system: Deaths Head SS guards, criminal kapo guards, and continuous harsh labor and beatings. Many of the prisoners were not even capable of uttering a complete sentence, let alone thinking a complete thought.

One evening I met a group of prisoners coming back from a work detail. There must have been almost 300 men trudging back from building a road in the forest. Most of them looked completely spent. Their clothes were torn and ragged, and many could barely walk.

I asked a question to the kapo in charge of marching the men back to the camp. "Kapo, where are you working these prisoners?"

He straightened up and answered, "Lieutenant, we have been taking down trees and building a road for the Germans in the nearby forest."

---

* General Paulus tried in vain to get his troops out of the Stalingrad Pocket where they were encircled by the Russian Army. Hitler refused to let him leave Stalingrad resulting in the defeat of the entire German 6th Army and the loss of almost 265,000 men. Less than 5,000 of these defeated soldiers ever made it back to Germany after the war. Paulus died in Dresden on the 1st of February 1957. He was 67 years old.

** General Konstantin Rokossovsky accepted the surrender of the German 6th Army on the 2nd of February 1943. He went on to crush the German Army Group Centre in Belarus and was on the banks of the Vistula River opposite Warsaw by mid-1944. After the war, he held various high positions in Poland and Russia. He died in Russia in August 1968 at the age of 71.

"Are you returning with the same number of prisoners you left with this morning?" I asked.

"We lost two from accidents or exhaustion, Lieutenant. I don't mean to be disrespectful, sir, but why do you ask? These Jews are all to be gassed soon."

I spoke loud enough so many of the prisoners could hear. "Kapo, all these workers are valuable to the Reich."

Then I continued. "Kapo, there has been a disaster for the Reich at Stalingrad this past winter. You should realize roads and bridges are very important to the smooth-running governing of Poland. Treat these valuable workers with respect."

I walked along with the 300 or so workers until they entered their "barracks." Their housing was more like chicken coops than barracks. One of the slave workers spoke up to me as they were going through the gate.

"Officer," he quietly called to me. "Please do not make any changes to our routine here at this camp."

"Why do you say that, prisoner?"

"We all dread changes," he replied quietly. "There is a saying here at Auschwitz, Lieutenant: 'When things change, they change for the worse!'"

"Has something happened recently? What is your name, prisoner? There will be no trouble."

"My name is Levi,* Lieutenant. Please do not say anything. My body is just healing from my last beating."

---

*   Primo Levi was an Italian Jew captured by the Fascist Militia in December 1943, in Turin and deported to Auschwitz. Fortunately, he survived and later wrote about his time in the camp titled "Survival in Auschwitz" published in English in 1996. Touchstone, Simon & Schuster, Inc.

"God be with you, Levi," I whispered to him as he entered his encampment area.

I spent the rest of the day looking for officers of my own rank with whom I could discuss disciplinary measures utilized at the camp.

I also wanted to visit the main hospital which I understood was over on block 21 of the camp. The labor camp was huge. I got directions to the main administrative office of the hospital *(Schreibstaube)* and met with the administrator.

The administrator gave me some information on the hospital structure. "All the doctors are Jews under the direct supervision of the SS Captains. Our chief selection officer is SS captain Joseph Mengele. He also does some research with twins and expectant mothers."

I tried to keep an open mind about most of the personnel I had met at Auschwitz, but I had never heard anything positive about Dr. Mengele. He abused his authority at the camp and abused his patients who underwent sketchy medical procedures. I put him on a list as a need for elimination if the opportunity of time and place ever became relevant.

24

A Visit to the Prisoners' Hospital (Häftlingskrankenbau or HKB)

As I walked through the hospital, it was painfully obvious the patients were not getting very good treatment. I asked to see the current administrator. Patients were often doubled up, two to a bed. Some were lying in filth. Many were laying naked on paper pads in pools of pus, blood, excrement, and urine.

SS Sturmbannführer Kurt Uhlenbroock* came out from his office and offered a wave of a Hitler salute.

"What can I do for you this morning, Lieutenant?" A cheerful greeting in such a macabre setting immediately put me on the defensive.

"Good morning, *Sturmbannführer*. I'm visiting from the Wehrmacht Research Center and would like to get some ideas for our infirmary in Peenemünde."

---

* Kurt Erich Uhlenbrook briefly served as an attending physician at Auschwitz. At his trial in November 1960, he was acquitted for lack of evidence. After the war, he operated a laboratory for drug testing and died at age 84 in Hamburg in 1992.

"What is going on at your research center, Lieutenant?"

"We are mostly researching various arms and fuels for the use in our war efforts against the Russians." This vague reply seemed to satisfy the Sturmbannführer.

He was still curious, but he offered to help. "I will have one of the orderlies show you around our facility. Remember, we do not have top-line equipment or medicines in this facility. In addition, we are short-staffed; most of our doctors are Jewish prisoners."

He then stopped one of the orderlies passing by. "Herr Klehr, could you please show the lieutenant our facility?"

"Of course, Sturmbannführer."

"Where would you like to start, Lieutenant? I suggest we skip the infectious disease block; it is depressing and neither of us needs a dose of typhus."

"What is your full name, Herr Klehr?"

"I am Josef Klehr,* and I have been here since 1941."

"Do you work in any particular area of the hospital?"

"You might say I work in all areas – especially where patients are very sick.

"I have implemented a way of reducing the number of ill patients at our facility who might be near death anyway."

He seemed proud of himself, so I asked him what I thought was a simple question.

"Oh," I inquired. "How do you accomplish a quick healing?"

---

* Joseph Klehr was a medical orderly at Auschwitz Prisoners Hospital from 1941 until it was overrun and liberated by the Russians in 1945. He devised sadistic methods of murdering sick patients by injecting phenol directly into the heart of his patients. His logbook indicated he had killed over 14,000 patients with these cruel methods. He was well-known for his abject cruelty.

"Lieutenant, you don't understand. Everyone in this facility will eventually wind up in the gas houses, unless they miraculously get better. Our facility is known as 'the waiting room for the crematoria!'"

"If they get better, they will go back to heavy labor in one of the camp projects."

I thought I would try one more time.

"Herr Klehr, what is your method of ridding the patients of their disease or broken bodies?"

"It is very simple, Lieutenant; I inject phenol directly into their heart. It is a quick and easy death for these Jews. They are deceased within five minutes."

His eyes seemed to dance at the prospect of taking more Jewish lives. His squinty-mad eyes and Satin-like smile displayed the zeal he put into his work.

My immediate thought was *I would like to choke the life out of this sadistic bastard right here in the ward.*

My reply included, "How delightful, Klehr. You seem to be following an excellent program of ridding these misfortune Jews from the Reich."

"Yes, Lieutenant, we do our best."

"Thank you for your valuable service to the Reich, Klehr; but I do have one question."

"I am at your service, Lieutenant."

"Who is the young, very pretty Aryan-looking girl I passed near the administrator's desk as I came into this block?"

"She belongs to Commandant Höss," replied Klehr.

"Do you mean he has his daughter here at the prison camp?"

"Oh, no, Lieutenant. When I used the word belong, perhaps I should have used a more accurate term. She is the commandant's sex slave."

"What?

"You've got to be putting me on, Klehr. How old is she, 15 years?"

"Her name is Cilka Klein,* Lieutenant. I believe she is 16 years old, or almost 16 anyway. The commandant took a liking to her as soon as she was tossed out of the transport. He happened to be at the selection desk and ordered her to come with him.

"Many of the other prisoners are jealous of her because she gets extra food and warm clothes in the winter. She is housed separately from the other prisoners and has many privileges denied to the other prisoners.

"From what I hear, she is continuously raped by the commandant whenever he likes."

All the disease and death in these infirmary wards were really getting to me.

"Are you telling me, Klehr, these four blocks of the infirmary – 19, 20, 21, and 28 – are basically just instruments of annihilation?"

"Lieutenant, let's put it this way: if you come into our hospital with a disease or injury – you may get better, but that would be a true miracle!"

---

* Cilka Klein did have special privileges at Auschwitz. However, those privileges came at a tremendous cost. When the Russians liberated the Auschwitz Camp, Cilka was labeled a collaborator, probably by the other prisoners. She was sent to Vorkuta, a brutal Russian prison camp where she endured ten years of further sexual assaults. Her life story is historically documented in a novel by author Heather Morris called "Cilka's Journey." This book is viewed as a sequel to Morris's best-selling novel, "The Tattooist of Auschwitz." HarperCollins 2018.

Miracle Doctors at Auschwitz

As I was leaving the infirmary block 20, I came across a woman whom I thought was a young nurse or orderly. She stiffened when I spoke to her.

"Miss, could you tell me if there are any prison doctors on this block in the infirmary?"

"Yes. Although I am the only woman doctor for this woman's infirmary section, there are other doctors in the prison."

Then I asked very quietly, but firmly, "Doctor, is there any place where we could talk without interruption for a few moments?"

She then beckoned me to follow her into a small office. The office was more like a small closet.

"This is where I write up my medical notes and make notations in the patients' charts.

"Could I ask why the SS would like to talk with me?"

"Thank you for speaking with me today, Doctor. I am visiting from a research center in northern Germany. I am interested in getting information on medical centers in the Reich, so I am better able to make recommendations at our facility."

She asked, "Is your facility a labor camp?"

"No. Our area of research is in developing fuels and armaments for the Reich. But we do have laborers from various camps.

"May I ask your name?"

"My name is Perl, Lieutenant, Doctor Gisella Perl.* Male prisoners threw me out of the cattle-car transport when I arrived here earlier this year. Dr. Mengele assigned me to the woman's infirmary after he learned I was a gynecological doctor."

"Are you only catering to the needs of the woman prisoners?"

"No, Lieutenant. Many of my patients have been injured in accidents or have had their bodies ravaged and raped by your SS, brutal kapos, or other male prisoners."

"Tell me about the injuries to the women prisoners, Doctor."

"Why would the SS have an interest in the injuries they have caused, Lieutenant?"

"Because there is always a chance I could talk with the commandant and see if conditions could be improved for the women prisoners."

"There is no chance for improvement in our conditions, Lieutenant. The commandant has even set up a block of the

---

* Dr. Perl came to Auschwitz after 4 days in a cattle car transport in March 1944. Dr. Mengele had advised her to send all the pregnant prisoners to him for special nutrition and treatment. After Dr. Perl discovered the "special treatment" involved experiments on live humans, and both mother and baby wound up in the crematoria, she performed live births and terminations in order to save the mothers. She moved to the US in 1951 and was convinced by Eleanor Roosevelt to practice medicine again. She had a successful practice on Park Avenue in New York City and delivered over 3000 babies. Dr. Perl passed away in Israel on 16 December 1988. She was 81 years old.

barracks here at Auschwitz for the very purpose of brutalizing and raping the Jewish female and young male prisoners. A few of the female victims of these attacks become pregnant. Once their pregnancies are obvious, the women's lives are in jeopardy.

"Many of these victims," the doctor continued, "will never be able to have children. Some will never be able to have normal relationships with anyone they might care about. A few will contemplate suicide, as I have on more than one occasion."

"Dr. Perl, you must know you are very needed here. These women would be in even worse condition if there was no one to look after them. If they became pregnant, it would probably mean a one-way trip to the gas chambers for the mothers and their babies."

"Why would you care?" The doctor asked me a pointed question.

"Doctor, you must know... *I had to choose my words carefully...* all the men who wear this uniform are not monsters. I would encourage you... no, I would implore you to continue to help as many women as you can."

"Why should any of us here at the camp trust anything you say?"

"Because, my Yiddish is as good as my German, doctor. And I will let you in on a little news."

"You speak Yiddish?" the doctor asked in complete surprise.

"Yes, I learned it well in school. But don't you want to hear some news from the front?"

"Please, Lieutenant. News at Auschwitz is not usually good news!"

"You may interpret this as you would like, but please keep it to yourself. I do not want the commandant to know its source.

"The Russians have encircled and defeated Hitler's Sixth Army at Stalingrad. I would not be surprised if the Allies or the Russians are here at this camp within a year."

"Liberation of this hellhole by the Allies would be a dream come true," was the doctor's comment. "Have you shared this information with anyone else?"

"Only one prisoner who had been recently whipped and beaten."

"Why?" I asked.

"I would like you to share it with one of my colleagues," affirmed Dr. Perl. He is another doctor here at the camp. We are only allowed to use our first names, so I only know him as Victor."

"I will ask Doctor Mengele to locate him for me."

"Oh! Please don't ask Mengele," the doctor implored. "Nothing good ever comes from contact with Doctor Mengele. He could make trouble for Victor or you.

"Since you seem curious about Dr. Mengele, I will give you an example of why you should never talk to him.

"When I first started here as a doctor to the pregnant women, Mengele asked me to send all the women experiencing pregnancy to him for better nutrition and care. After about a week of sending these pregnant women to him, I was passing by crematorium #1 and saw the SS beating the most recent pregnant women I had sent to the doctor. After these women were beaten with clubs by the SS, they were attacked by vicious dogs. They were then thrown into the crematorium like rag dolls - while still alive!

"Does this example give you enough reason to avoid the evil doctor?"

"Yes, Doctor Perl. I appreciate you talking freely to me. I will take your suggestion."

Although my depression deepened, I spent the rest of the day going through the wards or blocks of medical buildings. Even to the untrained eye, conditions in this particular hellhole were deplorable.

In one ward, I discovered rats just starting to eat a poor prisoner's toes. The patient was too ill to object or even care. I chased the rats out of the ward and placed a soiled blanket over the prisoner's lower body.

I noticed several of the cots had two prisoners on a single bed frame. The spread of infectious diseases must kill many of these poor folks.

The last bed I came to was empty. But the patient was curled in a ball on the floor and certainly deceased. It looked like he had shrunk to about half the size of a normal adult prisoner. I could tell by his facial hair, he was not a child.

I looked throughout the block for another doctor or block nurse, but no one was around. I thought, *tomorrow I will look up Victor to see if there were any more physicians working in this very sad excuse for an infirmary.*

It was getting dark outside. The only bright lights in the distance were around the camp's perimeter. The breeze from the east brought the distinct odor of burning flesh from the crematoriums. After walking through the wretched and horrible excuse for a hospital, I could barely place one foot in front of another. I was living my own depression. Thoughts of Ilsa were the only future I could contemplate to fight my sadness.

26

Physicians Who Heal

Although I was up early the next morning, there were several groups of prisoners marching off to labor projects either within the camp or just outside in the nearby forests. The sky was light with a promise of the approaching dawn. Fog hung in the gullies like grey veils in the camp.

The men in the prison labor groups resembled dark shadows in deplorable shape against a background of gray. My heart went out to them. Their workday began at 4:30 in the summertime; one hour later in the winter. Almost all prisoner work was mind-numbing and back-breaking.

I even felt guilty eating at the officer's cafeteria. I know these hard-working prisoners were getting barely sustenance nutrition. Their food resembled something I wouldn't have fed to animals.

Before going out on a day-labor detail, the prisoners were given a half liter of coffee substitute or herbal tea, but no food. No wonder most of the prisoners looked like a collection of skin and bones.

The midday ration for most prisoners consisted of three quarters of a liter of watery, often foul-smelling soup which had a very small portion of meat, four days per week, and some vegetables, mainly potatoes or rutabaga, three days per week.

In the evening, most prisoners were given 300 grams of often moldy bread along with a tablespoon of cheese or jelly. Occasionally, 25 grams of margarine or sausage were included, especially for prisoners assigned to hard labor. Many of the prisoners kept part of their ration for the morning meal in the hope it would not get stolen overnight.

I headed across an expanse of a trampled field overgrown with tired weeds on my way to the medical blocks. It was hot for this early in the morning. The sun was just up and burning off the dampness of the evening's dew. Admittedly, I wasn't in the best of moods after seeing the prisoner patients in the medical blocks yesterday. The low mist that hung in the air did nothing to improve my attitude.

I missed Ilsa. Even the thought of her and her tender touch brought a bit of a smile to my face as I entered medical block 28. The first orderly I came across suggested I look in block 19 for the doctor called Victor.

I backtracked a bit down a clay and weed-infested road and found block 19. There was a small green cross on the door, but no other notification it was a medical building.

I went to what I guessed was the admitting desk and asked, "Is there a doctor Victor here in this ward?"

The orderly prisoner jumped to attention when he looked up and saw my SS lieutenant bars.

"Yes. Of course, Lieutenant. Please wait here and I will bring him over."

A few minutes later, a wizened prisoner in what I figured was somewhere in his 30's showed up at the front desk. My guess was his stature had been humbled by many months of prison food and humiliation by the kapos and guards.

"I am Victor.* What can I do for you, Lieutenant?"

There was no fear in his speech or demeanor. His gaze was steady as he looked me in the eye.

"Victor, I am Lieutenant Ramsgrund. I am visiting here from a research center in northern Germany. Is there a quiet place we may talk for a few minutes?"

"Yes. Can the SS lieutenant tell me what this is about?"

"Of course. I would rather we were in a more private area."

He led me down a quiet corridor to what looked like a closet tucked in the back of block 19. The small room contained an overhead bulb dangling on a cord and a board across two small sawhorses which served as a cramped desk. There was a modest stool and a wooden box.

Victor grabbed the wooden box and motioned me to sit on the three-legged wooden stool.

"You will have to pardon the accommodations, Lieutenant. I do not get too many SS officers here in the infirmary. As a matter of fact, you are probably the first."

"You do not have to apologize for accommodations in this hellhole, Victor. What kind of a doctor are you?"

---

*   Victor Frankl was an Austrian neurologist who spent three years in 4 different concentration camps. While in the camps he developed an existential approach to psycho-analysis termed *Logotherapy* based on man's search for meaning in life. After the liberation of the Auschwitz camp, he was appointed head of neurology at the Polyclinic Hospital in Vienna where he wrote his most famous work, "Man's Search for Meaning" in nine days. He died of heart failure on the 2nd of September 1997 in Vienna. He was 92 years old.

After a considerable pause, he answered. "My area of specialization is in neurology."

"Where is your home?"

"My wife and I lived in Vienna before we were sent to the Theresienstadt concentration camp in 1942. My family has all been killed in the camps. My wife might still be alive, but I have no way of knowing; I do know I will see her again."

"I have to acknowledge, doctor, your attitude seems quite positive, considering the conditions here at Auschwitz."

"If I could trust the SS lieutenant, I would confide in you how I have survived. But I do not trust anyone who wears your uniform."

"Doctor, if I confided in you something that might convince you to trust me, could you keep it very confidential?"

"I don't know, Lieutenant. I have been here long enough to trust very few people. My background in psychiatry, however, has taught me to keep serious private conversations very private."

"I am about to divulge information to you that could get us both killed? Is that serious enough for you?"

"I would never," the doctor replied, "acknowledge to anyone that you are Jewish."

"How would you know my religion, Doctor?"

"In all my dealings with the SS, Lieutenant, I have never met any who has described this camp as a 'hellhole.' I will keep your private life, private. I assume there must be other reasons for you to wear our enemies' uniform. Do you care to trust me and tell me why you have joined the SS?"

"Well, if I can trust you not to acknowledge my sacred religion, I will explain the rest of my story:

"My parents sent me to Hitler Youth Camp when I was sixteen years in order to hide my Jewishness. My father is Swedish, and the SS seemed to like my Nordic features and recruited me from my engineering studies at the Technical Institute in Berlin.

"I obtained Italian citizenship papers for my life-long Jewish friend, and we were both recruited to a secret Wehrmacht base in northern Germany. The base at Peenemünde is being used to develop secret weapons systems that could turn the tide of the war for the Reich."

"What sort of weapons are being developed at this secret base, Lieutenant?"

"The army is developing long-range missile technology and warheads which could bring catastrophic destruction to the cities of our enemies.

"But now, Doctor, please tell me how have you been able to survive in this place for so long?"

"I listen, Lieutenant.

"One day one of the meanest guards, a kapo, came to me with a minor injury. These kapos were even more brutal than the SS guards. They liked to demonstrate their brutality in order to curry favor with the uniform you wear.

"I sewed up his face and told him it would leave only a hairline, almost invisible white-line scar.

"One day I was on my way to a work detail in another section of the camp and the same kapo started talking to me about his love life and matrimonial troubles. He really poured out his troubles to me.

"All I did, at first, was listen. Then I gave him an assessment of his character, and some psychotherapeutic advice for his marriage.

"Evidently, he was grateful. Whenever he oversaw doling out our meager rations, he would make sure I received a full measure or slightly more. In this camp, even slightly more, like a few more peas in your soup, can mean the difference between starvation and survival."

"Is this how you are surviving, Doctor?" I asked because I felt there must be more than a bit of food to help these poor souls survive.

"Yes, Lieutenant. There are a couple of other things you must do to survive this camp. You must always stay fit to work. You cannot get sick or lame. If you start to limp, you could get on a list to be gassed."

"Is that all of what it takes to survive in this brutal hell, Doctor?" I asked in order to pass on survival techniques to others here and at our research center in Peenemünde.

"Underlying everything, Lieutenant, is the individual's attitude and his faith in God. The prisoners must realize they have to take personal responsibility for their lives. And that each prisoner is unique and has a special contribution to make – not only in this camp, but in their own lives.

"I only pray this war ends before all of us are snuffed out in the harsh brutality that is Auschwitz."

It was at this point, late in my conversation with the doctor, that he wanted to mention something I might not have heard about.

"You might not be aware, Lieutenant, some of my patients have been shot by women who have curried favor with the Nazis." *

"What are you talking about, Victor?"

---

* For a full, well-researched history of German women in the Nazi killing fields follow the intriguing and chilling account of author Wendy Lower in "Hitler's Furies" from Mariner Books, Houghton Mifflin Harcourt, Boston, New York 2013.

"A few of my patients have witnessed young women from Germany who have traveled into Poland or other conquered areas. They work for the Gestapo or police units as secretaries or other office personnel.

"Some of these women have married Gestapo agents or SS officers and enjoy the status of women who are above the law. They steal Jewish belongings during 'shopping sprees' into the Jewish ghettos and have actually killed Jews while going about their 'business.'"

"Victor, it looks like the Nazis have infected our entire country and everyone in it!"

Surviving Auschwitz

After the first week of being at the Auschwitz camp, I was beginning to grasp the enormity of this killing machine. Commandant Höss explained to me the total capacity of the camp was approximately 140,000 people. This number included having the crematoriums run continuously 24 hours each day of the week including Sundays. There was a total of four crematorium complexes. Each crematorium could "process" up to 2000 people at a time.

The crematoriums seemed to create huge billowing clouds of black smoke that belched fire and gave the camp a shower of white ash if the wind was blowing back toward the barracks. It made me inconsolably sad to think this ash was the remains of European Jewry.

I told the commandant of my desire to learn more about the elimination process for all the undesirable people in the conquered areas. He told me to get in touch with one of the camp doctors, Dr. Nyiszli,* who was an assistant to Dr. Mengele.

I introduced myself to one of the SS guards outside of crematory #1, who led me to Dr. Nyiszli in the office beside the crematory.

"Good morning, Doctor. I'm Lieutenant Ramsgrund from the Army base near Peenemünde in northern Germany."

"What can I do for you, Lieutenant?"

"I need to bring back some ideas on your methods of liquidation of such vast numbers of prisoners in your facility and a little information on your medical experiments here in Auschwitz. I find it incredible you can eliminate trainloads of thousands of people each day in this one facility."

Dr. Nyiszli did not seem frightened or cowered by my presence. He looked me in the eyes when he talked.

"Lieutenant, would you like to see our operation?"

"First, I would rather you tell me about your procedures."

"Of course, Lieutenant.

"All the prisoners who have been directed to the left at the sorting tables are marched directly to the crematoriums. Most prisoners are dead within the hour they arrive here. Men and

---

* Dr. Miklos Nyiszli, a physician found himself at Auschwitz in 1944 when all the Jews from Hungary were sent to the camps after the Nazi invasion. He worked as a forensic pathologist for the Reich and lived next to crematorium #1. He was an admitted collaborator who helped Dr. Joseph Mengele with his medical experiments on twins and dwarfs by performing autopsies. He was liberated from the camps and continued to practice medicine, although he vowed never to lift a scalpel again. He died at age 54 in Oradea, Romania in September 1956.

women in good physical health along with mothers with twins and dwarfs are directed to the right."

Something puzzled me and I asked, "Why are the twins and dwarfs selected out of the extermination line?"

"Dr. Mengele is conducting some minor experiments on these individuals for important scientific studies."

"Are you helping Dr. Mengele with these experimental studies, Doctor?"

"Lieutenant, we have several hundred sonderkommando who are all Jewish prisoners here who take care of the bodies after they have been gassed. Many of them get injured or have medical problems. Basically, I take care of these prisoners and see that their medical problems are well-treated."

"Excellent, Doctor. But you haven't answered my question. What role do you play with the aid you are giving to Dr. Mengele?"

"It is a little difficult to explain, Lieutenant, but I shall try.

"After the experimental patients are euthanized, I do a complete autopsy with careful analysis of the findings and report these findings to the doctor.

"So far, Dr. Mengele has been favorably impressed with my work here as a forensic pathologist. I have done post-mortems on several prisoners, SS officers, and anyone whom the doctor has ordered me to examine."

"How are your circumstances here, Doctor?"

"Our housing, food, clothing, and medical supplies are as good as anywhere in the Reich. The problem is that all the sonderkommandos, including myself, will be killed at the end of our term."

"Why is that, Doctor?"

"Because the world in general, and European Jewry in particular, must never know what is going on in this place.

"If Jews were aware of their fate, before they arrived, it would be almost impossible for your SS organization to herd the Jews into these efficient killing machines.

"The sonderkommandos are only vaguely aware of their fate. After three or four months, the 400-500 sonderkommandos are told to report to the courtyard for resettlement at a rest camp. Once they are lined up in the courtyard, the SS machine guns them all. Their bodies are summarily burned in the crematoriums and the ash is dumped in the Vistula. Some of the prisoners' ashes are processed into soaps and fertilizer."

"It sounds very efficient, Doctor."

"Would you like to view the crematorium complex # 1, Lieutenant?"

28

A Tour of Crematorium Number One at Auschwitz

"Thanks for showing me your laboratory, Doctor Nyiszli. It looks very well-equipped!"

"You are entirely welcome, Lieutenant. As I am showing you around Crematorium # 1, I would like to comment on the only mistake our sonderkommando force has committed as long as I have been here. The error and surrounding issue have been cleared up, but I would appreciate confidentiality. Dr. Mengele is unaccustomed to any slip-ups concerning the liquidation of our prisoners.

"All of us who work in these crematoriums realize our days are numbered. I have lasted more than the usual three-month period, but I could be killed for even slight infractions."

"I will keep our conversations private, Doctor. Thank you for entrusting me with the information on the crematoriums."

"Lieutenant, this incident took place three weeks ago. I still have difficulty sleeping because I lived through it.

"This room we are in now is the undressing room.

"As you can see, there are hundreds of hooks on the wall for the prisoners to place their clothing after they undress. They are also told they must be completely nude before they go into the showers. They are told to remember the number on the hook so they may retrieve their clothing after the shower."

"The room is cavernous, Doctor. How many prisoners come through here at one time?" *I shuddered to think of the horror of having to undress in front of strangers and face the uncertainty of being gassed to death.*

"Each undressing room can hold up to two thousand prisoners. Often, they are reluctant to get completely undressed, so the sonderkommandos must beat a few with rubber truncheons; then they get more cooperative.

"Remember, we have to process up to eight to ten thousand people each day. Our crematoriums are functioning day and night. The only time we halt the cremation procedure occurs is if Allied or Russian planes are in the vicinity.

"The prisoners go directly from this room into the gas chamber. The inside of the gas chamber is painted a calming pastel green. The prisoners are told they are going into the shower room. They don't seem to panic until the last few are crowded into the room, and they realize it is far too crowded for bathing.

"The Zyklon B* gas is dropped down the four tubes in the center of the chamber as crystals immediately after they enter the

---

*   The I. G. Farben Company developed two types of Zyklon products during the 2nd World War. The name Zyklon came from the essential ingredients: cyanide, chlorine, and nitrogen. The cannisters the two products came in were identical except Zyklon A was a disinfectant; Zyklon B killed millions of people.

149

gas chamber. The gas is immediately released and fills the lungs with cyanide poison.

"The victims do everything they can to avoid inhaling the poisonous vapors. The prisoners climb on top of one another to try to reach toward the ceiling in order to catch a fresh breath of air. Within a few minutes, the nude bodies make a hideous pyramid of corpses to be cremated by the sonderkommandos."

"Isn't this form of liquidation pretty-much standard throughout the concentration camps in the Reich?" I asked.

The doctor held up one finger as if he had a further comment. "Lieutenant, shortly after the chamber was ventilated, a sonderkommando came running into my laboratory without knocking, which is most unusual."

"He was so out of breath; I felt the gas must have gotten to him. He almost broke the hinges off the door as he rushed into my lab."

"Doctor!" he yelled. "We found a young girl alive at the bottom of the corpses!"

I shouted. **"Bring her here to my laboratory and place her on the table!"**

"This sonderkommando was very excited to see one of his fellow Jews had survived the gassing. She was found at the bottom of the pile of bodies with her face pressed into the damp cement floor. Cyclon B does not react in the presence of humidity, and the girl was not killed by the gas.

"I rushed into the gas chamber and found the girl coughing and vomiting. The gas kommando men were in a state of panic. Nothing like this had ever happened in the gas chambers before. I carried her back to my table and administered a small amount of epinephrin stimulant to support her heart and circulation.

"Then the kommando men brought her soup and warm tea. They were treating her as if she were their own child. She was starting to sit up and the color was coming back to her skin. She said her name was Herta and she was eighteen years old. She told us her story.

"You have to understand, Lieutenant, this was something extraordinary for our crematoriums here at Auschwitz. No one had ever survived the gas chambers.

"As she told her story, my eyes filled with water. I knew her sad story was happening all over Germany and Poland, and indeed all over the conquered territories under the command of the Reich."

"What was her story, Doctor?"

Herta's Story

"**H**erta, our first and only gas chamber survivor," the doctor began, "was from Upper Silesia.* She was studying nursing. When the Nazis came to power in 1933, her family knew anxiety and fear from the Aryan German population. Gradually her family was forced to give up their clothing business. Little by little all their rights were taken away. Herta said her family was forced out of their home, which had been handed down in her family for generations, and had to live in two small rooms in the Jewish ghetto.

"Her family had to give up most of their possessions including their radio, silverware, clothing, and anything of value. She could no longer attend school, walk in the parks, or use trolley cars or railroad trains. She said park benches bore signs in large white lettering: '**STRICTLY OFF LIMITS FOR JEWS**'. Even store signs proclaimed in large letters: '**JEWS WILL NOT BE SERVED**' or '**GOODS WILL NOT BE SOLD TO JEWS.**'

---

* Upper Silesia, now part of Poland, was an early target of Nazi oppression of the Jewish population. The total population of approximately 100,000 Jews were rounded up, forced into ghettos, sent to concentration and death camps or murdered by the Einsatzgruppen death squads.

"Herta told us her family's ration cards were restricted so meat, vegetables, fruit, fats, and even clothing were forbidden. Since their Jewish temples had been burned down, they had to hold religious services in make-shift locations; but even then, Hitler Youth would often throw stones through the windows and disrupt their services.

"Herta related to us she was one of the fortunate Jews, because she worked in a hospital. She cried and whimpered while telling us many of her neighbors were marched out into the forest and made to dig their own graves. She told us how after digging their own graves, the neighbors and children were told to march past the ditches while the SS or the Einsatzgruppen* units would shoot the men, women and children. Then these poor slaughtered folks would tumble into the ditch which served as their grave. Often, the people were not killed at once but only wounded, so the Nazi's would just bury them alive.

"Herta spoke of being lucky as a hospital worker because her food and lodging at the hospital was somewhat better than the Jews living in the ghetto. She was the nurse working in the children's ward, or *Stionsschwester,* until early one morning.

"It was about five o'clock in the early morning on 23 February 1942." Herta told us, "I was awakened by a commotion and gunfire outside the hospital. As I looked out the window, the police were threatening all our Jewish hospital workers with rifles.

---

* Einsatzgruppen units were paramilitary or SS Special Action Groups organized by Himmler and Heydrich in 1939. These units would follow the German armies into Poland murdering national leaders and rounding up Jews for 'resettlement' - which meant murdering them in the forests!

"I immediately asked one of the policemen what was going on, but he lied to us by saying we were being transported to a work camp, and not to worry.

"A few days later we arrived at Auschwitz. None of us," Herta continued, "had any idea of what to expect. The SS guards in charge of our filthy barracks kept beating us with cudgels. Even the smallest children were not exempt from the cudgel."

I interrupted the doctor relating Herta's story by asking, "Even the children are beaten?"

"Oh yes, Lieutenant, especially if they are crying. Hungry children cry a lot. These children are quick fuel for the crematoriums. The younger children are usually thrown in first, often while still alive, and used for kindling for the larger children and adults. The more the children screamed, the more sadistic the SS would become.

"Herta complained the clothing provided by the guards at Auschwitz was crawling with flees and lice. The swarming insects tormented the prisoners and cause them to break out in pussy sores and bleeding scabs.

"Herta told us one of her close friends, a nurse, from the hospital fell during one of their forced labor projects. The guard came up to her, placed his heavy boot on her chest and asked: 'miss do you want to lie there and feel sick?' The guard then put all his weight on my friend's chest and stomped her with his steel-toed boot. You could hear her ribs breaking; blood flowed from her mouth. She died almost instantly."

"So," I asked, "you brought Herta back to life?"

"Yes, with the help of the sonderkommandos, Lieutenant."

"How did she escape the crematorium complex, Doctor?"

"Lieutenant, this sad story is about to get even more difficult."

"How much more difficult could it possibly get, Doctor?"

"About the time we had Herta rescued and back to life, the *Oberscharführer*, our SS overseer of the crematorium complex, entered my office and saw the young woman on my table.

"He would frequently come into my office to look over my work. He was the supervising SS officer for the Jewish Sonderkommando unit in the crematoriums.

"When Oberscharführer Muhsfeldt* came into my office and saw the young woman on the table he shouted, **'What is she doing here!'**

"It took me a minute to collect my thoughts, but I figured it would be best to tell him the whole story and the truth. He was so enraged; his hands and arms were shaking.

"When I asked if Herta could be brought back to the camp by the women who come and collect the clothing of the recently gassed prisoners, he again shouted, **'Are you crazy? The minute she returned to the main camp she would tell the first person she met what goes on in this place. We would pay for that information leak with our lives!'**

"The Oberscharführer then had some of the sonderkommando men carry the young girl to the hallway of the crematorium. Since Muhsfeldt didn't have the fortitude to kill her, he commanded one of the sonderkommando Jews to take care of the problem. I heard a loud **bang** report of a pistol. Herta was executed with a bullet to the back of her neck and tossed into the cremation oven."

---

* Eric Muhsfeldt was a German war criminal. He served as a non-commissioned member of the SS at the Auschwitz concentration camp as leader of the Sonder-kommando unit that would bring the gassed corpses of the prisoners to the to the crematoria. He was captured after the war, tried and convicted in Krakow and hanged on the 24th of January 1948.

30

A Snag in Getting Out of Auschwitz

At all the concentration camps Ezekiel and I visited, we heard equally terrible experiences. These killing machines have been the source of continuous nightmares for both of us. Auschwitz has been the worst because we saw thousands of men, women, and children wasting away on rotten food, harsh labor and continuous beatings with rubber truncheons and whips.

I sent a message to General Dornberger in order to let him know Sargent Carapezza and I had completed our mission and to see if he had an adequate workforce from the slave laborers we had provided to date. I also gave him a quick summary of what we had witnessed at Treblinka, Sobibor, and Auschwitz.

I gave the general a few graphic details so he could understand what we had witnessed firsthand.

His immediate reply was quite simple and predictable: "What you are telling me is not to be believed!"

I was working out of a small office in the administrative block of the camp in a building near the commandant's office. As I was getting ready to arrange transportation back to Peenemünde there was a knock at the door.

"Come in!" I called through the door.

A tall man dressed in a civilian suit of clothes and a fedora came into my make-shift office. He looked like Gestapo, but it had only been an hour since my message to General Dornberger.

He introduced himself. "Good afternoon, Lieutenant. I am Agent Burk from our Nordhausen office. Perhaps you don't remember me?"

My immediate thought was – how was it possible for the Gestapo to read military message mail?

"I remember you very well, Agent Burk. You and your fellow agent tried to arrest me and my colleague, Dr. Carapezza, because you lost a couple of Gestapo agents and their automobile somewhere near the secret rocket plant in Thuringia near Nordhausen."

"Yes, Lieutenant. We have not located Dr. Carapezza, but the agents and their automobile were found in the woods near the rocket center. Both agents had been murdered and buried near their automobile.

"The long arm of the Gestapo has been following you to Denmark, Sweden and all over Poland for the past few months. I am here to arrest you for their murder."

"Agent Burk, I would suggest you look elsewhere for your criminal."

"I need to place you in handcuffs!"

"If you remember, Agent Burk, when your lead agent, Agent Rikker, tried to place me in handcuffs at the Nordhausen office, it did not go well for him. Since it is late afternoon and I did not get a very excellent lunch, I would suggest you forgo the handcuffs. We should walk over to the commandant's office and see if we can sort this out."

"Very well, Lieutenant. But remember, we are in the middle of a very secure prison here at Auschwitz, and you should consider yourself under detention."

"Yes, of course, Agent Burk. I intend on being very cooperative. How long have you been in this camp?"

"I just arrived this morning and have not had a chance to get my bearings. The secretary in the commandant's office directed me here."

"Excellent! It is only a short walk over to the commandant's office. We will have to go between a couple of the prisoner barracks, but it should only take fifteen or twenty minutes to get there. This camp is very secure, so you do not have to worry about any attempts to escape. The camp is crawling with guards and SS. And besides, where would I escape to?"

My hope was Agent Burk was not familiar enough with the Auschwitz Camp to know his way around. I was also counting on his not being familiar with the electric fencing between the barracks.

"Right this way, Agent Burk. We will go between the prisoner barracks in order to get directly to the commandant's office."

I took a chance and grabbed my right-hand leather glove out of my desk drawer on the way out and placed it in my pocket.

While walking between the prisoner barracks and the electric fence, I could see an occasional prisoner making a trip to the latrine about twenty meters from the back end of the building.

It was cloudy with a slight mist in the air.

As we were traversing between the next building and the fence, I engaged Burk in conversation. "Tell me, Agent Burk. Has the Gestapo still been recruiting criminals for most of their dirty work?"

As I was talking and walking along, I put my hand in my pocket and slipped on my right glove.

"Of course not, Lieutenant! Whatever gave you such an outlandish idea?"

"I guess it just seemed to come naturally. Most of us in the SS look at the Gestapo as a criminal organization which prays on law-abiding German citizens."

"Just wait until you are under detention with Gestapo jurisdiction, Lieutenant. You will see how the Gestapo can obtain almost any necessary information from you. You will be very sorry you have disrespected me. I will have the commandant of this camp place you in one of these prisoner barracks. You will be denied food and water for several days. Then we shall see how brave you talk!"

I had just about enough of this fool. I saw a stick of wood in the weeds up ahead. I looked around to see if anyone was watching and brought my clenched fist down on the back of the agent's neck. His legs shot out from under him like a pithed and skewered frog. He went down like a sack of sand. I wasn't sure if he was dead, so I tossed him up against the electric fence and held him there with the stick I found in the weeds. His metal belt buckle sparked and the agent did a little jumping dance against the fence. I held him on the fence until I was sure he was gone.

No guards came so I called out to the prisoner who had just entered the latrine. The prisoner reluctantly approached the electric fence.

"Prisoner," I addressed him politely. "Could you help me with this gentleman?"

"I will try, Lieutenant. What can I do?"

"I am going to drag his corpse to your barrack. I would like you to strip him of his clothing and any belongings. These items will be yours to keep. Please destroy any items of identification. He is Gestapo.

"When is the next time for the selection truck to make a trip for the crematoria?"

"They come for selections every night," was the prisoner's response.

"Fine. Make sure his body is tossed into the next selection truck. The crematorium is actually too good a place for him. Make sure all identification is destroyed in the latrine."

31

Missing Ilsa

It was becoming obvious to me the Gestapo might be reading military messaging. If they could read military secrets, regular mail and phone conversations were never going to be confidential. I had to assume all my communications with Ilsa were going to be compromised. So, I decided to send her an innocuous letter which she would have to interpret.

> *Dearest Ilsa,*
>
> *It has been too long since I have seen you. I am hoping you are well. I have been visiting some of the re-construction camps in Germany and in the Conquered Territories. Our office is learning a lot about techniques for handling large crowds of people and medical procedures.*
>
> *It would be a joy for me to be able to see you in the upcoming weeks; I look forward to seeing you safely as soon as I can arrange leave.*
>
> *Lovingly,*
>
> *Jenz*

If there was any censoring of the mail, it was my hope this would reach her in Hannover within a week or two. I really missed the love of my life.

My next step was to leave Auschwitz with as little notice as possible. Even though most of the missile construction was now taking place in a large limestone cave, a factory constructed underground near Nordhausen, General Dornberger and some support and administrative staff were still in Peenemünde.*

I went directly to the commandant's office. His administrative assistant was at her desk. She was a plainly-dressed woman of approximately thirty-five years. Although painfully thin, she had a pleasant face and a disarming smile.

"The commandant has an appointment in about twenty minutes," supplied the administrative assistant. "If you are here for a short visit, he may be able to see you now."

"Thank you, Miss, I won't be but a few minutes. I just wanted to thank him for his kindness and hospitality toward me."

"I will see if he is available."

The assistant pressed a speaker button and announced I was in the outer office.

Commandant Höss came out of his office and asked, "What can I do for you, Lieutenant?"

This was a very dangerous man and I wanted to show him every military courtesy while keeping a neutral or pleasant expression on my face. I gave him a Hitler salute as he came out of his office.

"Good afternoon, Herr Commandant. I will be leaving this afternoon after I can arrange transportation to the train station

---

* The British had discovered the secret rocket base and bombed it on the night of 17-18 August 1943.

and would like to thank you and your very efficient staff here at Auschwitz for your hospitality. General Dornberger sends his regards and thanks for the Jew laborers we were able to send to him from this camp."

"I'm happy to help our war effort in any way possible.

"Oh, by the way, Lieutenant. Did Agent Burk get a hold of you?"

My quick response was, "No, Commandant. But if he is looking for me, I will be at our secret Wehrmacht base in northern Germany."

"Excellent, Lieutenant. I will have my assistant, Rebecca here, arrange for you to get a ride to the train station for your trip north. It is strange, however, the agent seemed anxious to contact you."

"Thanks again, Commandant!"

As the commandant retreated to his office and closed the door, it was obvious the knowledge of Agent Burk's inquiry hadn't troubled him.

I could tell by his assistant's Old Testament name that she was most-likely Jewish. With a little effort and a bit of style in her clothing, she would be an outright knock-out.

I felt ashamed thinking of her without her clothes. My thoughts of Ilsa flooded my mind and made me smile.

The commandant's assistant asked me, "Lieutenant, I could arrange a ride for you to the train station in Krakow for early tomorrow morning, would that be all right? There is a 9:30 am train to Warsaw for your trip north."

"Yes, Rebecca. An early morning ride would be most gracious of you. Tell me, does your name mean 'servant of God'?"

Surprisingly, she answered in Yiddish, "How would you know what my name means?"

So, I answered her in Yiddish, "My German education wouldn't have been complete without a knowledge of the Old Testament."

The surprised expression on her face gave me hope I would soon be on my way to see and hold my beloved Ilsa. Her absence from my life these past few months had been painful. I then thanked Rebecca and told her I would be in front of the officer's barrack #11 at 7am.

Getting Back to Peenemünde

My trip back to Peenemünde went smoothly and without incident. However, our train had to travel part of the time at night because of Russian raids on moving trains in eastern Poland. These areas were designated as Conquered Territories, but no one really knew how long they would remain under German control.

Traveling through the countryside of beautiful Poland, one could never imagine it was under attack from two evil powers. Poland was suffering in the vice grips of the Nazi Wehrmacht and the Red Army.

It was a pleasure to see my colleagues again, especially Ezekiel. We had dinner off the base on my first full day back and discussed many of the atrocities we had witnessed in the camps.

"Zeke, we have to remember exactly what we witnessed and write everything down. We must include names, dates, conversations, and even our impressions of the lives these poor people were suffering.

"We have to be very careful where we keep any of our records, notes, and descriptions of the camp conditions. If these writings were to fall into the wrong hands, it could go very badly for us with the Gestapo."

"I certainly understand," replied Ezekiel. "I'm pretty sure, I will never get over what we witnessed in Treblinka.

"I know Adiya and her sister, Chasha, will never be the same," said Zeke with some emotion in his voice.

"Adiya knew they were close to being put to death, but she has kept that knowledge from her sister until she is older or whenever this war is over.

"Jenz, I should tell you General Dornberger has ordered all officers to be at an all-command required meeting with Hitler's War Minister tomorrow morning. I'm not sure why he is coming to our remote base, but I hope he isn't making more demands on our staff. The general mentioned parade dress uniforms are required."

"Wonderful," I replied. "My guess is he would like to have the V-ll missile operational sooner, rather than later. We have to be especially careful with any interaction with this officer, since he could be very dangerous; and doubly careful with our efforts to slow down V-ll development.

"Any idea, Zeke, of the officer's background or name?"

"I believe his name is Speer.* And you may find this hard to believe, I think he is an architectural designer. He is also known to be close to our Fürher."

"He sounds like trouble, Zeke. I suppose there is no way we could avoid the meeting?"

"No, we have to make sure we are there. General Dornberger may have some pointed questions for us about the quality of life in the camps," emphasized Zeke. "How will we be able to answer those questions truthfully?"

My answer was a little convoluted, but I know Zeke got the idea. "We have to be direct and clear in our answers, but very careful not to show any bias toward the Jews or particular conditions at the camps. Perhaps, he won't ask difficult questions or he might ask us in private. If he knows or suspects what is going on in the concentration camps, he will probably ask us in private."

While we were finishing dinner, two well-dressed men came and sat down at a nearby table. Although they didn't appear to pay any attention to us, I whispered to Zeke "The two men who just

---

*   Albert Speer was a trained and gifted architect. First, he became Hitler's architect, then, over time Hitler came to trust his judgment. Of all the Führer's interactions with his officers, Speer was the only one who could be considered a friend of Adolf Hitler. Albert Speer certainly knew how the Jews were suffering under the Nazis. However, he was the only prisoner at the Nuremberg Trials after the war who showed any remorse and apologized for his actions. He also did not protest as too harsh his 20-year sentence he served at Spandau Prison. Speer was released from Spandau Prison in 1966. He died of a stroke in London on September 1st,1981. He was 76 years old.

came in and sat a few tables away, certainly could pass for Gestapo. Don't look over there, but they glanced at us when they sat down."

"You would think we would be used to these creeps by now, Jenz. After Treblinka, I don't think anything will really bother me too much again."

"Get ready to look relaxed, Zeke. The creeps are heading this way."

33

The Gestapo Catches Up with Us

It was an interesting arrest. Both agents were pretty beefy and at least six feet in height. Their suits looked stuffed with plenty of muscle mass. One of the agents headed for our table, the other went and stood at the only exit. As the agent approached, he unbuttoned his jacket allowing us to see his rather intimidating Luger pistol in his wasteband holster.

Both agents were dressed in dark suits with white shirts and plain-patterned ties. Their shoes were at a high polish with no noticeable scuff marks.

"Good evening, Gentlemen. I'm sorry to interrupt your meal, but I am Agent Krauthammer and I must ask for some identification."

"We will be happy to show you an identity card, Agent. But first," retorted Zeke, "could you please let us know why you need to know who we are while dining here?"

"We have it on good authority, Gentlemen, you are two individuals the Gestapo has been looking for throughout the Reich. Are you, by chance, Lieutenant Ramsgrund and Sergeant Carapezza?"

"Yes," Zeke replied. "We have been working at this Wehrmacht base for over a year. If you wanted to contact us, you just had to call our boss, General Dornberger, and he would let us know you were trying to reach us."

"Two agents were sent here last year," shot back Agent Krauthammer, "but they had an automobile accident and subsequent fire; they were lost in the fire."

I looked at Zeke and replied, "We are both very sorry to hear about your agents. But how can we help you now?"

"Lieutenant," the Gestapo agent declared, "We have also sent an agent from our Nordhausen office to speak to you while you were visiting the Auschwitz camp. However, he seems to have disappeared."

"I'm sure the sergeant and I are both sorry to hear about the loss or disappearance of your valuable agents, but how can we help? As you may know, the Auschwitz camp is a very dangerous place for anyone who isn't Wehrmacht or SS."

"I am sorry, Lieutenant, but the Gestapo has arrest warrants for you both. Agent Grinnell is waiting for us at the door, and two other agents are waiting for us in the van."

Fortunately, we had finished most of our dinner and I was still in a rather upbeat mood. Zeke, however, wasn't quite so pleasant. A flash of fear, then anger, registered in his eyes. He pointed directly at the agent and responded with a firmness I hadn't heard from Zeke: "Agent Krauthammer, give us a minute to finish and pay our bill. We will then walk peaceably to your van without causing any commotion. You may wait at the door, our only exit, with Agent Grinnell."

Zeke seemed to have the situation well in hand. I think after seeing what we saw at Treblinka, nothing was going to bother him too much anymore.

Zeke's direct toughness seemed to placate the agent and he went and stood by the only exit to the dining facility.

Zeke immediately asked me, "What happened to the agent at the Auschwitz camp?"

"He was the same agent, Burk, from their Nordhausen office. He was giving me a bit of trouble so he 'accidentally' bumped into an electric fence separating the barracks at the prison compound. I instructed a prisoner to strip his body of all clothing and identification and place him in the pick-up truck for a trip to Crematorium One at the camp. As the captured prisoners like to say in their gallows humor, he has probably escaped 'up the chimney' by now."

"Wonderful!" remarked Zeke. But do you have any suggestions for our current situation? Now they have four agents here to make sure we are taken into custody. It looks like they intend to place us in the back of a van and take us to the nearest Gestapo facility on the mainland."

"We will do our best not to be thrown in a Gestapo prison, but I think we should go peacefully to the van. Do you have any suggestions?"

"Well," replied Zeke. "Even though we are wearing civilian clothes, you know as a sergeant in the Wehrmacht I am required to carry a firearm."

"But Zeke," I queried, "neither one of us was prepared for this!"

"Let's quietly pay our bill," said Zeke. "I have placed my fully loaded Walther pistol in my ankle sock as a precautionary measure."

It was obvious Zeke was a very different man after our trip to the concentration camps. Perhaps it was because of him finding the love of his life. I wasn't sure, but I was certainly very grateful for his forethought.

We paid our bill and walked slowly toward the two agents at the entrance to the dining establishment.

34

A Horrifying Trip in a Gestapo Van

The Gestapo's Mercedes van was directly outside the entrance to the restaurant. It was parked as if the agents expected us to make a run for freedom. One of the agents standing outside near the passenger door actually had his pistol out and was waving it in our direction. He was yelling at us while making crude comments:

"You Jews get in the back of the van. Sit on the floor. The two seats are for the agents!"

I whispered to Zeke, *"let's wait until we are outside the gate before we make any moves. These idiots seem pretty serious."*

Zeke looked down at his left leg where there was an imperceptible bulge near the cuff. "Aren't you glad I thought to bring a little insurance to dinner?"

As a gesture of compliance and to show we were not hiding anything, we took off our jackets and put them on the floor to sit on.

The two agents in the front seat didn't even introduce themselves. I thought it might be good to judge their commitment to this arrest by whispering in the ear of the agent on the driver's side before I climbed into the van: *"the crematoria would be too good for you folks."*

It generated the desired response.

The agent became infuriated, red-faced, and slapped me quite hard across the face. I sensed the reaction and bent slightly out of the way and let the blow sound much harsher than it was.

Although I was going to have a welt on my left cheek, I responded in a quiet, but firm and measured tone. "Agent, you have just made a career-ending error. You must never again raise your hand or your voice to an SS officer."

"You swine!" was the driver's comment. He raised his hand for another blow. I grabbed his fist as it was flying toward my face and just held it while he finished his diatribe. **"You Jews will see how the Gestapo treats you when we get to our headquarters near Greifswald."**

I replied evenly, "Agent, I will have to include this incident in my report." I then squeezed his fist hard, but not quite hard enough to break his fingers. The expression on the driver's face let me know he felt pain.

This enraged the driver even more and he responded, **"I think you Jews are fortunate we haven't beaten you to a bloody pulp before we take you in for interrogation."**

I could tell Zeke was getting tired of being treated like swine. I saw him brush his cuff over his Walther PPK in his sock.

My response was meant to calm the driver down. I didn't want him to escalate the situation further. "Your future actions toward the sergeant and myself will dictate what I will include in my report."

The driver's comment was pretty cryptic, but delivered in a much calmer, almost subdued voice. "You Jewish swine can put anything you want in your reports. That is if you can still write after our colleagues finish questioning you at headquarters."

Zeke and I refrained from further comments or talking until we had traversed across the base and through the gate.

In a conversational tone, I made a suggestion to Zeke. "We should return to this area we are traveling so we could take in the views from the bluff overlooking the ocean." Of course, there was no bluff at the time, but the comment let Zeke know the exact location we were looking to put an end to this madness.

I thought a little conversation with Agent Krauthammer might lighten the mood for us in the back of the van.

"Agent," I started, "I am not sure you realize it, but the sergeant and I have a meeting tomorrow morning with Herr Hitler's Minister of War and Armaments. It is a 'command performance' meeting which we cannot miss."

The agent responded in a measured tone.

"You are both going to be under detention by the Gestapo for several days, perhaps weeks. I will send a message to your superior outlining the charges against you both. This message will serve as your excuse for missing your meeting with the Minister."

Then Agent Krauthammer decided to be a little more forceful; he announced in a rather loud and almost belligerent voice, **"The Gestapo has discovered you men are traitors to the Nazi Party and to our Aryan ideals. You will be held in detention and interrogated until you tell us everything about your Jew families and where they are hiding."**

We rode along the almost deserted road in the gathering twilight. Evening was quickly approaching; automobile headlights were on with the black-out shades covering the lenses. I mentioned to Zeke, "It looks like we are coming up to a beautiful stretch of scenery on the right overlooking the North Sea."

That was all Zeke needed. In one smooth motion he bent over, grabbed his PKK Walther from his sock, and squeezed off a round that went right through Agent Krauthammer's throat. **Bang!**

The agent looked up, coughed a great quantity of blood once, and slumped over in his seat toward Agent Grinnell. Blood was spurting from a neck wound. Agent Grinnell looked completely surprised as blood was covering his suit coat. Zeke's second shot followed his first by less than two seconds.

As Agent Grinnell turned to look at Agent Krauthammer, Zeke's second shot caught him directly between his eyes in the middle of his forehead. **Bang!** His head snapped back and clunked against the inside wall of the van. His eyes were fixed, unseeing, and wide open with surprise.

The agent in the passenger seat turned in his seat and was reaching for his Luger in his shoulder holster.

Zeke placed the barrel of the Walther up against the back of the passenger seat and fired two quick rounds into the agent through the seat. **Bang-Bang!** The force of the 7.65 mm. slugs threw the agent into the dash and to the floor.

The sound and smoke from the heavy slugs panicked the driver. He slammed on the brakes and turned the van onto the unpaved roadside. He was reaching for his Luger while trying to exit the vehicle. Zeke interrupted his progress with two quick shots in succession through the seat directly into the upper back of the agent.

Zeke, from a kneeling position, pumped his remaining two slugs into the driver through the back of the driver's seat. **Bang-Bang!** The force of the slugs hitting him in the back of his slumped forward head, forced the driver's face, or what was left of it, into the windshield. The entire dashboard and windscreen were awash with blood, tissue, and fragments of clothing.

The emotion that stuck with me most at the time and seemed truly amazing to me: Zeke was very calm and methodical. His facial expression was close to no reaction whatsoever. His facial features remained the same as in normal conversation.

My thought at the time was the camps, especially Treblinka, had hardened this mild-tempered man, who would never harm anyone. Here Zeke had committed the murder of four Gestapo thugs in lightning-quick action without so much as a moment's hesitation.

"Zeke," I asked. "Are you okay?"

"Never better, Jenz. These thugs got exactly what they deserved. I didn't like the derogatory way they spoke to us about being Jewish. It is this hateful and demeaning speech that is fomenting a lot of this anti-Semitism. I'm glad our boss, General Dornberger, isn't an anti-Semite."

"You picked up pretty quick on the code word 'bluff' after we traversed and exited the base."

"Of course, Jenz! I'm not quite ready to read your thoughts, but your suggestion was pretty clear for me.

"Now, how do we get rid of the van with four deceased Gestapo thugs inside?"

"This should be quite interesting, Zeke. We are very near the height of the next tide here on the North Sea. As you know, the tides are quite strong on the coast. If we weight the deceased Gestapo agents with rocks, and leave all the doors and windows open, the tide should take the van on the out-going tide. By leaving the doors open, this refuse will probably wash out and sink out to the bottom of the ocean."

"Let's find some small rocks and weight them down," exclaimed Zeke, almost enthusiastically. The wind was quite blustery with the surf crashing on the rocks below and against the cliff.

We weighted down the agents with rocks in their pockets and inside of their shirts.

We placed a fairly heavy rock on the accelerator pedal. I held on to Zeke as he threw the van into gear and I pulled him clear of the van as it rolled toward the bluff overlooking the North Sea.

We could hear the van crash and splash onto the rocks far below.

35

A Meeting with the Minister of War Production

It was quite a walk back to the base. The wind always blows strong on this northern peninsula. It was almost midnight but I don't believe we were noticed by any of the local population. The only lights were at the entrance to the base. The guards initially challenged us but put up no resistance once they read over the copy of our orders which I kept with me at all times in my officer's hat.

I know the tides and storms are very strong in the North Sea. It was my hope and prayer the waves and current would take the van with the dead Gestapo agents far out to sea. We had opened all the doors, gas tank and hood before driving it over the bluff overlooking the sea.

The next morning, I met Zeke in the conference room at 9:45. We were both apprehensive about the meeting with War Minister Speer. We didn't have too long to wait. The room filled up with about 80 officers and technicians; the quiet buzz stopped immediately when General Dornberger got up to introduce the Minister of Armaments and War.

"Gentlemen, good morning to you all. This morning I have the pleasure of introducing one of our brightest and hardest working leaders in the Reich.

"War Minister Speer is responsible for the development and production of all the armaments in the Reich including the army, navy, and air-force services. It is an honor to have him here today to brief us on the progress of the war and our response to our enemies. Let me remind all of you, this is a top-secret briefing. Failure to keep the proceedings of this briefing one hundred percent confidential would require immediate incarceration in a concentration labor camp under difficult conditions.

"War Minister Speer, the microphone is yours."

Enthusiastic clapping broke out from all the officers present.

When the applause tapered off, a youngish-looking, slightly balding, tall gentleman sitting in the front row got up to speak.

"Good morning, and Heil Hitler. It is a pleasure to bring you an up-to-date briefing from our Führer. I met with him yesterday, so this information is quite fresh and reliable. Our Führer sends his hearty greetings.

"First, Herr Hitler is not totally in agreement with the amazing work you are doing here in Peenemünde. He feels our resources could be better directed on more tanks, artillery shells, and bombs. I am not in total agreement with him, but I will lay out his thoughts for you.

"Here, I will go into some detail on armament development and production.

"A new bomb is being developed under very secret orders from our Führer. This bomb is so powerful it can level an entire city with one detonation. The power of this bomb comes from the splitting of uranium atoms. Our projection for the development of this destructive bomb is probably 1947 at the earliest, almost four years away.

"Unfortunately, the Gestapo has imprisoned many of our top scientists; other key personnel have fled the country to go to our enemies. In addition, some of our Wehrmacht recruiters have deemed it necessary to send many of our key technicians and scientists to the Eastern Front to confront the Russians.

"I have met recently with General Friedrich Fromm,* Otto Hahn,** and Werner Heisenberg, *** who briefed me on German atomic research. The major stumbling block to the development of this armament is the use of a cyclotron. This machine is not available yet in Germany. The only cyclotron is in Paris. The problem of security might be too big to overcome, at least at this moment.

"If the A-4 rocket being developed here could be operational, our Fürher would be greatly encouraged. This rocket could be used to deliver this bomb to the heart of our enemies.

"Are there any questions so far?" asked the war minister.

---

* General Fredrich Fromm was Chief of the Army and friend of the War Minister, Speer. He was executed by firing squad by the Nazis on 12 March 1945 for turning a "blind eye" on the conspirators after the assassination attempt on Hitler on 20 July 1944. His last words were: "I always wanted the best for Germany."

** Otto Hahn, is well known as the "Father of the Atomic Age, was a German scientist who discovered nuclear fission. He won the Nobel Prize in Chemistry in 1944. He died at age 89 in Gottingen, W. Germany in 1968.

*** Werner Karl Heisenberg was a German physicist involved with the development of Nuclear Research. He died of kidney cancer at his home in Germany on February 1st, 1976 at age 75.

General Dornberger stood and announced: "Our A-4 rocket currently under development will be ready for widespread use by 1944 as long as our current funding is maintained."

"If your technicians could make a movie film of an A-4 launch," commented the minister, "it might help our Führer to consider further funding for your project here, General. I witnessed the launch of the A-4 on the 13th of June 1942, along with Field Marshal Milch and General Fromm. We were very impressed by this technological development."

General Dornberger announced with some emphasis, **"Consider it done, Minister."**

Speer continued, "I would like to enlighten you gentlemen on three other recent developments which would directly involve your research here at Peenemünde."

"The first takes the V-I weapon and incorporates the propulsion mechanism into an aircraft for the Luftwaffe. Our air force has fought bravely against the 8th air force stationed in England for almost two years. Our jet aircraft, the Me-262* fighter plane, is slated for mass production in 1944. It flies almost two times faster than the Allied bombers and will be capable of shooting them down in large numbers.

"The second defense against the constant bombing raids by the Allies is a surface-to-air missile being developed under the code name 'Waterfall.' This is a rocket approximately 25 feet long

---

* The Me-262 fighter aircraft was the first manned jet aircraft in the world. Nicknamed *Schwalbe* (Swallow) it was fully operational by the end of the war. Development of the jet aircraft, unfortunately for the Luftwaffe, came too late to affect the outcome of World War II.

capable of carrying over six hundred pounds of explosive. It follows a directional beam up to a maximum altitude of fifty thousand feet and hits the enemy bombers with exceptional accuracy. It is still on the drawing boards, but the prototype works almost one hundred percent of the time. It is unaffected by day or night or by clouds, cold, or fog. I have encouraged Herr Hitler to put it into production immediately.

"In addition, we are developing a torpedo for the Kriegsmarine with tracking capabilities for the sound of enemy ships. This torpedo will follow their zig-zag motions for ensured destruction.

"These are some of the recent developments in armament production or proposals in our department."

"Please, I would be happy to take any of your questions."

I raised my hand after a short delay. Many of the technicians seemed reluctant to be noticed.

"Sir," I asked. "How long will it take to mass-produce the Me-262?"

"A good question, Lieutenant. We are waiting for the funding from Herr Hitler. He is very reluctant to fund anything looking like advanced technology. Sometimes I think he is stuck in the Great War Generation (WW I) which believes more artillery shells and bullets will win this war.

"It is a fact, however, unless something is done about the constant bombing of our factories and cities by the British and American bombers, our capability to wage war will be greatly diminished."

36

A Report to General Dornberger

A few days after the meeting with the Minister of War, Speer, I was surprised in the laboratory early in the morning by a visit from General Dornberger's adjunct, Sergeant Albrecht. I was still on my first cup of what was being passed around as coffee.

"Lieutenant, could you come with me to General Dornberger's office for a few moments? He would like a word with you."

"Of course, Sergeant. I will need to just cover my confidential information. Lead the way."

The sergeant led me down a long corridor to a spacious, but modestly furnished office near the back of the complex. He had me sit in a comfortable chair opposite the general's desk.

In a moment, the general came in from a small room adjacent to his office; I stood and he offered his hand for shaking hands. There was no Hitler salute.

"Good morning, Lieutenant. Thanks for coming in this morning.

"I wanted to especially thank you and your sergeant for providing us with almost three hundred new workers from the camps. There has only been one who does not feel comfortable here and may not fit into our rigorous schedule. Perhaps you would like to talk with her before she is sent back to the Auschwitz Camp."

"Who is that, General?"

"I believe her administrative officer said her name was Zivia. However, I'm not sure if that is her first name or last name."

"I will have a talk with her, General, as soon as I can later this morning."

"The prisoners you have sent us from Treblinka and Auschwitz have been hard-working and driven, Lieutenant, and equally important, healthy. I would like to thank you and your sergeant for finding terrific workers. The idea of sending families together, seems to be working out quite well. The workers seem much more content. I did have a couple of questions about your report, however."

"Is there something in the report we did not fully explain, General?"

"Lieutenant, you have reported all the prisoners at Treblinka are whipped, beaten, raped, and killed by gas. Did you mean they are all killed, or just the unruly prisoners?"

"General, some of them are allowed to live for a short period of time to work in the kitchen, cleaning the gas chambers, or cleaning the transports that bring the prisoners into the camp. But, in the end, the thousands of people from the ghetto in Warsaw are packed into cattle cars and murdered in the first hours of their arrival at the camp."

"Certainly, Lieutenant, your report cannot be correct. There must be some sort of screening process to pick out the educated scientists, technicians, and inventors?"

"Unfortunately, no, General. My sergeant and I did the only screening for technical people. Some of the young, pretty women were weeded out so the guards and officers could rape and defile them, but after the guards had their way with them, they were immediately sent to the gas chambers."

"What you are telling me in this written report is barbaric, Lieutenant. Were the conditions any better at the Auschwitz camp?"

"The conditions at Auschwitz were actually worse, General. Almost all the women, even pregnant women, children, and older people were immediately sent to the gas chambers and crematoriums. All their life-long possessions were stolen. The men and women who looked like they could work were sent to filthy, lice-ridden barracks and fed a barely subsistent diet of thin soup.

"Defenseless pregnant women who were expecting twins were subject to experiments by a doctor named Mengele. He also experimented on handicapped children, although I'm not sure what was the nature of his experiments."

"Lieutenant, this all sounds absolutely inhumane! Can all this material in your report be substantiated by your sergeant?"

"Of course, General. The sergeant and I were diligent and very accurate in every aspect of our reporting."

"Lieutenant, what has become of God-fearing Germans? Although I cannot put the blame on any one person, my belief is that Reichführer Himmler has had something to do with the decrepit condition of the camps.

"I don't feel comfortable sending this report to his office. Himmler has always wanted to worm his way into our research here at Peenemünde. This report could give him the excuse he needs to make mischief for us. For now, this report will go no higher. It will remain on a shelf in my safe.

"You are dismissed, Lieutenant; and thank you for your candor."

I went back to my desk and was looking over the plans for the A-4 rocket (which later became known as the V-II or the 2nd vengeance weapon). Zeke buzzed me on the intercom and ask if I had any arrangements for lunch.

"Vitali," I started, "I would like you to look up one of the prisoners from the Auschwitz Camp who came up on one of the busses with you. Her name is Zivia; however, I'm not sure if that is her first name or surname. I would like her to meet with both of us outside of the detainee's cafeteria in one hour. We can take our lunch after we meet with her."

Zivia and Zeke were out near the entrance of the cafeteria where the enlisted men and detainees took their lunch. I pointed to them both and motioned them to follow me to the next building where I knew there was a small conference room where we would have some privacy.

As soon as we sat down, Zivia started being difficult.

"And what does the SS want with me now?" she barked.

I held up my hand, palm side out for her to stop talking.

But she persisted. **"Is it time for some sort of SS gang rape, or are you just going to slap me around until I break down?"**

At that point, slapping her around a bit did come to mind. However, I asked Zeke to speak up by pointing to him.

"Miss," Zeke started in a very reasonable and quiet tone. "Everyone who wears this uniform is not a monster. We brought you here in an effort to save your life.

"Both the lieutenant and I know you would like to get back to your native Poland and locate your friends, loved ones, and family. But you have to understand, Poland is a very dangerous place right now. All of Germany, indeed, most of Europe is not safe for Jews."

Then I spoke up. "Zivia, I put you on the bus to this secret rocket base because you led me to believe you had something to contribute. Now you have a choice. You can work to improve the conditions and work at this base or you can be returned to the Auschwitz Camp. Your time there would apt to be very short and end up with you being murdered by gas and being cremated. No one would know of your existence."

Finally, Zivia spoke in a normal tone of voice. "It is just very difficult to work for a regime that has destroyed my family, my city, and my country."

"Both of us," Zeke spoke up, "have lost friends, family, and neighbors to the Gestapo. We are very well aware of what this regime is capable of inflicting on decent Germans and the Polish population. All we are asking you is to work with a certain attitude and know this war cannot go on forever. The Nazi forces in the East have had a change of circumstances. Until this war is over, your chances of survival and reuniting with your friends and family are much better here, working for the enemy.

"Please, Zivia,* go take your mid-day meal; and believe me when I say this. Your food here at this Nazi army base is considerably better for you than anything you would ever see in the Auschwitz Camp.

"In addition, and this is not meant as a threat, your attitude and behavior have been noticed at the highest level at this Wehrmacht base. If you are not fully aware of the danger you are in, let me assure you, if you continue with a lot of negative social behavior, within one week you will be escorted back to the death camp."

---

* Zivia. See page 121.

37

A Chance to See the Love of My Life

I desperately wanted to see Ilsa before the Christmas holidays. I knew it would be almost impossible to get leave at this stage of the war, especially since I had a pretty good idea of what was happening to General Paulus and the Sixth Army in Stalingrad. I wrote to my dear Ilsa to see if she could come to Peenemünde. I discussed the situation with my immediate superior and it was arranged to get Ilsa lodging in the married officer's quarters. There would be no cost for the lodging, but she would have to pay for her own transportation to and from our rocket base.

Ilsa arrived at the end of November. It was wonderful to be able to spend some time with her after work. Zeke, Ilsa and I would take lunch and most dinners together. I didn't trust the Gestapo, so we kept most conversations very general and quiet in our room and in the officer's dining area.

When we were alone, we talked about how most of our manufacturing facilities had moved to the Nordhausen area to avoid further attacks from the British. I told Ilsa that Zeke and I would have to be moving to the new facilities there next month.

We also discussed the progress of the war and our plans for after the war. Ilsa said because of the Allied bombing of the major cities in Northern Germany, including the airplane manufacturing facilities in Hanover, living near the city was dangerous and unnerving.

Although Ilsa's family home was outside the city, the bombs were often too close for comfortable living. If it was a cloudy or rainy nighttime raid, often the bombs would fall outside of their designated drop area. In addition, the wind would sometimes carry the bombs far from their intended target.

Ilsa talked about one raid on the 9th of October 1943, just last month. This raid brought terror and destruction to the airplane and rubber manufacturing plants in Hanover.

"Over 700 planes attacked the industrial areas of our city. The oil refineries, gun manufacturers and the metal-fabricating plants were targeted. The raid lasted from one in the morning until just before two o'clock, almost an hour of continuous terror bombing of Hanover. My parents and I stayed in the cellar all night; the house was continuously shaking. At one point we were afraid the ceiling or the entire roof might collapse.

"The next day was as dark as night, even though the sun was an orange ball in the sky." Ilsa continued. "My parents are considering a move to my grandmother's summer home in Denmark, just to get away from the bombing and smoke."

I tried to comfort Ilsa, with calming words and caresses. Talking about the end of the war seemed to make her feel better. She also brought up the topic of having a family. I told her, "Germany might not be the safest place to bring up children after the war, but I very much want to spend the rest of my life with my dearest friend and if God blesses us, children would be a wonderful gift."

The conversation seemed to calm her down because she started undressing me slowly. I wanted to make sure the room was secure, so in addition to locking the door, I pulled a heavy chest of drawers in front of it.

When she was about halfway finished undressing me, I suggested we finish undressing and get into bed.

"I'm sorry, Jenz," she replied. "It has been many months since we have been together, I have to get used to your wonderful body again."

She did give my privates a brief squeeze as she pulled off my trousers. She could tell I was getting a little excited.

I went to start unbuttoning her shirt. She stopped me saying, "I can undress myself, once I get you into bed."

She then stripped off my underwear and, in a firm, but friendly voice, declared, "Now you, sir, get into bed."

She started to undress herself in a slow, almost glacial, pace. She bent over, put her hand on my chest, kissed my stomach, and pinched my nipple very gently, but firmly. I was on fire.

"Please hurry," I stammered. "It has been a long time since I have held you!"

She retorted, "It has been a long time since **I** have held **you;** and I'm looking forward to being in your arms all night."

She kept finding little things to do. After folding her clothing, she looked at her nails, brushed her hair, and rearranged her shoes. I kept moving around on the bed and she recognized I might be going over the edge.

She finally said, "Relax, Darling; aren't I worth waiting for?"

I knew what she was doing. She knew she was driving me crazy with desire.

She very slowly pulled back the covers and slipped in beside me. She could tell I was very excited.

"I love holding you, Ilsa. It seems like it has been such a long time. This last assignment has taken Zeke and me to places which have been difficult to describe and even more difficult to understand."

"I know these past few months have been difficult for everyone in Germany, but tonight let's just talk about us," cooed Ilsa.

She was shaking a little, perhaps because of the coolness of the room, or because of a little nervousness about being together again. My entire body was quivering. My dear Ilsa was trembling as she said, "Dearest Jenz, I want to be with you forever. I am so sorry I shared you with my friends back while you were at Hitler Camp. I never wanted to; my friends talked me into it."

I ran my hand down her back to her buttocks. She whimpered slightly, then moaned, "Oh Jenz, it is so good to be back in your arms."

38

A Knock on the Door

Ilsa and I were sleeping deeply and soundly. I was in dreamland thinking about what a wonderful woman Ilsa had been for me. She seemed to be able to anticipate my every thought. We were both very happy.

All of a sudden, my eyes were instantly opened. Something had awakened me. I listened for a while and heard nothing. I lay there quietly wondering what could have disturbed my sleep. The room was pitch-black with just a sliver of light coming from underneath the door.

Then I heard it. Someone was trying to quietly turn a key in the door. Was it an intruder? I quietly slipped out of bed. I could detect shadows moving under the crack between the door and the floor. There was a definite chill in the room. Ilsa was sleepily awakening and asked, "Jenz, what is it?"

I put my finger to my lips and whispered in her ear, "Darling, someone is at the door. Please do not move or make any noise. Quietly get up and slip under the bed from the side away from the door. I want whoever is there to think we are still sleeping."

I dressed quietly, including my officer's coat, boots, and leather gloves. I had no idea who was on the other side of the door, but I wanted to be ready no matter who it was. The Gestapo usually knocked loudly late at night. And yet, there it was…

Knock, Knock, Knock, in quick secession. It sounded like something metallic was hitting the door. My immediate thought was … the barrel of a firearm!

The metallic sound on the door was somewhat unnerving, but nothing compared to what happened next.

There was a **crash** against the door and **the door flew open!**

But only a few inches, because the bureau blocked the entry.

Two burly men, one of whom was rather beefy looking, eventually forced their way into our room. After sliding the bureau to one side, they both looked angry. Light filtered into the room from the corridor. The one with a pistol in his hand was almost awkward looking, tall and ugly; the other wasn't too tall, perhaps five and a half feet or so, but had hands the size of dinner plates.

The one with the pistol was closer to six feet. He declared as he pointed his weapon at me, "You are under arrest. We are from the Greifswald Gestapo office. We demand to know what happened to our agents and their vehicle. They were sent here a few days ago to arrest you and Sergeant Carapezza."

I spoke up in a calm and almost soothing voice. "Agent, I am not sure what you are talking about. Furthermore, I have no idea where your agents could be located now."

The ugly agent cocked his pistol and aimed it at my face.

I should explain myself. There are two predicaments that can get me a little peeved. The first is a drop in my blood sugar. Supper had been a little on the light side, because I wanted to be over with it and alone with Ilsa. I would have been fine, had the agents not interrupted our sleep.

Although I was a little annoyed about being awakened in the middle of the night, nothing makes me more cantankerous than a cocked pistol thrust in my face.

Agent Ugly had three things going against him at this moment: First, he had awakened us in the middle of the night, exacerbating my problem with my good humor and low blood sugar. Second, he made the mistake of pointing a loaded and cocked firearm at me. And third, he was being extremely impolite toward me and my best friend in the world hiding under the bed.

"Agent," I advised him, "I would suggest you never point a loaded weapon in the direction of any SS officer in uniform. Your actions here this evening could be a career-ending mistake. Furthermore, I am a little on the hungry side; it is best not to disturb me when I'm hungry."

Then Dinner Plates hands started to raise his voice and stutter. **"You, …you, Lieutenant, are the one who has made a career-ending error. You Jews have done something with our agents and their vehicle. We need to know where they are, NOW!"**

I came to the conclusion there was no sense in debating these two despicable pieces of trash any longer. I did not want their yelling to disturb other guests sleeping in the barrack. If I grabbed for his weapon, it could discharge.

I certainly did not want to take the chance of a stray bullet going anywhere near my dear friend and love of my life.

"Sirs," I started, "let me try to explain something to you."

I thought it best to keep them talking in a subdued voice while a distraction came to my mind.

"Gentlemen," I said in a low, very calm voice. "You know these rooms are monitored by speakers through the phones. The conversation goes directly to the duty officer at the front desk."

Dinner Plates shot back, **"There was no one at the front desk when we came into the quarters."**

He was still much too loud and I knew I had to do something to shut them up.

I decided to raise their blood pressure and anger them so they wouldn't think through what I was about to do.

In a demeaning tone, I responded. "The night duty officer makes rounds throughout the officer's quarters specifically to keep out **creeps** like you two."

Right after that little soliloquy, I nudged the door shut with my shoulder and stepped a little closer to Agent Ugly.

As I closed the gap between us, the agent raised the pistol and waved it in my face. He had underestimated my reach, however.

I quickly grabbed his pistol by placing my thumb behind the trigger with my left hand. My right elbow came up and slammed into his left cheek. I could hear the crunch of his infraorbital bone below his eye.

With my left hand and arm, I brought his pistol under my right armpit with the muzzle facing in back of me. I then wheeled on my right foot so the muzzle was aimed at Agent Dinner Plates.

I released my thumb guard hold on Agent Ugly's trigger and placed my forefinger over Agent Ugly's trigger finger and fired two quick slugs into Agent Dinner Plates.

The first slug went through the agent's throat approximately in the vicinity of his Adam's apple, directly through his larynx. The second slug caught him under his jaw as his head snapped back from the first chunk of lead and did not exit his cranium.

By placing the firearm under my armpit, the sound was muffled somewhat to sound like two quick coughs, but still annoyingly loud.

As Agent Ugly dropped his pistol, my arm went around his neck. I squeezed hard, heard his vertebrae snap, his temporal bone being crushed, and then proceeded to squeezed his breath and life out of him.

Poor Ilsa was terrified. Her head popped up from the other side of the bed when she heard the firearm discharge.

"Are you okay, Jenz?" she asked.

"Let's just say I'm a lot better than the two creeps on the floor."

Ilsa stood and viewed the two very dead Gestapo agents beside the bed.

"*Mein Gott im Himmel,* Jenz, what happened?"

"They came here looking for trouble, and they found it!"

"What will we do with them, Jenz? Do we have to call anyone?"

"First, we are going to crack the window in order to get rid of the gunpowder odor. Then we will wait a few minutes to see if the noise aroused any interest from our neighbors.

Hopefully, most of the folks in the quarters here are sound sleepers. After about a one-hour wait, we will load them one at a time into their automobile trunk and drive them to a drop-off spot. I think I know of a good place."

We quietly opened the door and brought Agent Ugly out to his car trunk wrapped in a sheet. Agent Dinner Plates had the keys in his pocket. We took him out to the trunk of their car and placed him on top of the other agent.

I drove the agent's automobile out the back gate with Ilsa following me. This would allow less suspicion when we came back in just one automobile through the front gate quite early the next morning.

We drove to the bluff where the van and the four agents disappeared into the froth below.

I put both agents in the front seat, weighted down their bodies with rocks in their pockets, lowered the windows and put the car in gear for the short trip over the edge. I said a silent prayer asking for God's forgiveness.

"Will the car ever be found?" asked Ilsa.

"I don't think so," I replied. "But it might be a good idea for you and your family to move to your grandmother's summer home in Denmark because of the constant bombing."

I put my love on a bus the next day to start her journey back to Hanover.

39

A Surprise Note from the Commanding Officer

The next morning Ezekiel and I were notified that the general, who was in charge of the entire base at Peenemünde, Major General Walter Dornberger, wanted to see the both of us together. We couldn't help but get a bit nervous. Zeke was almost apoplectic. He thought we would just be arrested and executed by firing squad, if we were lucky.

I have to admit, the firing squad was a distinct possibility. But then Zeke cautioned, "Let's at least go to the meeting with an open mind. We can always prepare for the worst. I would, however, like to see Adiya once more before we meet him."

I wasn't sure if Zeke had been changed by Treblinka or Adiya; either way, he was a changed man. His attitude was even better than mine.

I admit, it was a grey overcast day; even at midday the amount of daylight here in northern Germany was limited. Perhaps the gloom was affecting my mood.

"Zeke, we have to face up to the fact, that the general might have discovered our cover. The Gestapo has probably been investigating us for a while now. It would not be unusual for them to contact the head of leadership at this base to get additional information on the scientists and personnel who are working here."

Later in the morning, we received our second shock. The general's sergeant came to my work-desk with a hand-written envelope and said, "Lieutenant, the general would request you and Sergeant Carapezza meet him at the address in the enclosed sealed envelope this evening."

Both of our names were on the outside of the envelope with a note under our names: *Hand Deliver.*

"Please notify your sergeant because he wasn't at his desk when I went into his office area."

I immediately rang Sergeant Carapezza on the inter-office phone, but there was no answer. Then I remembered he was interested in seeing Adiya before meeting the general, so I immediately opened the envelope.

The note from the general read: *Lieutenant Ramsgrund, Sergeant Carapezza: Please be advised to meet me this evening @ 1800 hours inside the entrance to the Klinikum der Universität, Universitätsumedizen, Ferdinand-Sauerbruch-Strasse, 17489, Greifswald. Civilian Dress. Gen. Dornberger.*

When I located Zeke, he was in quiet conversation with Adiya in the antiroom in front of the cafeteria. They were the only two people in the room.

Adiya was stunningly beautiful, even in her work clothes. I didn't have to fantasize about how she looked without her clothes; I had already seen her without her clothes at Treblinka. I immediately felt a little ashamed of myself and greeted them with a warm hello.

I was probably the only person on the planet who wouldn't get a perturbed look from either of them while they were in deep conversation. They both offered me a chair. "Please join us, Jenz," said Zeke.

"Here, sit between us," chimed in Adiya.

I apologized for interrupting them, but handed Zeke the note as I sat down.

Zeke studied the note for about a minute. He commented, "What do you think this means, Jenz?"

"I wish I knew, Vitali."

"Do you mind if Adiya reads it.? She knows we have a meeting."

"Not at all. But please, Adiya, keep the contents confidential. It will be much safer for all of us if this is kept very secret."

"What is your best guess, Jenz?"

"It is a little worrisome the general wants to see us in such a short time period. It is encouraging the meeting is off-base and in civilian attire. There will probably be no listening devices in the hospital.

"However, and I certainly do not want to alarm either of you, but, if he wants us arrested and gone forever from the secret rocket center and the Wehrmacht, this might be an opportune time and place to be rid of us forever."

Zeke had a more positive opinion. "First, we have little choice but to attend the meeting, no matter the consequences. And, second, although the general always seems to make each decision 'by the book,' he has also had an almost paternalistic attitude about his scientists and officers under his command.

"We should make ourselves ready to catch the three o'clock bus to Greifswald!"

"Vitali, I am going to leave you two alone for a while. I'm going to wrap up my work for the day and change into a suit for the meeting.

"I will meet you at the front gate for the three p.m. bus for Greifswald."

40

A Curious Meeting at the Hospital in Greifswald

Zeke and I were not only apprehensive and worried about meeting with the commanding officer, but also resigned – because there was really nothing we could do to affect the outcome of a face-to-face meeting with the general.

We took a bus from the base to Berthold-Beitz-Platz in Greifswald. The bus let us off directly in front of the main city library. Since the bus ride only took a little less than an hour, we decided to go into the library to think-out exactly what we were going to say to the general based on what he wanted to talk about.

We went to one of the library conference rooms, but our conversations only enhanced our sense of foreboding. We had no idea exactly what General Dornberger wanted, or if we were going to be arrested. We decided it would be better to just respond as best we could to any accusations or predicaments we might run into.

We walked the three and a half blocks to the Klinikum main entrance. During our walk, we were met by some icy stares from citizens not used to seeing military-age men walking around in civilian clothing. We saw no evidence of Allied or Russian bombings; the streets were clean and well-kept. The cloudy day brought an icy wind off the Baltic Sea.

Inside the entrance to the Klinikum, we introduced ourselves to an older woman at the desk; she told us to wait, and someone would be with us shortly. She directed us to sit in a waiting area off to the right of the main desk area. Although very polite, she gave us a rather quizzical look.

The pleasant surroundings and plush chairs did little to ease our discomfort. The hospital had a mixture of odors which did nothing to allay our sense of trepidation and unease. There was a whiff of cleaning products mixed with a distinct medicinal smell. We were almost fifteen minutes early so we sat down to wait for something to happen.

After a few minutes, a middle-aged man in a white clinic coat appeared at the front desk. The woman at the desk pointed in our direction. Zeke whispered to me in an almost too-loud breath, "My Gott, Jenz, they are going to do medical experiments on us!"

My retort was, "Relax, Zeke. This isn't Auschwitz." *I just wished I was one hundred percent convinced of my response.* I knew this meeting presented a danger to both Zeke and me, but neither of us had any idea of how to avoid the whole problem. Were we about to meet the Gestapo, Doctor Mengele, or something even more dire?

The White Coat took us to a bank of elevators, extended his arm for us to enter first, and pushed the top button. Unfortunately, I could tell what Zeke was thinking: *Great, they are going to throw us off the top floor and claim an accident!*

White Coat again extended his arm for us to get off ahead of him and led us down a corridor with lights gleaming off the polished tile floor. It was a little like being led into an operating theater.

Zeke and I looked at each other; our facial expressions showed uncertainty and dread. The situation was a little disconcerting because White Coat never uttered even one word.

White Coat stopped in front of a room with a sign announcing Executive Dining Room. He opened the door and White Coat ushered us in with a wave of his arm. The door made an audible click as it closed behind us. Part of me wanted to immediately turn around and check if the door had been locked; White Coat had disappeared.

The room appeared empty. The subdued lighting, plush carpeting and beautifully appointed walls with elegant spotlighted paintings of seascapes were in stark contrast with the rest of the almost too clean hospital. It took a moment for our eyes to adjust to the subdued light.

The handsome furniture was polished to a mirror-like shine that exuded opulence in an age of scarcity in the Reich. The lavishly appointed seating was plush and comfortable-looking. There was only one person seated with his back to us in the middle of the room at a table with a white linen cloth covering the highly polished surface.

Major General Walter Dornberger turned and rose to greet us as we walked over to him. He extended his arm and shook hands with Zeke and me. There was no Hitler salute and no Heil Hitler greeting.

He offered, "Gentlemen, thanks for coming. My apologies for the meeting space. My colleague is in charge of this hospital and assured me there were no listening devises or other interruptions that would disturb our meeting. He was the one who ushered you here.

"I will get right to the point. As you know, we lost one of our eminent scientists during the air-raid bombing on the night of August 17th- 18th* last summer. This raid, by the British, is forcing our now not-so-secret facility to move to an underground gypsum mine near Nordhausen, Germany. Reichsführer Himmler tells me the facility and base office housing should be ready next month on the 1st.

"Unfortunately, the British air raid also killed Dr. Thiel** and his family. They were taking shelter during the raid in a slit trench in front of their home in Karlshagen. The bomb explosion killed the doctor, his wife, and their two children.

"The loss of Dr. Walter Thiel will be difficult to replace. He and other scientists were the driving force in our space exploration program with the A-4 rocket motor. Although we have had many launch failures, the rocket is becoming more reliable.

"Now that the motor for the A-4 is becoming better tested and more predictable, Reichsführer Himmler seems to want a more prominent role in our rocket development as a war weapon. Dr. Thiel disagreed with the Reichsführer, and tried to resign from the program the day before he was killed."

---

* The raid by the Royal Air Force, on the night of the 17th-18th August, 1943 destroyed much of the launching and testing facilities at the secret rocket facilities at the Wehrmacht base at Peenemünde. The army moved the base out of the reach of the Russian and Allied bombers to the geographic center of Germany near the town of Nordhausen.

** Dr. Thiel was a key scientist at the secret rocket base in Peenemünde, northern Germany. He was one of the first space exploration pioneers to be inducted into the International Space Hall of Fame in Alamogordo, New Mexico, USA, in 1976.

I decided to ask a question by raising a finger with the query. "General, who do you think can replace Doctor Thiel?"

"A good question, Lieutenant. Dr. Thiel and I were not getting along too well with the Reichsführer. Dr. Thiel complained Himmler was spending too much time trying to direct our research and his presence actually was slowing down our progress."

41

Avoiding Disaster

"General, surely there is a scientist in all the Reich, who could replace the expertise of one of our key personnel," I asked.

"Yes, Lieutenant, but many of our scientists have fled to other countries because of the programs set in place by our Führer and Reichsführer Himmler. I have asked Dr. von Braun* who he

---

* Wernher von Braun was the co-designer of the V-II Rocket. He defected to America at the end of WW II along with several of his fellow scientists under a code named "Operation Paperclip." This group of rocket engineers and scientists helped develop the US Space program and the Saturn V Rocket responsible for the US moon landing on the 16th of July, 1969. Dr. von Braun retired as a vice-president of Fairchild Industries in January, 1977, and died from pancreatic cancer on 16 June, 1977 in Alexandria, Virginia. He was 65 years old.

would suggest. He commented, 'It would be wonderful if we could get Dr. Einstein* back from America.'

"Our best guess is with Einstein leading our nuclear program, our possession of an atom bomb would be sometime in 1947. Our Führer and Himmler are so anti-Semitic it is a little like prosecution of a war with one hand tied behind our back. Many of our best scientists are Jewish and among the missing. Himmler has basically run them out of the country or imprisoned them.

"Himmler even placed von Braun under arrest earlier this year, when I was off the base, just because he felt he was too invested in space travel and not in weaponizing the A-4 rocket. In addition, now the A-4 rocket is being perfected with successive excellent test results, Himmler seems to want to take credit of our progress."

"What could we do, General Dornberger, to help ensure Himmler does not slow the development of the testing of the A-4 rocket motor?"

Zeke looked at me as I asked the question, because he knew we were doing everything we could to slow down or delay the rocket's actual launch date.

---

*   Dr. Albert Einstein was a German-born theoretical physicist. He was visiting the United States in 1933 when the new German government was elected. Since Einstein disagreed with the newly-elected German government headed by a confirmed Nazi, he decided to stay in the United States. Although he objected to the use of nuclear weapons, he alerted President Roosevelt of the German progress in developing an atomic bomb in 1940, and encouraged nuclear research in America. He remained in the United States and taught at Princeton University until his death at age 76 on 18 April 1955.

The general responded in a serious tone. "Please, gentlemen, avoid contact with our Reichsführer. He is an extremely dangerous man."

Then he hit Zeke and me right between the eyes with his next statement.

"Because of all the Gestapo inquiries at our base, he may suspect you are both Jewish!"

A look of abject terror flashed across both our faces before the general raised his hand off the table, palm out and interjected. "I don't care about your religion. I do care that you help run our base and the new facility near Nordhausen with professionalism and efficiency."

Both Zeke and I assured the general we would do our best to keep our departments running smoothly. But then I asked a simple question. "Sir, how did you come to know Vitali and I were Jewish?"

General Dornberger then announced, "I have several Jewish officers and scientists working for the Wehrmacht. None have been disloyal to the Reich.

"I consider the Gestapo organization, as it has evolved, to basically be a criminal organization. Each time these criminals have enquired about you two individuals, nothing has come of it. The agents of this organization seem to disappear, or lose interest in pursuing either of you. Their interest was my first clue, you were probably Jewish.

"I will confide one piece of information to you gentlemen of which you may not be aware. I was taken prisoner in the Great War in France. It was two young Jewish men, much like yourselves, who saved me from execution and helped me survive those difficult years. Ever since that time, probably before you were born, I have felt a family's religion is a private matter between the family and God.

"The second definitive clue, was your report on the labor camps in Poland. I thought at the time I read over your report, nothing like this could be happening in our country. So, I called the commandant of each camp and asked some pointed questions. I was wrong. Your report was, unfortunately, right on target. Innocent Germans and Poles and their families are being murdered in alarming numbers. A country this corrupt and debased does not deserve a world leadership position, let alone to win a major war.

"The defeat of the Sixth Army at Stalingrad last winter was the defining blow for the Reich. Our Führer would not allow General Paulus to withdraw in a timely manner after being surrounded. The result was a loss of almost two hundred and fifty thousand men with all their equipment.

"Many divisions from our western and southern fronts have been shifted to counter the Russian threat, leaving our entire country vulnerable."

With this rather shocking statement, the general pointed to the kitchen door. A waiter in the window immediately came toward our table with covered trays containing heaping plates of hot food, and asked us for our drink order.

As soon as the waiter departed, the general warned us. "I think it is obvious, now, why I wanted an off-base meeting. Nothing about this meeting or its contents can ever be discussed with anyone at any time. Is that clear?"

In unison, Zeke and I ensured in a quiet, but firm tone, **"Yes, Sir."**

42

The War Comes Closer to the Reich

As Zeke, and I, along with most of the rest of the personnel at the Rocket Center had moved to the Nordhausen area, it was pretty clear the Russians had gained a foothold on the Eastern Front. Operation Barbarossa* had come to a complete and utter halt with the defeat of the Sixth Army during the cruel and brutally cold winter at Stalingrad in late January of 1943.

General Eisenhower had authorized a massive build-up of ammunition, food, and essential supplies to Stalin's forces helping to ensure the success of the Red Army.

Everyone in senior leadership involved in the development and manufacturing of the V-I and V-II missiles at the gypsum mine near Nordhausen was even more nervous when the German Army

---

* Operation Barbarossa was the code name for the German invasion of the Soviet Union. It began on the 22nd of June 1941.

led by von Manstein* was defeated at Kursk** in a famous battle of artillery and tanks beginning on the fifth of July, 1943 to August first, approximately 280 miles southwest of Moscow. The battle represented the first successful summer battle by the Red Army.

In June of 1943, I remember Ezekiel asking me an important question. "Jenz, in your estimation, how long will it take for the Red Army to get to the Vistula?"***

"That's an excellent question, Zeke. It depends on the development of our defenses and probably the use of advanced

---

* Eduard von Manstein was a German Field Marshall who commanded the Wehrmacht on the Eastern Front. He disagreed with Hitler on many strategic orders for the war effort and at one point was quoted as saying, "Can't someone fire five bullets into that man's mouth?" He was convicted for war crimes in 1949 but only served 4 years of an 18-year sentence. He passed away in Munich in 1973. He was 85 years old.

** Kursk was a decisive victory for the Russian Army. They deployed 1.3 million men and women, 3600 tanks, 20,000 artillery pieces, and 2792 aircraft. The German response was hampered by Allied bombing of its' major cities, the Allied invasion through Italy, and the threat of Allied landings in France. It was a decisive Red (Russian) Army victory beginning their final march into Berlin in the spring of 1945 and ending with the unconditional surrender of all German forces.

*** The Vistula River, although in Poland, was considered by Germans at this time as part of the Reich. The battle of the Vistula, in January, 1945 was another decisive victory for the Red Army. The German Army was outnumbered 5-1. In another 15 days, the Red Army had advanced to the Odor River, a mere 43 miles from undefended Berlin.

weapons, like the V-II.* We have done everything possible to slow the development and production of these weapons, and we have to be cautious in our new center here in Mittelwerk.

"My further concern is the development of the atom bomb discussed with us by our Minister of War, Speer. The combination of the V-II missile and this particular bomb would be a war-winning combination for the Reich, but an absolute catastrophe for the rest of the world. We must do whatever is necessary to make sure we can slow or halt the further development and testing of the missile."

"Jenz, be very careful. Between the Gestapo and the scientists at our new location, we have to really be on our guard. I'm reasonably sure the Gestapo has an office somewhere near Nordhausen, and could well be watching us, or listening to our every word."

There was a bit of "war hysteria" in the air. The civilian population of nearby Nordhausen was very aware of the pain the Red Army was capable of inflicting on our citizens if they invaded our country.

One late fall evening Zeke and I thought we would try a little break from our routine of taking dinner at the cafeteria mess hall. The food wasn't nearly as good as the on-base cafeteria in Peenemünde. We were out walking to our automobile and away

---

* The development of the V-II rocket-powered missile, the world's first long-range ballistic missile, was fully operational by the summer of 1944. Over 3000 of these missiles were launched against the Allies, primarily London and Antwerp, before the end of the war killing an estimated 9000 civilian and military personnel. However, over 12,000 Jewish forced laborers died while testing and manufacturing these missiles.

from any possible eavesdropping by the Gestapo when Zeke said something that made me ponder our efforts.

"Jenz, I think we have done all we can do to ensure the Vengeance Weapons are not a deciding factor in a victory for the Reich or for the Nazis. Although the V-II* is a monster weapon at over five stories tall, von Braun initially developed it for space travel."

"Yes, Zeke, but it can travel over 200 miles in five minutes without detection and it is indefensible. And, the Reich is building over 3000 of these super-sonic weapons."

"I believe you are correct, Zeke. Our 'improvements' with the electrical system and fuel mix have made the rockets less accurate and more complicated. We can hope the development of the atom bomb is only a pipe-dream for the twisted Nazi mind!"

"I agree, Jenz, it is a very dangerous weapon, but it cannot carry enough destructive power to justify the expense of the rocket – unless you factor in the possibility of the atom bomb being secretly developed and made ready to ride this monster."

"There is one thing we could do, Zeke, but I agree, it is too dangerous now to try to alter the fuel or electrical systems."

"What do you suggest, Jenz?"

"I think we have a working relationship with General Dornberger. I am going to send him a memo proposing we move some of the V-II missiles to our base in northern Denmark at

---

* The V-II Rocket, the first truly guided missile, was 46 feet tall and developed 55,000 pounds of thrust. It traveled five times the speed of sound and could deliver a one-ton warhead 120 miles within 5 minutes. The missile was designed to land within a ½ mile of the target. In reality, accuracy was limited to within 5-10 miles of the target. Its main use to the Wehrmacht was as a terror weapon.

Aalborg. Simply altering the range of these monsters would put them in an ideal position for targeting London or Moscow. Our enemies would never know where the missiles came from or what sort of weapon actually caused the destruction.

"In addition, you and I could get a few of these monsters out of circulation, by somehow making them non-functioning once we get them to the Nazi base at Aalborg."

"Let's discuss possible actions over dinner in Nordhausen."

43

The Gestapo follows us to Nordhausen

"Zeke, I hate to bring this to your attention, but there has been a black sedan following us for the last few miles since we left the base. Don't turn around, but get a look in the mirror."

"You might think it has Gestapo written all over it, Jenz. Should we try to lose them?"

"I'm pretty sure they would just harass us at dinner or in some other public place, Zeke. Although we are in civilian clothes, did you bring your insurance weapon?"

"I did happen to load it and pack it in my sock."

"Terrific, let's pull over on a desolate stretch of road in a wooded area and see if they stop with us or just keep going. There could be a logical explanation for them being behind us."

As we pulled to the side of the road, it looked like the black sedan was going to drive right by us. However, as it was passing us the driver slammed on the brakes and pulled directly in front of our automobile.

Four men got out of the car!

One was carrying a long gun. Zeke said, "I think it might be a shotgun." The other three had drawn pistols. It was getting dusk and the shadows made it difficult to recognize anyone or determine the type or model of the long-gun.

Zeke leaned toward me and, in an attempt at humor, said, "This might be difficult to explain to the general."

"With four of them in the automobile," Jenz continued, "I'm not sure if they want to take us into custody or just murder us on this lonely stretch of roadway. Let's err on the side of caution and not let these criminals shackle us in any way. I will get out of the car first and talk with them. Perhaps you could stay in the car until they make their intentions clear.

"I will stay with you in the car as long as possible. Please cock your pistol, but keep it out of sight until the last minute. I would recommend taking out the long-gun criminal first."

"Be careful, Jenz; they don't look at all friendly."

As I looked back on this incident, it reminded me of a movie I had seen later in the States. I had a "Bonnie and Clyde" moment, even though at that time I had never even heard of those bank robbers. I certainly didn't want Zeke and me to mirror their outcome and demise!

Zeke had placed his hat in his hand and it neatly concealed his pistol.

I got out of the car and asked in a firm voice, **"What can I do for you gentlemen?"**

Trying to be friendly was an obvious mistake.

The tallest criminal, probably their leader, cocked his pistol, aimed it at my face and yelled, **"Get down on the ground and don't move!"**

My mother had always warned me not to try to make friends while I was hungry. This unfortunate idiot was trying to arrest me while I had an empty stomach. I was going to try to explain to him I always get a little testy when I'm hungry, but he looked like he might not understand.

So, I pointed to the flat ground out on the road and took a step closer to the tallish Gestapo agent with the cocked pistol. This put me within reach of his firearm.

"Would you like me to lie down on the paved road?" I said while pointing to the road behind the Gestapo agent.

Ezekiel sensed what I was doing and exited the automobile holding his firearm in his right hand covered with his hat.

"Fine," he yelled. "Just get down on your knees and then flat on the ground!"

He glanced at the flat road behind him as he was yelling at me. He must have considered how close he was to me, because he started to step back while yelling.

His backward glance was all the time I needed.

My right hand flew to his firearm and my little finger lodged between the firing hammer pin and the bullet. He pulled the trigger, but my finger wouldn't allow a discharge of the firearm.

I shoved the barrel of the pistol under his chin, re-cocked the pistol, and squeezed his finger holding the trigger.

Bang!

A large chunk of the back of his head flew off.

During this commotion, the criminal with the long gun started to swing the weapon in my direction. Zeke put a chunk of lead from his "insurance weapon" directly into long-gun's left temple. The sudden jolt to the head caused a discharge from his long-gun. The explosion of the shotgun took the lower part of the right leg off at the knee of one of the other agents.

That agent was down and writhing on the ground. What was left of his lower right leg was a mangled mess.

I pulled the side-arm from the agent who had yelled at me while he was headed to the deck in a heap.

I placed one quick round into the chest of the last agent standing and then carefully placed a lead bullet into his brain and another round into the back of the head of the agent writhing, whimpering, and pleading on the ground. At the time I was thinking of just putting him out of his misery. If I had waited another couple of minutes, he would have bled out through what was left of his lower right leg.

We placed all the dead agents in the trunk of their automobile and drove it deep into the woods. After covering it with brush, we headed back to our car on the side of the road.

As we drove slowly through Nordhausen, very few people were about. Although it was still early evening, none of the restaurants or shops seemed open. It was a cool fall evening, but not cold enough to keep everyone inside. We went back to the small eatery where we had eaten lunch in the spring, but the small sign for the "Gashouse Restaurant" was no longer in the window. We decided to try knocking on the door.

44

A Surprising Dinner in Nordhausen

A prolonged but gentle knocking brought the owner's very pretty sixteen-year-old daughter to the door. I'm not sure she recognized us at first; we were out of uniform. She started to tell us they were closed at night. Both Ezekiel and I had enjoyed a very nice, if meager, lunch there last spring.

The daughter's name was Greta. At our first visit to her father's restaurant, she had begged us to take her with us because of the family's fear of the Russians invading their country. Everyone in the little town had by now heard about the disastrous battle at Kursk and knew the Russians, led by Marshal Georgy Zhukov[*] and Marshal Ivan Konev,[**] were almost to the Vistula River and on the march to Berlin.

The Wehrmacht (German Army) had a total of 450,000 men who were defending against the Red Army of 2,203,000 men

---

[*]   Marshal Georgy Konstantinovich Zhukov, was the general leading the Red Army to the 1st Belorussia Front in the Warsaw area of Poland.

[**] Marshal Ivan Stepanovich Konev, was the general leading the Red Army to the 1st Ukrainian Front in the south.

and women hungry for revenge. The Red Army also had almost 14,000 heavy artillery pieces and over 2000 Katyusha Rocket Launchers (also called Stalin's Organs) against the German Army's approximately 4000 artillery pieces.

Zeke asked a question in a very gentle voice. "Are you Greta?"

A look of surprise and astonishment came over her face. At first, she looked confused, and then asked: "Do I know you?"

"Greta," Zeke replied in a caring but quiet voice, "we had lunch here last spring when you and your dad were working the restaurant. Remember, you asked us to take you with us when we were talking about escaping the Reich?"

"Oh!" she cried. "Of course. I recognize you now. One of you was wearing the SS uniform at the time. Have you come to take me with you?"

"Greta," I emphasized with some quiet firmness. "We came to try to get a little dinner at a local restaurant. It would be impossible for us to take you with us, but we do have some information for you and your family to escape before the Red Army arrives in Nordhausen.

"Why," I asked, "are all the eating establishments closed at this hour?"

"Please come in." Greta opened the door wide for us and we entered what was once a cozy dining room.

"Very few places are opened for eating now because no one can afford to eat out at a restaurant. And many of the local townspeople are trying to make a way to flee ahead of the Russian invasion into our country.

"I will talk with my father and see if we can prepare a light supper for you both. **But, please tell me, why is there so much fear about the Russian Army?**"

There was no meat in the thin onion and vegetable soup, but we did enjoy a hard, dark bread for dinner. When we soaked the bread in the soup, it was quite delicious. We were grateful Greta and her father could provide us with a meal.

I then tried to explain why it would be a good idea for the families to move ahead of a Red Army invasion. It was obvious, Greta, her father, and probably most of the townspeople or German citizens hadn't heard of the Einsatzgruppen* groups that terrorized Poland, Belorussia, Upper Silesia, Czechoslovakia, Hungary and all the population on the Eastern Front in Russia.

"About two years ago, when the German forces were invading Russia," I explained to Greta and her father, "there were two very anti-Semitic Nazi leaders who were instrumental in setting up what were called 'Special Action Groups'. These groups would force any Jews living in the conquered areas, mostly cities, to move into usually the poorest areas of a city and confine them to a Jewish ghetto. These ghettos were the most cramped, cold, and least desirable living spaces in the cities. The Jewish population had to give up their homes, most of their possessions, and their health and safety when forced to move into these cramped and undesirable quarters. Then the local Nazi victors would attempt to starve them to death.

"The abandoned Jewish homes would then be looted by the local population."

---

* Einsatzgruppen were "Special Action Groups," first organized by Himmler and Heydrich in 1939. They were to follow the German Army into Poland and round up Jews and force them into ghettos; in addition, they were to murder any local and national leaders. When the Nazis invaded Russia, the Einsatzgruppen were used to "resettle" (exterminate and murder) Jewish men, women, and children, by forcing them into mass graves and shooting them. Also, see p. 153.

"Your description of these 'Special Action Groups' makes them sound absolutely inhumane!" chimed in Greta's father.

"That's absolutely horrible!" shouted Greta.

"When starving the Jews to death wasn't too effective, because this form of brutality would take time, the Nazis forced the Jews out of the ghettos and onto cattle car railroad transports. The transports took them to death camps where they were killed by gas. I'm talking about completely innocent men, women, children and the elderly. In addition, many prisoners of war from the Russian Army and people from all over Eastern Europe were similarly killed by gas. Then their bodies were burned in the crematoriums or buried and covered with lime."

"How could people do these things to other human beings?" cried Greta.

"Zeke and I have discovered two specific horrific instances where the Russian vengeance and reprisals would be understandable, and in some cases perhaps even justified."

"You have to remember," Zeke reminded Greta and her father, "Russians in general, and the Red Army in particular, have a very disorganized society. Not only is their army undisciplined, but also extremely fearful of their leadership.

"Their army comes from a society which has nothing: no education, no property, and incredible poverty. Fear of their officers' retribution rules their actions.

"For ninety-nine percent of the men and women in the Red Army, stealing a watch from a dead Wehrmacht soldier would give the aggressor more value than any possession he could have accumulated in his lifetime in Russia.

"Please, let me give you two appalling examples of why the Russian Army is thirsty for revenge."

45

Horror at Babi Yar

"**I**n the fall of 1941," I began, "as the Wehrmacht swept into the Ukraine, they came to Kiev, a thriving city in the southern part of Russia. The city had a large Jewish population, Greta, which stood in the way of the Nazi ideal of an Aryan utopia for the Conquered Territories.

"The Nazis conquered Kiev on the 19th of September, 1941. On the 29th and 30th of that same month, the Jews living in Kiev were rounded up and taken to a ravine on the northern edge of the city. Included in this mass round-up were teenagers, like yourself, Greta, and many younger children as well as adults and the elderly Jewish residents of Kiev. If the elderly were too ill to walk, they were shot in their beds.

"The Jewish residents were brought into the ravine, called Babi Yar.* In this ravine they were executed, shot, and murdered by the SS, Einsatzgruppen, and the local police."

Greta's father then asked, "How many people were killed in this ravine, sir?"

"An accurate accounting of how many Ukrainians and Russians were put to death is difficult to ascertain. However, during those two days in September, 1941, the body count for the innocent men, women and children of Jewish residents of Kiev was in excess of 33,000.

"Over the next two years, the Nazis used this ravine as a killing zone or execution place for Russian prisoners of war, gypsies and anyone else from the area they deemed undesirable.

"An additional massacre occurred in another Russian city, Odessa** a little later in the fall. However, I should emphasize, Kiev and Odessa were only two of many cities and towns throughout Eastern Europe brutalized with mass killings by the Nazi war machine.

"In Odessa, the mass murder of the Jewish population occurred in the late fall of 1941 and the winter of 1942. Before the

---

* The Babi Yar Ravine became the killing zone for the Jews and many Red Army soldiers of Kiev.

   Wendy Lower's "The Ravine," Houghton Mifflin Harcourt, Boston, New York, 2021; is a well-researched account of the horror Jewish families experienced in the Ukraine in the 1940s. "Murdering mothers with their children is the ultimate evil." P. 96 of Lower's book.

** Odessa, Per Order of the Occupying Nazi Command 7 November 1941: "All men of Jewish origin between the ages of 18 – 50 years, report to the city prison within forty-eight hours. All residents of Odessa and its' suburbs are required to notify the authorities of any Jews or men of Jewish origin. Failure to notify authorities would require the residents to face the immediate penalty of death."

war began, Greta, the city's Jewish population was over 200,000 people. All of these Russian Jews were living in relative harmony and at peace with the rest of the Russian population.

"In response to a Red Army bomb explosion, which killed the Romanian occupying general, the occupying force of the SS and Einsatzgruppen began the execution of Jews and anyone else suspected in the act of the sabotage bombing.

"Over the next few months, the German and Romanian occupiers of Odessa broke into the homes and apartments of the Jewish population and hanged or shot to death anyone found in the residence, even women and children. Some estimates indicate up to 22,000 city residents were murdered that fall and winter.

"Does this massacre of so many innocent people, Greta, give you some idea why the Red Army may not feel too kindly toward the German population living in the area?"

"Of course!" emphasized Greta and her father in unison. Then Greta's father asked a question. "Is there anyone in the Reich who could lead us out of this horrible war and secure peace with our neighbors?"

Zeke responded with a quick answer. "The Wehrmacht has several generals who could end this madness. The only one I would completely trust is General Rommel.*

---

* Irwin Rommel had a unique leadership style. He was sympathetic to the plight of the Jews and civilians in Germany. He fought in the front lines right along with his men. Toward the end of the war, he saw the need to eliminate Hitler. For his part in the plot to assassinate the Führer, he was given the choice of suicide by cyanide or a trial and death and humiliation of his family. He was forced by Hitler to choose suicide. The story, perpetuated throughout Germany was that Rommel was killed by strafing from an Allied fighter plane while riding in his jeep.

"From what I understand, he is a skilled tactician, fearless warrior, and has a sympathetic heart," continued Zeke. He is known for protecting civilians – including Jews – from the horrors of the Nazi idea of placing undesirable populations, who might disagree with Hitler's philosophy, into concentration camps. As far as I know, he has never joined the Nazi party. He could lead Germany to peace.

"Do you think General Rommel could lead us out of this war?" asked Greta's father.

My reply was rather simple. "If it were not for the Gestapo, Rommel might have a chance. However, Hitler and his henchmen use the Gestapo to quell any dissent. Sadly, Rommel would never have a chance to save his beloved country."

"But what will happen to our family?" Greta's dad spoke up. "Greta and I only have each other. Her mom died from the typhus last year."

Zeke spoke up. "We would recommend you both leave and head west toward the Allied lines at least one month before the Red Army comes into Nordhausen."

Just at that moment, there was a loud banging on the door. **Bang…Bang, Bang!**

46

Knowledge of the Real Enemy

"**W**ho could that be at this time of night?" exclaimed Greta. We are not expecting anyone!"

Zeke and I had the same instant thought. "It could well be the Gestapo," whispered Zeke.

Greta's dad jumped to his feet. "Quick! Take your plates and hide in the kitchen. There is a back door if you have to flee, or there is a root cellar off to the right with stairs down to an enclosed dirt storage area."

Zeke and I quickly gathered our dinnerware and crept into the kitchen.

Greta's father called out, "Just a minute, I am coming."

There was another knock at the door, louder than the first.

Bang. Bang-Bang!

Greta's father proclaimed, "Please do not break down my door," as he opened it a pair of brutish men barged into the room.

"**We are here on official business,**" proclaimed the first oaf. He was a bit overweight with close-cropped hair starting to gray around the temples. He flashed a wallet with a badge attached. His face was contorted with a anger.

The second churlish official, who was nearly bald, pointed a finger at Greta's dad and shouted, "We are from the Gestapo. We have a report of two strangers entering this house about an hour ago. We are looking for two men who might have something to do with the disappearance of a team of missing Gestapo agents. Tell us immediately where they are, or things will not go well for you."

Greta spoke up. "We have had no strangers visiting us at this address. Please, feel free to look around as much as you would like!"

The churlish agent, who came in second, was quite muscular. He slapped Greta's dad hard across the face and threw him into a chair. The chair and Greta's father sprawled and crashed onto the floor.

Greta let out a scream. "**Stop!**" She cried out. "**Why are you hitting my father? We are law-abiding German citizens; we have done nothing wrong!**"

The taller agent then pulled out his pistol and waved it at Greta and her father. "Tell us immediately where the two strangers are hiding, or we will have other ways to convince you to tell us."

The bald agent started searching the house. He returned after a few minutes proclaiming, "They are not here!" He was sputtering his words with angry-looking eyes.

"Then we will have to force you to tell us right away what you know about the two men who entered this address within the past hour," shouted the balding agent.

The two Gestapo agents proceeded to tie the wrists and ankles of Greta's father to a sturdy chair. Then they tied Greta's hands behind her back and threw her onto the couch with the warning, "If you make a sound, you will both be killed."

Greta started to protest, **"You cannot do this to law-abiding German citizens!"**

Slap!

The overweight taller agent put some muscle behind his open hand and struck Greta across her face.

"Take that, you pretty one!"

She was crying softly on the couch. Her face was already swelling, her nose was bleeding, and her eye was swelling shut.

"What are you planning to do to us?" she whimpered.

"After we cut off your garments, we shall each rape you in front of your father," offered the balding agent as he produced a knife and held it in front of Greta's face.

Zeke and I were hiding on the stairway going down to the root cellar. I asked Zeke if his insurance pistol was loaded. He nodded in the affirmative.

I slipped out the back door and came around to the front door. The home had been bravely cared for, but there were some outward signs of dilapidation. The paint was starting to peal in several areas and a few of the shingles were missing.

I could hear muffled voices inside and heard the slap to Greta's face. I wanted to burst into the room, but I wasn't sure Zeke was in place.

Greta screamed as her shirt and skirt were cut and torn off her body; she lay mostly nude on the couch. Her father was crying.

I knocked softly on the front door.

47

Epiphany!

It was pitch black outside; it took me a few minutes to find my way around the house to the front door. I hesitated a few moments until I was relatively sure Zeke was in position.

I could hear Greta being pushed around and threatened as her clothes were being torn and cut off her body. I tried desperately not to let my emotions get control of me, but I was getting enraged.

I knocked softly on the front door.

Knock, knock…knock, knock.

"Hello. It's your neighbor. I thought I heard a woman screaming. Are you folks okay in there?"

I started to rattle the front latch and feign entering the home.

A male voice yelled out to me. **"Do not come in, this is official business!"**

The bald agent had started to molest Greta, and I could hear her crying. I didn't burst in because I wanted Zeke to take out the larger of the two agents with his "insurance firearm."

In the meantime, Zeke had crept into the dining room. He took careful aim at the pistol-waving agent and placed a lead round directly behind his ear.

Bang!

That was my signal.

I burst into the room and grabbed Baldy off Greta as his fellow agent tumbled very dead to the floor.

The bald agent was stronger than I first estimated and he squirmed away from me. Now, after seeing his fellow agent dead on the floor, he panicked and tried to scuttle away from me and find his pistol.

Unfortunately for him, it was hard for him to get too far very fast with his trousers around his ankles. It was almost comical to see him try to hurry away from me with his trousers half on and half off.

As he toppled over, my boot caught him under his chin. The kick might have ended his life, but I didn't want to take a chance of him becoming a future problem. I stood him up and placed him in a choke hold. I could hear his neck and lower jaw breaking as I squeezed any remaining life out of him.

I put my jacket over Greta; she was whimpering uncontrollably. Zeke found a sharp knife in the kitchen and was cutting her restraints off her wrists.

He then shifted his attention to Greta's father, who was also so traumatized he couldn't speak for several moments.

I went to the kitchen to see if I could find anything to warm up for them to drink. I couldn't find any tea or coffee, but there was a little soup left in a pan. I heated it up with a little water and brought it out to Greta and her father. It seemed to settle them a little.

As he calmed down and stopped whimpering, Greta's father asked a question. "Is this what law-abiding Germans have to suffer during this conflict?"

Zeke spoke up. "Unfortunately, sir, this is just the tip of a very large iceberg for our beautiful country. Many of our citizens have had their homes, all their possessions, and their lives lost to Nazi brutality."

"Is the war responsible for all this destruction of our society?" asked Greta's father.

"The war is a symptom of our Führer's greed. Our leaders have brought destruction and pain to our country because they are greedy and are not looking out for citizens' rights and concerns," was Zeke's comment.

Greta spoke up. "Thank you so much for ridding our home from these terrible agents. What do we do with them now?"

"It would be expedient," I suggested, "to bury them in your root cellar, but I'm afraid more agents might come looking for them."

"Zeke and I will take them in our automobile, it is parked at the end of the block. We will dispose of them on our way back to our base near the gypsum mine."

I wasn't sure where the agents had left their automobile since I didn't see it when I drove our car back to Greta's home.

After loading the two dead agents in the trunk of our automobile, I felt I should warn our hosts.

"Greta, you and your father should make arrangements to leave this place and make it to the Allies' lines as soon as possible. You will have a much better time being under the American-controlled section of Germany and away from the Russian-controlled areas. The American Army has many different types of soldiers. Some are Black-American, some Latin-American, and even a few Asian-American. Do not be fearful. They will treat you much better than the Red Army.

"What Zeke and I have uncovered, by eliminating some of the Gestapo agents, is a network of terrorists who have infected Germany. Once the German people discover that hoodlums have taken over the government, the tide of this war should turn.

"It is quite obvious now the Gestapo is looking hard for the two of us. We hope we can outmaneuver them until we can do one more project for the Reich."

I certainly could not let Greta or her father know I was in the process of getting permission from the general of our research center to ferry some of the very dangerous V-II missiles out of Germany to a Nazi base in Denmark.

"However, you and your father now know the real enemy of the German people. Unfortunately, you have met them in your own home.

"Once the majority of God-fearing Germans come to the realization of the exact nature of the enemy, this conflict will be over."

Zeke and I thanked Greta and her father and gave them all the money and firearms from the dead agents. They might need all the cash they could get in order to flee the Russians.

We still had to make it back to the research center after disposing of the trash in the back of our automobile.

There was a complete black-out in Germany by this time in the fall. Most of the leaves were off the trees and there was a distinct chill of the approaching winter. Fortunately, we were able to bury the dead Gestapo agents off the road under some rocks, brush, and leaves.

When we returned to the research center, we got word the Allies had formed a decent foothold in Normandy and a large part of France.

48

A Plan to Exit the Reich

Zeke and I thought long and hard about finding a way out of Nazi Germany while still performing what looked on the surface as helpful service for the secret rocket research center. We felt a certain loyalty to the center and the scientists, especially Dr. von Braun and General Dornberger.

In the fall of 1943, I received orders to investigate the Nazi airbase in Aalborg, Denmark. These orders were issued because Hitler had read my report which discussed the advantages of utilizing the air base in northern Denmark as a missile launching site for the V-II ballistic missile. My report had gone up the chain of command from our Chief of Operations, Herr Frits Gosslau*

---

* Dr. Frits Gosslau received his PhD from the Technical University in Berlin in 1926 in Aeronautical Engineering. He was involved in the development of the V-I and V-II missile programs for the Reich. He died in Bavaria at age 67. See p. 28.

then to Dr. Ernst Steinhoff,* from the Guidance, and Telemetering Devices Laboratory, and on to General Walter Dornberger, who discussed the proposal with Hitler.

Although General Dornberger thought enough of the plan to bring it to Hitler's attention, Zeke and I had only two goals. First, we wanted to get as many of these monster missiles as possible out of the Reich. We thought we could render them incapable of firing if we could get them away from the watchful eyes of Nazi technicians. And second, both Zeke and I thought our chances of exiting the Reich and getting into neutral Sweden were much better from Denmark.

Fuel for the V-II missiles was a combination of an alcohol-water mixed with liquid oxygen. The propulsion laboratory had discovered this combination could produce the most explosive controlled thrust of 55,000 lbs. to lift the rocket to a height of 50 miles before guiding it toward its target.

Our plan was to get the missiles out of the Reich. Perhaps the fuel for the propellant, or the warheads would be difficult to get up to northern Denmark. This was going to be our final trip to

---

* Dr. Ernst Steinhoff graduated from the Technische Universität Darmstadt in 1940 as an aeronautical engineer. He was a member of the von Braun rocket team that developed the V-I and V-II rockets. He surrendered to the Americans after the WW II and came to America under "Operation Paperclip." In 1958 he was awarded the Decoration for Exceptional Civilian Service to the U.S. Rocket Program. In 1979 he was inducted into the New Mexico Space Hall of Fame.

Operation Paperclip was the secret code name which brought 1600 Nazi scientists and aeronautical engineers to America after the war to aid with the U.S. space program.

Denmark, and we hadn't planned on returning to the Nordhausen rocket facility. Of course, plan disruption is rather the norm in the military.

While Ezekiel and I were discussing our exit plans, there was a gentle knock on the door. It wasn't a hard knock like the Gestapo uses in the middle of the night to wake up and disorient its victims. It was a soft, almost gentle knock.

Ilsa and I had married during my last trip to Denmark and Sweden, but I couldn't convince Ezekiel to stay with my relatives in the Stockholm area. Before answering the door, I whispered to Zeke, "I hope this isn't the convincing argument I should have used to insist you stay with my uncle in Sweden and out of the Reich."

Knock, Knock – **Knock.**

There it was again. A soft, but persistent knock at our laboratory door.

Zeke and I had drawings and computations all over the laboratory. Since we were the only two working in these make-shift quarters, we thought nothing of leaving the top-secret designs of the V-II rocket motor out while we were working.

I called out to the door, **"Come in, Sergeant!"**

Instead of our tall sergeant coming through the door, the door opened only halfway.

There standing in the half-opened doorway was a shy sixteen-year-old girl from Nordhausen.

"*Ach, Mein Gott im Himmel,* Greta! How did you get into this secret base?"

"My father drove me here and told the guard his niece wanted to see her father, Lieutenant Ramsgrund."

"Oh, my dear Greta! Do you have any idea how dangerous it is to come on to a German Wehrmacht base without authorization?"

"How could your father let this happen to you?"

"It broke my father's heart to bring me here. But he brought me because he loves me. He felt I would be safer here than anywhere near the Red Army. He said we would contact each other after the war, if we survived.

"Lieutenant, I really have no idea how dangerous this base is to me. But... I do know it is a lot safer here than being raped multiple times by uncouth, undisciplined, and disgusting Red Army infantry soldiers. My father knew I would be safer with you two men.

"Besides, I am a law-abiding German citizen, what could happen to me on a secure German army base?"

"Well," Zeke spoke up. "We could all be shot for treason, breach of secrecy, or some other made-up charge. You have to understand, Greta, the Gestapo does not need to follow German law. The Gestapo can arrest us, torture us, and shoot us in the back of our head for any reason. Most law-abiding Germans who are arrested and detained by the Gestapo at # 8 Prinz Albrecht Strasse, in Berlin are never seen again.

"Although you may not have heard of Gestapo tactics, even the mention of the address of # 8 Prinz Albrecht Strasse* brings abject fear and trepidation to most law-abiding Berliners.

---

* Gestapo Headquarters in Berlin. Passersby's could hear the shrieks and moans of German citizens being "questioned." The torture included electric shock to the genitals, rape, burning with cigarettes or a blow torch, removing fingers, one at a time and, near-drowning experiences.

"Remember, Greta, the SD* are everywhere. Often, they could be your neighbors, friends, or acquaintances. This 'intelligent' arm of the SS would provide the SiPo** with almost any information to have you arrested."

"Well, here I am," announced Greta. "My father told me to work with you both and do whatever you want me to do in order to secure safe passage out of the Reich; and to stay with you until after the war is over.

"I will do whatever you want me to do including getting you meals, running errands, and moving items for you. Many high-ranking officers have aides, I'm sure. I will be yours."

---

* SD or Sicherheitdienst, was the intelligence agency of the SS.

** SiPo or Sicherheitpolizei were the security police with unlimited power to arrest anyone in Germany or the Conquered Territories during the Nazi era; they did not require a valid reason.

49

A Small Complication
Leaving the Reich

"Greta," I addressed her sternly. **"The Wehrmacht does not indoctrinate sixteen-year-old girls into the military as aides!"**

"Then," she answered quietly but with firmness, "I will become an eighteen-year-old male aide for you and Mr. Zeke."

"And just how do you propose to change your gender and feminine looks?"

"I will cut and color my hair and darken my complexion. If you get me a small male uniform from army supply, I will make it into a uniform for an eighteen-year-old male soldier. I will wear tight underwear to flatten my breasts."

"Zeke," I said with some exasperation. "Will you talk to her and explain how crazy this entire scheme of hers is for her long-term health?"

Zeke took me aside and asked in a quiet tone: "Is her request any crazier than what we are attempting? Do you recommend she try to play 'nice' with the Red Army?"

"Zeke! You're not making our decision any easier. How are we going to get this past the general?"

"Well," ... Zeke hesitated for a few seconds, "we shall have to tell General Dornberger the truth: we have decided to hire an aide, in addition to our technical sergeant, to help us with some of the technical and social issues for transfer of the missiles to the Aalborg Luftwaffe Base."

"I'm not sure," I cautiously replied, "I could tell the general anything like that without making some incriminating facial gestures or just breaking out laughing."

"I will inform the general, Jenz, and pick up a small uniform this afternoon. We will have to keep her hidden away somewhere until we have the missiles loaded on the train."

My immediate thought was exasperation. I could see us all lined up against a wall and being shot. But then I reluctantly acquiesced, saying, "She will have to stay in the office here or sleep on the floor of my officer's quarters. We will wait to see how her gender transformation goes before we can let her into the dining area.

"Zeke, while you are looking for a small male uniform, see if you can pick up some dark dye for her face and hair. Greta is going to be a significant complication to our smooth exit from the Reich, but we will have to act as if she or he is a normal part of our exit plans."

Later that evening, I found Greta in our back-office diligently cutting apart and sewing while actually remaking an enlisted Wehrmacht uniform into her size. She was wearing a very tight male undershirt which helped to flatten and disguise her developing breasts.

She had finished taking in and shortening the trousers and they looked like a pretty good fit. Her hair had gone from light blond to dark brown and her complexion was about three shades darker. I almost didn't recognize her.

"Greta," I remarked, "Your transformation is quite convincing!"

"Thanks, Lieutenant. I still have a way to go, but I'm getting there. I am going to fix my shoes to make me appear a little taller. Are there any specific insignias for military aides?

"By the way, please address me as George, my male name, from now on. I want to get comfortable using it."

"Okay, George. You might also try speaking in a little deeper voice if you can do it without sounding ridiculous."

Zeke and I spent the next three days solidifying our orders and getting the missiles ready for transportation to the Aalborg Luftwaffe Base.

We had to make one more trip to the gypsum mine to inspect the final construction and packaging for the transport of the missiles and to check on the living conditions for the workers.

As I was explaining to Zeke the hazards of another visit to the manufacturing facility, to Zeke, Greta, (or George as she wanted to be called), interrupted our discussion.

"Lieutenant," she chimed in, "I think it would be important for your aide to go with you on this 'inspection visit.'"

"Absolutely Not!" I shot back. "The visit and inspection are dangerous enough for Zeke and me. You would complicate our safety; the mine is a very dangerous place. In addition, I cannot let you react poorly to the trauma the prisoners could be experiencing and the horror they are going through."

"Lieutenant, I promise I would not say a word. I will take notes on what we see and write down anything you think is important. I will keep a good record of our visit for future reference."

Since I was unsure of the placement of Gestapo listening devices, I suggested we take a break from the back office and take a walk around the base. It was getting late in the afternoon and I was thinking it might be time to test out Greta's disguise in the cafeteria. In addition, the off-green walls were starting to close in on us.

I had a lot of things going through my mind. In addition to our safety in the gypsum mine factory, there were reports of German losses in Africa* and the Allied invasion of Sicily.** Many of us in the Wehrmacht wondered why bad news on the battlefield took several months to reach us. With Allied victories in North Africa and Sicily, all of us wondered what was going on after the Allies had landed in Italy.***

While out walking, I felt a bit outnumbered. Zeke and Greta wanted to try eating in the cafeteria for the evening meal. If the dining experience went without problems, I agreed to let Greta accompany Zeke and me to the assembly tunnel in the mine.

---

* The German campaign in Africa collapsed in May 1943, with the encirclement of several hundred thousand Italian and German troops in Northern Tunisia. The British had broken the Nazi secret code which proved critical in the Allied victory.

** Sicily was attacked by the Allies under the command of Lt. General George S. Patton and General Bernard Montgomery on 10 July 1943. The campaign ended in Allied victory on the 17th of August, 1943.

*** Italy underwent Allied invasion on the 3rd of September 1943 under the command of British General Montgomery. Later that day the Italian government agreed to an armistice with the Allies. The Germans, however, were determined to defend Italy without Italian assistance.

I didn't think the Gestapo had listening devices out in the paths around the buildings at the new facilities for the rocket base, but we still kept our voices subdued. There was a light mist falling from clouds darkened by wind and rain. It looked like a possible storm coming off the Hartz Mountains to our east.

50

Camouflaging the Missiles on the Train

It took the help of over two dozen technicians to get the missiles painted with camouflage paint and trucked and loaded on the train. The missiles were heavy (just over 25 tons loaded) and quite large – over five stories tall. Three of the monsters would just fit in one open railroad transport car. The stabilizing fins had to be loaded separately. Two crane loaders were used for each missile. In addition, heavy camouflaged tarps were placed over the missiles in order to keep the secret load safe and away from the prying eyes of the Allied bombers all the way into our Denmark Luftwaffe base at Aalborg.

Each missile was a destructive monster. The detonation of one warhead would leave a crater 20 meters (66 feet) wide and 8 meters (26 feet) deep and eject almost 3000 tons of shrapnel into the air.

I had strongly suggested Zeke stay in Sweden on our last trip, but he persisted, "If you need to go back to the rocket base to make sure the missiles are transported safely to our base in Denmark, then I will help you and meet you in Nordhausen in a few days."

Many of the rail lines had been smashed by Allied bombs and many rail cars and engines had been abandoned. Also, we had to travel through most of Germany at night because of the constant threat of Allied or Red Army aircraft strafing attacks. We stopped during the day in the forests for rest and to eat our cold food packed for us by the rocket base cafeteria.

As we neared Hamburg, we could see the red glow in the sky from the frequent bombings. Occasionally the sky would light up like a lightning strike from an explosion. Our country was being ground to dust by stubborn politicians who couldn't understand that further resistance was useless.

Sometimes we could hear the Allied bombers as they raced toward their targets in the interior of our country. Industrial cities of Hamburg, Dresden, Frankfort, Schweinfurt, Bremen and Munich were certainly on the list of cities to incur Allied and Red Army wrath.

Now that the Allies had developed fighter aircraft that could accompany the Flying Fortresses* on their bombing runs, most of Germany was unprotected in this stage of the war. The Allies had what we Germans called *der Gabelschwanz-Teufel* (Fork-Tailed

---

* The Flying Fortress, otherwise known as the B-17, was developed as a heavy bomber by the Boeing Aircraft Company for the US Army Air Force in the 1930s. In the early part of the German bombing campaign, Allied fighter aircraft did not have the range to accompany the giant bombers on their missions deep into German territory so the B-17 was heavily armed with 30 and 50 caliber machine guns.

Devils) or P-38* fighter aircraft which was more maneuverable than our *Würger,* (Shrike in English) or *Focke-Wulf 190.***

Occasionally we would spot dogfights over the countryside as German and Allied aircraft tried to knock each other out of the air. We could hear the distant droning of the heavy bombers, which only specks in the sky at 30,000 feet. But their presence spelled doom to any heavy industry involved in the war effort.

Our progress north toward Denmark was halting, and even though the days were short and the nights were long, our progress was agonizingly slow. Sergeant Albert, our rocket technician, was getting frustrated with traveling at night only. I told him we could speed the progress after we were in Denmark because we wouldn't have to take so many detours and we could travel by day.

Our train had seven open cars for the missiles and stabilizing fins and two cars for our food and supplies. We slept in one of the supply cars. We also carried two armed guards, and of course, our aide, Greta. I will say Greta, or George as she now preferred, was unobtrusive and for the most part, stayed out of our way.

Dawn was breaking to our east. We were traversing farmland and looking for a forest or secluded area to spend the day about 40

---

*   The P-38 Lightning Fighter Aircraft, developed by the Lockheed Corporation, had twin tails bridged by a central boom; it was fast (over 400 mph) and highly maneuverable. The twin turbo supercharged engines turned out 1000 hp each.

**   The Focke-Wulf 190 was the German premier fighter aircraft. This aircraft became the backbone of the *Jagdwaffe* (Fighter Force) of the Luftwaffe during WW II. The top speed of the *F-W 190* was over 450 mph but diminished maneuverability at high altitudes (above 20,000 feet) limited its effectiveness against the Allied high flying heavy bombers.

kilometers south of Hamburg. I was filling out some paperwork forms when we heard an explosion in the air somewhere high above us. There was dense cloud cover so visibility was limited but we could hear the desperate whine of aircraft engines biting the atmosphere for survival.

Ezekiel shouted, **"Jenz, look behind us!"**

There low on the horizon was an obviously seriously injured B-17. One engine was missing along with about a third of one wing. Fire was coming out of the adjacent engine. The aircraft was laboring to stay at tree-top level and it looked like the pilot was trying for a crash landing on the farmland we were traversing. The aircraft was on fire and coming directly at us. It looked like a ball of fire coming across the horizon over the landscape.

Shepherding the wounded Flying Fortress was a smaller fighter plane the P-38 Lightning. This aircraft was extremely dangerous.*

The Lightning must have been out of ammunition. It looked like it might make a strafing run on our train, but it only buzzed us at close range. As it flew overhead, the Flying Fortress crash landed in a huge explosion of dust, farmland dirt and flame. It landed with the one good wing touching first and spun into a wide circle.

The B-17 must have been about out of fuel because there was no secondary explosion on impact. We could see some of the crew hastily exiting the burning aircraft.

---

*   The P-38 carried four .50-caliber machine guns as well as a 20-mm cannon in the nose housing. Both were extremely accurate and could hit targets up to 1000 yards away.

51

Saving an Allied Bomber Crew

"**E**zekiel," I shouted, "Let's see if we can save any of the crew. Bring the fire extinguisher and I'll grab a couple of blankets!"

Our guards for the missiles were already ahead of us brandishing their rifles and shouting at the crew escaping from what was now a flaming inferno.

By the time Ezekiel and I got to the crash site, our two guards riding with us on the train had the crew face-down in the dirt after firing a few rounds into the air. The aircraft had thrown up a five-foot-deep furrow of dirt and debris around what was left of the burning aircraft.

I shouted to the guards who looked like they were about to execute the airmen. **"What are you doing?"**

The first guards shouted back, **"Lieutenant, we have to shoot these Terrorfliegers** (terrorist flyers), **they are baby killers and child murderers!"**

"**Sergeant**," I said with some authority behind my voice, **"These airmen are now the responsibility of the Reich. They will not be harmed. They could prove valuable to our country! Get your fingers off the trigger mechanisms."**

"But Sir!" complained the guard, "These men have been bombing our homeland and killing our people."

"I am Lieutenant Ramsgrund of the SS. Stand down or accept the most severe consequences!"

Both guards seem to hesitate a bit but then lowered their rifles.

"George and Vitali, please see if any of the flyers are injured."

The co-pilot was severely injured when the port engine exploded and shattered the canopy. He was also badly burned. The pilot had some burns and shrapnel wounds, but could move about. One of the waist gunners was dead and the turret gunner beneath the plane had to be dead. There was no way out for that unfortunate soul.

We collected the survivors into a circle. Unfortunately, the aircraft was a mass of fire and black smoke and the whole area was too hot and dangerous to try to extinguish with a hand-held fire extinguisher. Zeke sprayed some of the flame retardant powder on the smoldering co-pilot's clothing, then helped him out of his flight jacket.

The black smoke was my most immediate concern. Within ten minutes the engulfed plane and smoke brought a small open caravan of two trucks from one of the Hamburg suburbs with four Wehrmacht soldiers. They stopped about 50 meters from the burning aircraft near our circle of wounded airmen.

The sergeant in charge informed me he would take the prisoners to a prison camp deep in Germany. I inquired, "Where would you take these men, Sergeant?"

"They will be incarcerated at the Buchenwald Camp,* Lieutenant."

The Buchenwald camp would be a death sentence for these captured flyers.

I spoke in a firm, but moderate tone to the sergeant in charge of the "rescue party."

"Sergeant, these men are enemy combatants. They are under my protection and control. They will be taken prisoner and transported by our train to a prison camp in northern Germany."

"But Sir," the sergeant protested, "Shouldn't these men face the ultimate penalty for their actions against our homeland?"

"Yes!" I replied in a firm and more assertive tone. **"These men are now under the control of the Schutzstaffel, (SS), Sergeant, and I would strongly advise you alert your superiors of this fact!"**

Our technical sergeant in charge of arming the missiles came over to me and in a quiet conversational tone asked me, "Sir, we are on a secret mission. Does it make sense to bring along a group of Allied prisoners to our base in Aalborg?"

"Can you think of a better bargaining chip with the Allies, Sergeant?"

After loading up the prisoners on the last car on the train, we did our best to tend to their injuries. We spread sulfa powder on the burn victims and bandaged up their most serious wounds.

---

* Buchenwald Concentration Camp, established in July, 1937, was one of the largest slave-labor camps within the borders of Germany. It eventually held almost 280,000 prisoners. The book by Tom Clavin, "Lightening Down," St. Martin's Press, 2021, provides an excellent description of the horrendous conditions for Allied Air Force personnel imprisoned at Buchenwald during World War II.

Greta and Zeke were terrific in calming down the prisoners and looking after their needs. They needed water and we shared some of the dark bread we had on hand. Zeke's English was more than acceptable.

The pilot addressed me after the guards had left. "Lieutenant, what are you planning on doing with us?"

"Captain, it is important for you and your men to listen to me very carefully."

I addressed them in English as best I could.

"Your men are now under the protection and control and prisoners of the SS. As you can see, you will be treated fairly and in accordance with the Geneva Convention."

I looked around the transport rail car to make sure no one else was listening before I continued.

"I realize it is your duty to try to escape from this train as we progress through northern Germany. I would strongly suggest escape would be foolhardy in this area near Hamburg. You would likely be shot on sight or turned over to the Gestapo.

"Our destination is northern Denmark. As you know, Denmark is now a German state. However, if you were to escape in Denmark, your chances of success would be much greater. In addition, if you wait a bit, you might be able to take your wounded with you.

"It is my suggestion that you wait for escape when your wounded are feeling up to traveling, and we get into a more favorable country for your survival. Our train can make a stop in the country, or just outside of a Danish city, where your wounded can be tended at a hospital, or you can make your way to Sweden.

"However, if you try to escape in Germany, I will not be able to help you and you will probably be shot by our own guards or the local population. Many of my countrymen are not favorably disposed to Allied flyers.

"We are unfortunate in only carrying mild pain-relieving medication for your wounded, but I assure you circumstances could be much worse, especially if you attempt an escape."

"Sir," the pilot continued, "I understand and appreciate your adherence to the Geneva Convention, but by your uniform and demeanor, you are a member of the feared SS. Why are you being kind to us and suggesting we escape at a more favorable time?"

"Captain," I informed him. "We are on a special mission for Germany. Your aircrew is not our priority. We will continue our mission without interruption, as long as your crew is cooperative. Any further interruption in our mission from you or your crew would not be looked on favorably by my guards.

"Is my English clear enough for you and your crew?"

"Yes, Lieutenant, I think we understand."

Crossing into Denmark

Our crossing into Denmark wasn't as smooth as I had originally predicted. Much of the Wehrmacht was on high alert since the Wehrmacht's incursion into the Ardennes* had not had the hoped-for result for our Fürher. As long as the inclement weather continued, our tanks and troops were successful. The moment the weather improved, our troops and armament were exposed to Allied aircraft and continuous strafing and bombing.

The weather had cleared and was decidedly colder as we entered Denmark in January 1945. The Wehrmacht went through our train and I had to let them look under the tarps. The guards were amazed at the size of the missiles. One of them commented, "Mein Gott, we must be winning this war with weapons like this!"

---

* The Ardennes Counteroffensive occurred from the 16th of December, 1944 until the 25th of January, 1945; also known as the Battle of the Bulge. This incursion into the Allies' position was the German Army's attempt to capture Antwerp and drive a wedge between the British and American forces.

I had to remind the Wehrmacht inspector. "Sergeant, any mention of our secret mission or these missiles would make you immediately eligible for the firing squad."

We had placed the flyers in rope restraints to assure the border guards the prisoners were under the control of the SS. I actually gave the pilot several lengths of rope and instructed the flight crew.

"Please make the ties look convincing to the Nazi border guards, but be careful of your injured crewmen."

The border guards questioned me extensively about the prisoners at the crossing near Flensburg, Germany, just before we crossed the border into Denmark. The weather had turned bitter cold with a stiff wind under clear blue skies.

The head border guard gave me a bit of trouble with the prisoners.

"Lieutenant, these criminals should be in the custody of the Gestapo for extensive questioning!"

I assured the guards. "These prisoners are under the control of the SS and I will deal with them appropriately as soon as I complete the Führer's orders. I want to remind you and your fellow border guards; further delay will result in consequences if we are unable to complete the Führer's orders."

The border guards were shown every courtesy from Zeke, Greta, and me while they were poking around on the train. They left with a reminder.

"Be careful, Lieutenant, these terrorist flyers can be very tricky."

After we had crossed the border and were on our way into Denmark, I untied the Allied flyers. One of the crew, I think he was the navigator, had a broken arm. We hadn't realized his injury sooner, but while tied up he was in considerable pain. Freeing the aviators from their rope restraints did wonders for their trust in Ezekiel, Greta, and me.

As we were passing through the city of Haderslev, I told the flight crew we would pull into a railroad siding outside the town of Kolding or the nearby Fredericia. I informed the pilot and crew to not travel as a group, but to go as small groups of two or three. I suggested the wounded travel by bus to the hospital at Fredericia.

If stopped by the Danish or German authorities, I suggested they tell the truth, but indicate their plane came down in Denmark and urged them to never mention our transportation by train out of Germany.

My English wasn't the best, but I think I got my points across to the flight crew. One of the crew asked me a question in German. "Where might we go where we could avoid the chance of meeting up with the Gestapo?"

"It is a relief," I continued, "to hear one of your crew speaks German quite fluently. The German language might help get you through any checkpoints for traveling to the hospital and to Odense on your way to Copenhagen.

"Keep in mind, Copenhagen has the central office for the Gestapo. You should be able, after everyone has healed up some, to get past the Gestapo and over to Malmo, Sweden.

"Anyone dressed in a dark suit with a fedora could well be Gestapo. To be safe, trust as few people as possible. Anyone looking to curry favor with the Gestapo or German authorities could turn you over to the Wehrmacht."

I quietly informed the pilot, as we came into a railroad siding in Kolding, that the back door of the rail car would be unlocked for a period of half an hour after nightfall while we refueled and I instructed the engineer on our future progress to Aalborg.

The pilot asked me again about our kindness for letting them escape into Denmark. "Lieutenant, I want to thank you and your men for saving our aircrew from certain death from your guards."

"Captain," I spoke in as clear English as I could muster, "landing your plane with survivors in a burning aircraft with half of its engines inoperable was very professional and a brave act of flying. Killing your air crew would do nothing to shorten this foolish war.

"I would like your full name and call number of your aircraft in case I am ever asked about this incident after hostilities have ceased."

"Certainly, Lieutenant. I am Philip Oskar Ahlin of the 5th Army Air Force. My plane is, or was, the 'Flying Betty' named after a famous movie actress, Betty Grable."

"Thank you, Captain. I will give you a short update on the war and its progress."

I informed him about the Allies being close to crossing the Rhine River and the Red Army with General Zhukov located at the Lower Oder River in the East.

"In addition," I commented, "your SOE* has done an excellent job of interfering with Nazi plans to build a superbomb."

"What superbomb?" replied the pilot. "And what is the SOE?"

"You will have to ask your SOE people, Captain. Their information will be much more accurate than anything I could tell you.

---

* SOE or Special Operations Executive was the highly secret British spy organization begun 22 July 1940. This group of spies was responsible for destroying the Nazi Heavy Water plant in Norway and ending the Nazi hope for developing the Atomic Bomb.

"Captain, this foolish war cannot last another year. Our Wehrmacht has made many mistakes in the East, including an attempt to invade Russia in the winter months. However, our biggest mistake is letting a small minority of Nazi goons take over our country.

"This political group of Nazi thugs has imprisoned, killed or caused to flee our country many of our most prominent scientists, political and cultural leaders, innovators, church leaders, and anyone who disagrees with the Nazi philosophy of a 'Master Race.'

"The extent of what the Nazi's have done to their own people and the innocent people in the conquered territories, or occupied states may never be known. We have lost an entire generation to this war and the crematoriums. What is worse, we will never know or probably understand the full extent of our loss.

"Sergeant Carapezza, my aide George, and I hope your crew finds your way to safety and to your home and families without too much further delay."

"Thank you, Lieutenant. Our flight crew will be forever grateful."

53

The Gestapo at the Aalborg Luftwaffe Base

It took Sergeant Albert, our rocket technician, almost three days to get the missiles unloaded and properly stored in a facility within the Luftwaffe base at Alborg. When the unloading and storage were complete, I strongly suggested to Sergeant Albert we would fire the missiles toward the preselected targets only if absolutely necessary.

"Sergeant," I reaffirmed, "let me make a couple of points very clear. You are to keep the firing codes and launch mechanisms separate and out of the hands of anyone else associated with these armaments.

"If the guards ask about the prisoners, they are with the Danish authorities. I want the guards to return on the train back to Germany. Please inform either Sergeant Carapezza or me if there are any inquiries from individuals in or associated with the Gestapo.

"You have orders to stay with the missiles until you are needed to activate and fire them. Be aware, there are no warheads loaded into the missiles at this time. Under no circumstances should you let these armaments get into the hands of the Red Army. They would use them against our own people. Destroy the missiles, before you let them fall into the hands of the Red Army.

"If the Allies arrive here first, you may be assured they would capture the technology, but not use these weapons against us. If you have to surrender, surrender to the Allied Army, not the Red Army."

"Lieutenant," the sergeant spoke up. "Do you really feel our defeat is inevitable?"

"I'm really not sure, Sergeant. But I do know our political leaders are morally bankrupt, stubborn, and not very bright. This is a bad combination for victory. Our Fürher has had several attempts on his life, one is pretty widely known. Unfortunately, he has purged many of our best officers including General Rommel.

"The hero of the African campaign, Oberst Claus von Stauffenberg, * was shot by firing squad shortly after his attempt on our Führer's life at Wolf's Lair last July.

"The Führer has used this assassination attempt to purge thousands of people he feared might disagree with him. Included in the purge were two of the von Stauffenberg brothers.

"Unfortunately, this purge of high-ranking officers will decimate the leadership and morale of the Wehrmacht. Excellent leadership is required for a good outcome in times of war.

"Our nation should have made peace with the Allies before going into Russia. However, Sergeant Albert, all of our nation's

---

* Claus von Stauffenberg earned the German Cross in Gold for his courage in the African Campaign in Tunisia on 8 May, 1943. In the Africa campaign he lost his left eye, his right hand, and two fingers on his left hand. He was killed by firing squad shortly after his attempt to assassinate Adolf Hitler during operation Valkyrie on 20 July, 1944.

mistakes cannot be blamed on our leaders. It is the German people who never should have brought war to our beautiful country. Too many of us are living in fear of the Gestapo and the SS."

"What are we to do now, Lieutenant?"

"All of us should work toward the day that these missiles are never fired. Peace will eventually come to our nation.

"However, Albert, notify Sergeant Carapezza or me if the Gestapo starts to ask any questions."

"Yes, Sir!"

Everything seemed to be going smoothly at the Aalborg Luftwaffe Base until late one evening.

I was going over reports on the war progress when I heard the outside door of our officers' housing residence fly open with a bang. With a howling wind coming across the base, it wasn't inconceivable the wind could have slammed the door open. The only other explanation possible was the typical late-night visit of the feared Gestapo.

My immediate concern was to call Ezekiel on the phone two rooms away and down the hall.

"Zeke! We may have a visit from our 'friends' in the Gestapo."

"I heard the door bang," said Zeke.

"Let's prepare for the worst, Zeke. Pack your 'insurance' in your sock and prepare to meet any intruders who may show up here late this evening. Please leave your phone line open so we can tell if either of us are being interrupted."

Almost immediately I heard a loud knock with a metal object on Zeke's door.

Bang, Bang...Bang seemed to echo down the hall and over the open line.

54

Gestapo Intimidation

I could hear the Gestapo bursting into Zeke's room and yelling at him to give them information on my location.

Slap!

I could hear them strike Ezekiel. That did it for me. I finished putting on my uniform, including my boots and leather gloves.

I quietly left my room and quickly walked down the hall to Zeke's room. The door was still partially open so I could see the two goons starting to slap Zeke around. There were two of them. The one working Zeke over was beefy and around six feet tall. He had bushy hair greying around the temples and looked to be in his late 40s.

The second agent looked to be younger, perhaps in his early 30s, about the same height as 'Bushy Hair', but with a wiry build. He was pretty much completely bald except for some whispery strands over his ears. I smiled inwardly because he almost looked like a cartoon character.

I pushed the door fully open and filled the opening with my six-foot, four-inch frame and asked a simple question in a commanding voice.

"May we help you, Gentlemen?"

Bushy Hair snapped his head around and commanded, "Lieutenant, come in and sit down. We have been looking for you two."

Every drop of blood seemed to drain from Baldy's face, but he was the agent holding the pistol.

As Baldy turned toward me, his pistol swung around and pointed in my direction.

I reached out, grabbed the barrel of the Lugar, and directed his aim toward the bed.

Bang!

Baldy had squeezed the trigger as I deflected his aim. I immediately wrenched his wrist backward taking the pistol from his hand while breaking his trigger finger in the process.

"Ow, you broke my finger!" he shrieked.

The other agent looked like he was ready to charge me so I aimed the Lugar at his head. He immediately backed off but started spouting his authority.

"Do you two realize we are the Gestapo?" Bushy Hair sounded pretty high and mighty – almost confident, even though I was holding the pistol.

"Yes." I tried to sound calm and collected.

"When I entered the room, I asked how we could help you. Then, you turned on me and leveled a firearm at me. Let me ask again. How can we help you?"

"Baldy, you sit on the bed or I will break more than your finger."

Bushy Hair started to spout how the Gestapo was in charge and not restrained by German law.

"You both are in big trouble," Bushy Hair continued in a voice too loud for my liking. **"Our department has been looking for you both all over Germany, Poland, and now in Denmark. We need to question you both about the loss of some of our agents."**

"Unfortunately," I replied, "Sergeant Carapezza and I do not have time for your ridiculous questions. We have been on a mission from our Führer and need to return to Germany."

"Sergeant, please relieve these men of their handcuffs and any other firearms they may possess and secure their hands snugly behind their backs."

Bushy Hair started to protest. **"You cannot order us around; we are the Gestapo and have jurisdiction here!"**

I pressed the barrel of the pistol to his forehead and asked Zeke to make sure his handcuffs were nice and snug on both of these criminals.

In a firm voice, I reminded him, **"Look, you idiot. You are not in charge here anymore. You are both under detention by the SS. You will be taken back to Germany for trial."**

Bushy Hair cried out, **"You cannot put us on trial, we are above the law in Germany!"**

"Unfortunately," Zeke reminded Mr. 'Bushy Hair', "you are not in Germany anymore."

"Zeke, let's get them comfortable in the boot of the automobile. I will get a blanket for warmth for these two criminals.

"You can't put us in the trunk of an automobile," argued Baldy. **"We would be frozen by the time you got to Germany!"**

I leveled the Lugar at eye level with the balding criminal on the bed.

263

"You're both either in the boot, or your brains are scattered around this room. Who's first?"

Fortunately, neither criminal gave us too much trouble as Zeke and I squeezed them into the boot of our automobile. I threw in the blanket, but I knew it would be useless to keep them from freezing to death.

My comment to Zeke was, "Let's get packed and get Greta out of bed for a journey out of the Reich."

Ezekiel asked, "Jenz, are we going to have trouble crossing the border?"

"We will have to dispose of the frozen criminals in the back of the automobile somewhere in Denmark, well before the border, Zeke. If we are stopped by the authorities on the Danish side of the border, we can use our orders to hopefully justify an incursion into Sweden."

"Let's get Greta and head for the border."

"Do we have a target destination for this evening?" asked Zeke.

"We should be able to pass Randers and Aarhus this evening and in the Vejle area by early morning. A lot depends on the roads not being too icy. There is a deep fjord in the City of Vejle where we can say goodbye to the rubbish in our boot.

"The next day we should be able to pass Fredericia and get over to Odense to Nyborg. From Nyborg, I believe there is a causeway or ferry to Halsskov. From there we should be able to get a bus to Copenhagen."

55

Some Difficulty Leaving
the Reich for Sweden

Zeke was pretty tired from driving most of the night so I told him I would drive the rest of the way. We were stopped in a beautiful park in Vejle, Denmark. The sun was just brightening the horizon into a beautiful red-orange-yellow glow. I think sunrise was around 9:30 at this time of year.

The rubbish in our trunk was frozen solid. We filled their pockets with small rocks and placed larger rocks underneath their shirts and gently floated them out of the canal. The outgoing tide would take them to their final resting place.

The act of getting rid of two Gestapo agents didn't seem to bother Greta. She had experienced enough trauma from the two agents who invaded and terrorized her at her home for a lifetime of discomfort whenever the Gestapo or SiPo were mentioned.

Our next stop was Fredericia. We were all getting a little hungry so we stopped at a small hotel on Krügersvej Street in Sanddal, just south of the city. The hotel was able to serve us breakfast and before long we were on our way to Odense. The roads were clear, so the traveling was relatively smooth.

We arrived in Copenhagen just after four in the afternoon. It was completely dark and we were all tired from our drive from Aalborg. Zeke had a suggestion.

"Perhaps it would be best to avoid any interaction with the authorities this late in the day while we are trying to catch the ferry to Malmo, Sweden."

"Good suggestion, Zeke. Let's see what we can find for lodging for the evening."

My SS uniform and Ezekiel's Wehrmacht uniform raised some eyebrows in Copenhagen, but we were able to get two rooms at a hotel in the Kastrup section of Copenhagen on Englandsvej Street. It was quite obvious to us that most Danes were not thrilled with the Nazis occupying their country.

The next morning, we drove to the landing where the ferries left for Malmo, Sweden. We had debated leaving our automobile in the lot because the Gestapo would eventually find it and trace us to Sweden, a neutral country. In the end, we left the car in the far corner of the lot. We decided the Gestapo would have trouble finding us as civilians in the Stockholm area.

The next morning, we had an interesting interaction with the German authorities at the ferry landing.

At the disembarkation desk, we were confronted by German authorities in uniform.

"Lieutenant, what is the nature of your visit to Sweden?"

"We are traveling to visit relatives after completing a mission for our Führer, Constable."

I spread out our orders for the official to read.

After reading over our orders, the official signaled another police officer over to secure his opinion of our orders.

The name on his badge read "Ahlbrecht." He seemed quite officious and puffed up with his own self-importance.

"What is going on with the three of you?" His tone of voice helped me understand where he was coming from.

He was an official that intended to give us trouble.

In a very soothing voice, I replied calmly. "Herr Ahlbrecht, my sergeant and aide will be going to visit relatives in the Stockholm area since we have completed our mission for the Führer. We will then be returning to the Reich in one week."

I couldn't have been any nicer to this bumbling idiot. I even handed him a copy of our orders for confirmation.

Officer Ahlbrecht's next sentence placed me and Zeke on high alert.

"These orders look legitimate enough, Lieutenant, but how do I know you are not just fleeing the Reich to avoid a disaster if the Russians continue their advance."

I had to tone up my language a bit to get this creatin's attention.

"Officer Ahlbrecht! You should know that this kind of defeatist talk is not tolerated by the SS."

Ahlbrecht seemed ready for a fight. I decided not to challenge him further until he asked, "Lieutenant, I will need to question you individually about your travel. I will need to start with your aide."

Much of the blood drained from Greta's face, but she stepped forward to answer any questions.

"No, Lieutenant, I will need to take each of you to an interrogation room in order to record your responses. If you are cleared to my satisfaction, you may proceed to the gate for ticketing and boarding."

"Unfortunately, Agent Ahlbrecht, my aide cannot be isolated from my sergeant or me." I pointed to my head to indicate George might have diminished mental capacity.

"However, we will not interrupt or comment on your questions to him during your interview."

Ahlbrecht seemed to relent and replied in an officious tone. **"Fine, the three of you follow me."**

He led us down a wide corridor with rooms for interviews branching off from both sides.

We entered an interrogation or interview room about twelve by fourteen feet with a tile floor and suspended ceiling. The lighting was harsh fluorescent and glared off the pale-green walls. There was a table with a Formica top and two sturdy wooden chairs. It all looked a little intimidating.

The constable took a chair and told George to sit in the other available chair. He motioned for Zeke and me to stand off to the side.

Immediately, the official started with an aggressive tone.

"So, young man; what have you been doing in this protectorate of Denmark since you entered?"

"I have been helping the lieutenant and the sergeant on their secret mission for our Führer, Sir."

"I'm sorry, corporal, but I don't for a minute believe you. How old are you?"

"I have just turned eighteen years, Sir. I assume you have read our orders?"

"Of course, I have read your orders! After some consideration, I have judged them completely bogus and false!"
Slap!

The official stood up and struck Greta so hard across the face, he knocked her off the chair. She went sprawling onto the tile floor.

Zeke took a step forward but I held up one finger as a "wait" signal. Zeke stepped back to the wall with me.

This official had obviously learned some Gestapo tactics and smoothly drew his pistol while waving it at Zeke and me with the warning, **"Stay against the wall if you know what's good for you!"**

Zeke and I said nothing while Greta was getting back on her feet and into her chair.

My father's words about avoiding fighting, flooded back into my mind.

I then in a soft and kind voice asked the official, "Sir would you like to read a cover letter from our Führer that might help to clear up our intentions here in Copenhagen?"

The official growled in an unfriendly voice. **"Let's have it, Lieutenant, it's probably bogus also!"**

I slowly walked over to the bombastic official while opening my uniform jacket in order to get out papers for the idiot to look over. As soon as I was within an easy distance to him, I dropped the papers on his shoes.

As Ahlbrecht look down, I brought my fist in sharp contact with the back of his neck as hard as I was able.

Crack!

I could hear his cervical vertebrae break as I brought my weight on my closed fist with my leather glove on the back of the swine's neck. His head snapped up and he looked at me with incredulous and dying eyes. I then picked him up and squeezed his neck in a chokehold to make sure he was done bothering us. I could hear his facial bones, mandible, and hyoid bones crack as I applied continuous pressure for about a minute.

Zeke had immediately latched the door to avoid any interruption.

Greta then asked a reasonable question without a hint of panic. "Lieutenant, what are we supposed to do with this individual now?"

There were no closets or hiding places in the interrogation room.

"Zeke, quick. Stand on the table and see if the hung ceiling will support his weight."

The wires suspending the ceiling looked too light to support this overweight bureaucrat. However, the pipes above the ceiling looked pretty sturdy, hopefully, strong enough to hold the weight of this bloated criminal.

"What we need to do, Zeke, is loop my belt over the strongest looking pipe. We can then loop my belt through his belt and buckle it after we hoist him above the ceiling."

The whole operation took us less than eight minutes to get Ahlbrecht up to the ceiling, suspend him securely to the pipes, and replace the ceiling tiles. It took Zeke and me to hoist the corpulent idiot to the rafters.

I leaned over and whispered to Greta. "This is how we make bad men disappear."

She smiled and unlocked the door.

We proceeded to the ticketing booth and boarded the ferry for Malmo, Sweden. The bus trip to my relatives in Stockholm went smoothly. We stayed with my relatives near Stockholm until April, except for my one brief return to the rocket center in the gypsum mine near Nordhausen.

Hostilities throughout the Reich ended in May.

56

Observations from Small Town America

When my wife, Ilsa, and I first came to America the freedoms we found were a little difficult to understand. For the first time in our lives, no government agency seemed to care about any financial transactions we were contemplating. The Gestapo wasn't questioning our neighbors about our religion. No one seemed to care about our religious affiliation. Ilsa and I both attended synagogue and church, depending on our plans each week.

Our first impression of America was a collection of small towns with the occasional city. The sky was pure blue. There was no haze or smoke from burning cities or bombings. The people seemed genuinely happy.

As we were blessed with children, we brought them to our local Methodist church in Sudbury Center and the local synagogue. I'm not sure they ever enjoyed either, but they never complained too much. We wanted both children to get the most out of each religion, just as Zeke and I had growing up.

Firearms and ammunition were available at the local hardware store or could be purchased directly from catalogs. In Germany, the Nazis confiscated all firearms. Jews were not even allowed into many of the stores that use to carry firearms. Having a firearm in your home was an extreme offense. You could be arrested, fined, and, if you were Jewish, sent to a concentration camp. There were many cities, towns, and villages in America where having a firearm in the household was encouraged. In Kennesaw, Georgia, it is on the city charter: every household has to own a firearm.

Our family enjoyed the freedom of just walking around the center of town or hiking through the woods and pastures in back of our home. We would fish in a small stream at the bottom of our hill. Pantry Brook would yield pickerel and small trout.

None of the park benches in town had signs restricting Jews from sitting on them.

Not only were the local residents friendly and helpful, no one even commented on our accent or asked questions about our origins. I will admit, I never made too much of my former position in the SS or my dealings with the Gestapo. Ilsa, Greta, Zeke, and I thought the less said about what we did in the war the better. We wanted to put the Nazi nightmare behind us.

After Ilsa and I got married in a Lutheran church in Stockholm, Greta wrote to her father and said she was going with us to America. This was news to Ilsa and me.

We never actually adopted her but Greta's last name was the same as ours on all her papers when we entered America. Ilsa and I thought of her as a little sister; Zeke thought of her as a bit of a pest, but he was so happy with Adiya and Chasha he never said anything.

Zeke finished his engineering studies in Berlin at the Technical Institute and married the love of his life, Adiya. He adopted Chasha and they eventually moved near us in Marlboro, Massachusetts.

I still shudder and tear up when I think how close Adiya and Chasha came to the gas chamber at Treblinka.

Whenever we had the chance, on Sunday afternoons we would meet at the Wayside Inn in Sudbury for a relaxing dinner. By this time, Ilsa and I had two boys and Greta. One son wanted to join the Merchant Marine and eventually became a captain sailing for Maersk Shipping Lines.

Ezekiel, Adiya, Ilse and I often used these Sunday afternoon get-togethers to discuss and pray for our gratefulness for living in a free and independent nation. The contrasts and similarities of some of the nightmares of the Holocaust were discussed in somewhat hushed tones and never where we could be overheard. The Nazi political deeds and cruelty of the 1930s and 40s would cause nightmares for all of us.

The Nazi Nightmare in America

Ezekiel and I would often discuss some of the similarities we lived through in Düsseldorf with some of the tragedies we witnessed or heard about in America.

Almost every month there was some bit of news about an anti-Semitic comment or incident in America. Compared to what Zeke and I lived through in Düsseldorf, most of these anti-Semitic incidences were of minor concern. There were no late-night "knocks on the door" from the Gestapo, or visits from the SiPo authorities.

However, on the 27th of October 2018, a deranged anti-Semite went into a synagogue in Pittsburgh, Pennsylvania and killed eleven worshipers and wounded six other people. Several of the killed and wounded from the Tree of Life Synagogue were Holocaust survivors. This shooting was probably the worst anti-Semitic incident I had heard about since coming to America. The U.S. president, President Trump, and some of his family who were Jewish went to the synagogue to express their horror and condolences to the congregation.

In the months and years that followed the shooting in Pittsburgh, other anti-Semitic problems were evident in America,

Europe, and Australia. In our state of Massachusetts, at least the state government was doing something to limit the exposure of houses of worship to terrorist and hate crimes.* The $2.9 million grant went to thirty Jewish nonprofits and other houses of worship as part of the money to defray the cost of metal detectors, surveillance cameras, lighting, fencing and new locks.

When I talked with the American Jewish Committee in 2022, their comment was "close to 25% of American Jews had experienced some form of anti-Semitic behavior in the past year."

There also seemed to be quite a bit of anti-Asian discrimination with some serious crimes against the American-Asian community. In general, there seemed to be a rise in crime all over America.

Ezekiel and I would discuss how the political situation in America compared with different situations we lived through growing up in Düsseldorf in the 1920s and 1930s. Many of these comparisons gave us concern that America was losing some of its democratic and inalienable rights (rights that cannot be transferred or taken away by legislation).

It was almost like our new country was developing habits we had fled from in Germany. America seemed to become more socialistic. It was disturbing that America was becoming a country of takers.

Ezekiel and I saw the rise in the call for universal health care or a single-payer system, the call for universal free college, and universal regulated income in order to equalize income regardless of skill or educational level. All of these programs called for big government solutions, much like we experienced in Nazi Germany.

---

* "Synagogues Get Money to Increase Security," by Christian Wade, Statehouse reporter for North of Boston Media, 11 October, 2021.

The Covid-19 pandemic that swept across America and the world only seemed to deepen the central government's hold on the American people. The rise in lawlessness, riots and looting in some of America's largest cities, border insecurity and prejudice against people of different backgrounds were all deeply concerning to Ezekiel and me.

A recent, rather dramatic incident occurred in New York City. A college psychology student approached a family of young children playing in their neighborhood. This 21-year-old female adult college student spit at an eight-year-old child and yelled at him and his two siblings, **"Hitler should have killed you all! I know where you live. And we'll make sure we get you all next time."** The female college student has on her Facebook account that she is studying to be a guidance counselor!*

It is hard to understand how a well-educated female could attack small children in such a hateful, malevolent and vicious tone while actually spitting on her victims. The incident illustrates hate is not too far from the surface for many normal-appearing people in this country.

We had seen what rapid inflation had done to Germany when Zeke and I were quite young. In the early 1900s, as late as 1914, the value of the German Mark was approximately 4.2 Marks to 1 US dollar. Less than 10 years later the German Mark was worth 4.2 trillion Marks to 1 US dollar.

Rising inflation, a rising homeless population on American city streets, and armed violence against police, minority groups,

---

*   The Hate Crime perpetrator, reported by the Daily Mail on 29 January 2022, was a student at a local college. She has been arrested for endangering and menacing the life of a child.

and Americans in general, were topics of great concern for Zeke and me. We discussed the night in 1938 when we interrupted thieves in Bucherer's jewelry store in Düsseldorf. We both hoped the small businesses in our hometown of Düsseldorf and all over Germany had survived the Nazis.

When Zeke and I tried to assess the problem of inflation for our families, we saw nothing very encouraging. The current president seemed to be following an agenda which included something euphemistically called "The Green New Deal."

This "Green Deal" looked to Zeke and me like it could cost trillions of dollars and wreak havoc on many industries in America including energy, transportation, and industrial production. Both of us were very concerned the increased taxes and government printing of extra dollars could result in runaway inflation, severe recession, or depression for our adopted country – just as had occurred in Germany, leading to the Nazi party's election victory.

Ezekiel and I have been doing a little research on our current leader, President Biden. He has been in public life for over 50 years and neither Zeke nor I have been able to come up with a shred of evidence of any meaningful accomplishments for this political figure and leader of the free world.

Both Ezekiel and I are getting on in years. However, if our discussions are put on paper, our joint notes and efforts will be written down in another treatise, "Traitors in America." Ezekiel and I hope this new effort will become completely unnecessary with an improving economic and political climate.

58

Author's Personal Notes

The reader must understand the contents of "Traitors in the Gestapo" and this sequel, "Traitors in Treblinka," are works of fiction. All the characters are real except for the protagonists and their families. Some of the ancillary characters, especially those in the Gestapo, are fictitious examples of real-life criminals. Some of the heroes and survivors of the Holocaust have been "fit" into the storyline.

For example, Zivia was a true women's hero of the Polish underground, but did not take part in the rocket development at Peenemünde. She was a symbol of hope and encouragement for many victims of Nazi criminal behavior during the Holocaust in her country.

Many of the physicians who survived horrible conditions during their illegal and unlawful incarceration during the Holocaust, including Drs. Victor Frankl and Gisella Perl, represent true heroes of their professions. Working under conditions so dire they are almost impossible to accurately describe, these clinicians prevailed and went on to lead productive, influential, principled, and even decorous lives.

Both "Traitors in the Gestapo" and this sequel, "Traitors in Treblinka" contain scenes of sexual content and violence and may not be suitable for younger readers. Including sexual content and violence is a way for the reader to get an idea of what it was like growing up in Germany in the 1930s.

The violence is used to describe the Gestapo as probably the greatest criminal element in all the world's history. The Nazis, including the Gestapo and the SS, have committed crimes that affect all of us, including future generations. As I indicated in the dedication, our tragedy is ongoing and unending.

The sexual content is a little more difficult to understand without knowing about a program instituted on the 12th of December 1935 called "Lebensborn."* This program was originally instituted in order to improve the falling birth rate in Germany and provide SS wives with encouragement for having more "racially pure and healthy children." The program screened for healthy women who could prove their "racial purity."

The Nazis felt that personal character traits like loyalty and bravery were inheritable and could be promoted through the process of selective breeding. This abominable program was the way the SS hoped to raise a population of "racially elite" German population to conquer and populate the rest of Europe and eventually dominate the world.

Of course, the whole plan, devised by the head of the SS, Heinrich Himmler, a former chicken farmer, was based on very shaky or no science.

The *Lebensborn* program was based on whimsical wishes. The entire program eventually degenerated into kidnapping of

---

* *Lebensborn*, meaning 'Fountain of Life,' was a program initiated to promote the growth of Germany's Aryan population.

"Aryan-looking" children from the conquered territories and placing them in "good" German households.

In addition, Himmler's Aryanization program was shown to be completely ridiculous and absurd when a black American, Jesse Owens, excelled and won four gold medals at the 1936 Olympics.

The Lebensborn children were initiated into the SS and led a cushy life of good food and excellent education. They were told they were elite human beings, and they were going to inherit the world.*

The "baptism" of the Lebensborn by the SS included a ritual of holding a silver dagger over the child, next to a Swastika Flag, and a candlestick made at the Dachau concentration camp. The dagger was held over the baby's head while the mother pledged her allegiance to Hitler for herself and her child. This bazaar ritual was for the "perfect" Aryan children.

If the Lebensborn children were deformed in any way, the less-than-perfect children were killed or sent to concentration

---

* Anni-Frid, one of the singers from the very popular "ABBA" band was a Lebensborn child. Anni-Frid Lyngstad achieved monumental success. At the height of the band's popularity, they were earning more than the Swedish automobile company Volvo. She was fortunate because her mother moved to Sweden when Anni-Frid was young (Norway didn't want these "Nazi rats"). Tolerance of Lebensborn children was much better in neutral Sweden. Later in life, she met her biological German father, Wehrmacht Sergeant Alfred Haase.

The Yiddish word for father is "Abba." It is the authors' speculation the bandleader may have chosen to honor our Father in heaven or to remember the father she never had, in addition to their first name initials.

camps. Unfortunately, even today, it is not routine for babies with known defects in the womb to make it to full term in Germany.

The total number of Lebensborn children in Norway and Germany numbered approximately 20,000. However, another approximately 200,000 Aryan-looking children were kidnapped from conquered countries all over Europe and placed in "good" or "normal" German homes.

The Nazis didn't care if you were married or not; as long as you produced Aryan children for the Reich. This was the atmosphere Jenz lived through when he met young girls and women at Hitler Youth Camp in 1936. This should help the reader understand what Jenz, a rather naive, tall Aryan-looking male sixteen-year-old, was up against during the summer of 1936 at Hitler Youth Camp. The fact that he was actually Jewish, may not have mattered to any of the women he met.

This novel is not meant as a voyeuristic view of the Gestapo or the SS. Everyone should understand that the Gestapo was a criminal organization praying on innocent Germans and anyone disagreeing with Nazi doctrine.

The SS was a group of "elite" Hitler henchmen who will go down in history books as misguided, depraved, and disgraced killers.

"Traitors in Treblinka" is meant as a snapshot of history in a readable form for contemporary individuals to get some feeling for the horror, deprivation, and revulsion of Nazi acts during the Holocaust.

Stealing a family's possessions and homes wasn't enough for these criminals, they had to kill whole families together so parents would witness the suffering and destruction of their own children. Children had to witness the suffering and horrible demise of their own parents and loved ones. This is probably the cruelest form of genocide.

Healing may take centuries.

59

The Author's Family History

In the 1870s the author's Swedish ancestors traveled to America and settled in Massachusetts. The reasons they chose to live in New England were two-fold. The coast mimicked much of the country they had left: rock-strewn coastlines with occasional beautiful beaches. Also, they were assured of employment at a Norwegian's factory near Worcester, Massachusetts, that employed many men from Sweden. The Iver Johnson Arms and Cycle Works was expanding and had moved to Fitchburg, Massachusetts. The company needed more extensive facilities to meet the demand for reliable, safe, and inexpensive handguns, and classic well-engineered bicycles.

The three Swedish men who came over together, were Misters Rehnquist, Ramsgrund, and Ahlin. There was a reason they came across as a family group. These three men had married three sisters from Stockholm, Sweden. Mr. Ramsgrund had a son who was the grandfather of the main fictional character in this novel. A branch of the Ahlin family became interested in dry-goods marketing in 1899. Today, under different ownership, the Ahlen's department stores are plentiful in Sweden.

The author has served in the United States Navy as a dentist on the USS Kitty Hawk from 1969 to 1971 in Vietnam. *"Traitors in the Gestapo"* is his second novel. His first novel, *"Overrun, The Battle for Firebase 14,"* was about some of the author's experiences in the Gulf of Tonkin and in the country of South Vietnam as a U.S. Navy dentist in 1969. His first two books were dental textbooks, *"Maxillofacial Orthopedics: A Clinical Approach for the Growing Child,"* Quintessence Books, 1984, and *"An Atlas of Dentofacial Orthopedics,"* with Dr. Marc Saadia, 1999, published while he was teaching at Harvard University, School of Dental Medicine.

The author's son Konrad is a research engineer at Georgia Tech Research. Konrad and his wife Katie and son Keayon live in Kennesaw, Georgia. The author's daughter Verity and her husband Harry are living in Richmond, Virginia. Verity has her master's degree and is working for a small business incubator company; Harry is pursuing his doctorate in pharmacology. Dr. Ahlin has practiced dentistry for over fifty years in Gloucester, Massachusetts.

60

Credits to Very Deserving Authors

My thanks to the many authors cited in this work for their in-depth research and detailed explanation of some of the horror and paralyzing pain inflicted on the innocent men, women, and children of the Holocaust. Without these authors' astute research and testimony, this novel would never be written.

I would also like to thank United States Naval Officer Michael David Rubin for his many comments on this work and my previous work, *"Traitors in the Gestapo."* His insightful perceptions in the prologue of this work are very appreciated.

My deep appreciation to Ms. Martha Maas for her expert editing of the manuscript. Any errors and omissions belong to the author.

Jeffrey H. Ahlin, CDR, DC, USNR
Gloucester, Massachusetts
Spring, 2022

CPSIA information can be obtained
at www.ICGtesting.com
Printed in the USA
BVHW071253270922
647892BV00002B/127